When the Saints Go Marchin' In

The Winsome Ways of Miz Eudora Rumph

Volume Four

To
Mary!
Happy Reading
to my special friend!
Catherine Ritch Guess
¡Miz Eudora!
August 19, 2011

BOOKS BY
CATHERINE RITCH GUESS

EAGLES WINGS TRILOGY
Love Lifted Me
Higher Ground

SHOOTING STAR SERIES
In the Bleak Midwinter
A Song in the Air

SANDMAN SERIES
Old Rugged Cross
Let Us Break Bread Together
Victory in Jesus

THE KATRINA LEGACY
I Know Who Holds Tomorrow

- - - - -

In the Garden　　　　*Church in the Wildwood*
Tis So Sweet　　　　*For the Beauty of the Earth*
Be Still, My Soul　　　　*The Friendly Beasts*
Because He Lives

THE WINSOME WAYS OF MIZ EUDORA
In the Sweet By and By
Precious Memories
Beautiful Star of Bethlehem

CHILDREN'S BOOKS
Kipper Finds a Home
Rudy the Red Pig (Rudy el Puerco Rojo)
Rudy and the Magic Sleigh

MUSICAL CDS
Musical Sculptures and This Is My Song

When the Saints Go Marchin' In

The Winsome Ways of Miz Eudora Rumph
Volume Four

CATHERINE RITCH GUESS

CRM BOOKS
Publishing Hope for Today's Society
Inspirational Books~CDs~Children's Books

CRM BOOKS, PO Box 935, Indian Trail, NC 28079

Visit us online at www.ciridmus.com

Printed in the United States of America
ISBN (10 digit): 1-933341-36-X
ISBN (13 digit): 9781933341361
LCCN: 2010931526

To

Michael Ritch Purser,

my own
wee Irish blessing

ACKNOWLEDGMENTS

To the residents and business owners of Smackass Gap and Clay County for your continued acceptance and support of Miz Eudora.

To Mary Langley, Miz Eudora's personal Smackass Gap tour guide.

To Mary Fonda of Clay County's Moss Memorial Library, and her wonderful assistants Deborah and Judy, who make research a wonderfully fun learning experience.

To Paula Deen's Lady & Sons Restaurant in Savannah, GA, and Renay Perkins, the store manager, who was most instrumental in making Miz Eudora's St. Patrick's Day trip so much fun. And especially to Bobby Deen for making all the ladies feel so special, and for putting up with Miz Eudora.

To the following businesses of Savannah, GA, for making our weekend there an event to remember, and for the special St. Patrick's Day treatment: Inn at Ellis Square, Shannon Winery, Rob and the Haunted History Tour and Foody Tour, Mom & Nikki's Soul Food, Polk's Fresh Market and Wright Square Cafe.

To Jimmy, the pianist, and to all the waiters and staff at Vic's on the River, my favorite Savannah hang-out. Thank you for letting The Savant Sisters bop in and entertain your crowd when we're in town!

To Dirty Harry and Slick Willie in Savannah, you know who you are!

To my "Forrest Gump" friend, I LOVED the chocolates!

To the infamous dance team, I had no idea you guys were so famous. THANKS for allowing Miz Eudora to "move and groove" with you!

To Carly Lutsky, my real-life "soul piano sister" and the other half of The Savant Sisters, and to Keith, the extra set of ten fingers.

To Froggy Bottoms, Northfield, MN, for the delicious food, enjoyable stories and especially the "tall, dark and handsome" waiter - can't wait until my next visit!

To St. Olaf College for an inspiring week filled with incredible professors and heavenly music. It was a most enriching experience, and obviously quite inspiring in *many* ways!

To Fran Holmblad, one of the dearest souls I know; and to three of my PAUMCS friends, Lea Matthews, Gail Johnson and Denise Poetter - what a treat to spend time with all of you on your turf in MN, especially with no snow on the ground!

To my "Traveling Queens" sisters, for lots of fodder and good times, to Barbara Brooks Taylor and Deborah Rodgers Farris for keeping Miz Eudora as "in line" as possible and for being my "forever friends," and to all of you for your continual support and help with **everything**!

To Doris Weaver and Doris Loudermilk for helping my spark of an idea for Christmas in August...Smackass Style burst into flame and become a reality! And to all of you GA ladies who helped this mission become a "novel" experience!

To the dear husbands of my many friends and readers who allow their wives "to go traipsin' off" with Miz Eudora on her wild adventures. There will be a star in your crown, too!

To Peyton Trexler and Lydia Hill for your cunningly delightful inspiration, and to Jane Cress for keeping me "in touch" with "the neighborhood" of St. John's Lutheran Church, Concord, NC.

To Melanie Griffin and the Sweet Pickle Bakery & Deli, Kannapolis, NC, whose giant cream horn is DIVINE! ; and to Vera Drye for introducing me to the Sweet Pickle.

To Shirley of Shirley's Soul Food, Toccoa, GA - You will definitely be in that number when the saints go marchin' in! Thank you for your unique ministry for the homeless!

To those of you who allowed me to "borrow" your personna for one of my characters, MANY THANKS! And to Mr. Grover Swicegood, my hat's off to you! You have the hardest job of all keeping Miz Eudora, and especially Mabel, under control.

To dear friend and photographer Mark Barden for capturing "all" the many sides of Miz Eudora!

As always, to my wonderful family - You are my greatest blessing in life!

A Special Word of Thanks

There is a very dear person whom I would be greatly remissed if I did not thank and offer *many* words of dedication. Peggy Linn, of Charleston, SC, is the greatest "manager" in the whole world. Your help and encouragement, not to mention all the fun times and ideas, made this book a reality. Our St. Patrick's Day adventure in Savannah stands out as one of my greatest memories ever! Not only that, you have made it possible for the Savant Sisters to bring fun and laughter to many people in lots of places. Carly and I would have never been able to do what we do without you. There had to be one "sane" one in the bunch, and God obviously handpicked you for the job!

God truly blessed me when He brought you into my life, and now, in your battle with cancer, may you always know you are loved and appreciated more than words can tell.

Oh, and as the manager of the Savant Sisters, this note of appreciation comes with a whole pot of four-leaf clovers. You need all the luck you can get in order to deal with those two!

Love You, Peggy Linn!

A Note from Catherine

We, as human beings, all have a tendency to want to take things into our own hands. Some of us are even what people call "control freaks." That would greatly describe the situation that unfolds in this fourth volume of "The Winsome Ways of Miz Eudora Rumph." Mabel decides she wants to be in charge of the music program at First Church, Smackass. Miz Eudora, in turn, decides to be in charge of making sure Mabel is *not* in charge of the music program. And since no age group holds the market on wanting to "be in charge," this story even includes one young lad who decides to be in charge of what time the congregation gets out of church on a Sunday morning. (That's one many of us would like to control!) Oh, and last but not least, there's the wife in that same chapter who is a control freak. Most husbands would agree they have one of those.

But in the end, as this story goes, there comes a time when we must "let go and let God." When we bow out and do that, we often discover that His way was best after all. We also usually find out His way was in play the whole time and we were simply "in the way."

Enough for the lessons learned in this book. I'll bet you thought these books for solely for laughter and pure enjoyment. However, the circumstances in which Miz Eudora and Mabel find themselves is not so different from some of us in our everyday lives. In fact, most all of these stories either happen to me, or someone close to me. You can't make up stuff this good!

Having said that, it's time to thank all of you for being such wonderful readers and supporters of Miz Eudora. I hope to meet many of you in my travels, for you are the support that keeps Miz Eudora alive and my writing muse going. So now, sit back and watch the shennanigans of the "control freaks" contained in these pages and you may just see a glimpse of yourself somewhere along the story. Oh, and I usually invite you to sit back with a glass of tea -- sweetened, of course--but in recognition of all the "goin' green" in the following pages, I invite you to try a glass of green tea.

Lastly, I wish many blessings for all of you. Therefore, as you encounter each day, may you not only stop to smell the roses (wild and otherwise!), but look for the four-leaf clovers along the way!

Luck of the Irish,
CR?

When the Saints
Go Marchin' In

PROLOGUE

COME SPRING AND summer, there is a lot of green in Smackass Gap. In fact all of Clay County, like its neighboring counties, is then splendidly robed in a glorious shroud of green from all the trees and shrubs covering the mountainsides, and the lush grass of the pastures and valleys. Not to mention the kudzu, of which there is also plenty, but of which we don't like to discuss.

The verdant color becomes even more strikingly vibrant when the farmers plant their fields and gardens. Then there are more greens. The folks here raise lots and lots of greens: turnip greens, collard greens, mustard greens, creasy greens. You get the picture. If the vegetable has "greens" in its name, they raise it.

Miz Eudora is no different. She raises an abundance of crops in her huge garden each year, and amongst all the vegetables are plenty of greens. It's too bad she doesn't also have a hearty stand of shamrocks in and around all those greens. Had that been the case, she might have been blessed with the "luck o' the Irish." Instead, all she was blessed with was Mabel's presence, and in her way of thinking, that was about as unblessed—"unlucky"—as she could be.

Had that also been the case, there would not have been this installment in "The Winsome Ways of Miz Rumph." And it wouldn't have been my fault that the events, which subsequently occur, in this volume ever transpired. I won't go into any further explanation of that. It will be best said in the pages of the book.

To get on with the story, I have "come to learn" that Smackass Gap is just about one of the most naturally picturesque—and brilliantly colorful—places on the face of the earth. When the lush green of spring and summer is gone, the fall colors set our mountains ablaze, a beauty that is doubled by the reflection of bordering trees in the water of Lake Chatuge, as Chunky Gal Mountain stands proudly reigning as Queen of the Hills. When the winter takes its stance, should there be a lack of luster brought on by the snow or icicles hanging from all our evergreen trees, one of our local businessmen takes care of that by brightening up the spirits of everyone around with his annual New Year's Possum Drop over at Clay's Corner in

Brasstown, just up—or down, depending on how you look at it—the road from Smackass Gap. So living in Smackass Gap is a magnificent array of wonder—most of the time from wondering what's going to happen next between Miz Eudora and Mabel—even in spite of the kudzu.

Oh, and about the kudzu, I've decided it's a lot like Mabel Toast Jarvis, the sister-in-law of my neighbor from across the road, Miz Eudora Rumph. It's simply there, and there's not a whole lot you can do about it. The more you try to do about it, the more predominant it becomes as it literally takes over everything. You can try anything you want, but you can't get rid of it. Some people say it is in the pea family, some people say it came from Asia, some people say it got its North American start in the North Carolina mountains by some farmers planting it for forage or soil stabilization. All I can absolutely verify is whatever it is, and wherever it came from, it's a downright nuisance, and most people have little use for it, except to throw out an explicative—or a long row of them—regarding it once in a while. Like I said, it's a lot like Miz Eudora's description of Mabel. (And just so you know, that happens to be greatly akin to the opinion Mabel shares of Miz Eudora.)

Enough. It's time to get on with what's currently happening between those two. For those of you who are already familiar with Miz Eudora Rumph, you need no explanation. For those of you who are getting a glimpse of her for the first time, in order for you to grasp the full flavor of Miz Eudora and Smackass Gap, I'll do my best to tell the story using her vernacular.

Best wishes,

Sadie Callaway

GLOSSARY OF
MIZ EUDORA'S SPEECH HABITS

afraid - a'feared

because - 'cause

can't - cain't

could of - could'a

going to - gonna

I came to - I come to

ing - in'

seen - see'd

sure - shore

that's going to - what's gonna

was - wuz

wasn't - wadn't

we were - we was

would of - would'a

what's happening - carryin's on

You get the picture!

ONE

A Snake in the Grass

"THAT MABEL!" BLURTED Miz Eudora Rumph as she came "huffin' and puffin'" up my front steps. "She's nothin' but a snake in the grass." Even from inside my house, where I stood inconspicuously watching and listening to her, I could tell by the way she tromped onto the front porch, with more vigor than usual, that the day was off to a good start. *Scratch the word "good,"* I told myself as she paced a couple of times across the porch's floor boards, not bothering to knock on the door. *Let's just say it's off to a start.*

Her head, lowered a bit, was tossing ferociously from side to side. She reminded me of a dog when it has an old rag, or some such, and is giving it a good shaking. Actually I thought that analogy quite appropriate for, in this situation, Miz Eudora was the pit bull and Mabel was the rag. At least that's the way it appeared to be on this day. There were days when Mabel was the pit bull and Miz Eudora was the rag. Those were the days when everyone in Smackass Gap, and even some areas around, took cover. On days such as this particular one, you might also wish you had taken cover, but it was usually more fun to keep your head peeking out barely enough to see what was going to happen.

For me, though, I didn't need to keep my head peeking out to see what was going to happen. Don't ask me why, but I had already foreseen trouble on the horizon. And if you've happened to read the three books that precede this one, you've seen it coming too. It's like that smoke, billowing out of the smoke stack ahead of a train that's "comin' 'round the bend," to let you know it's on its way. Only in this scenario, the smoke was billowing out of Miz Eudora's ears and the bend was my front steps.

As she continued to "huff and puff" like "the little engine that could," I decided I'd better mosey on outside before she self-destructed via combustion. I cautiously carried my watering can out to the front porch, under the pretense of caring for my two new shamrock plants, and feigned surprise at finding her there. "Good morning, Miz Eudora!" I welcomed her. "Isn't it a 'beaut' of a morning?"

"Don't know a thing about this morning, beautiful or otherwise," she spouted, the proverbial steam still rolling from her ears. "All I know is that Mabel is a snake in the grass and I wish she'd slither right on out of here so none of us would ever have to look at her again." She took a seat in her self-assigned rocker on the front porch and began to rock with such force that I feared she might spill back over the railing and onto the ground below.

I quickly rushed to "fetch" her a large stoneware mug of coffee, grateful I had unintentionally made it extra strong this morning. All of a sudden my earlier act, of putting nearly twice the amount of coffee necessary in the coffeemaker, seemed an omen instead of a grave mishap. Having come to that conclusion, I feared the only "grave" thing about this morning would be what happened to Mabel if she showed up within the next little bit.

I stared as Miz Eudora guzzled down the contents of the mug and slammed it on the small patio table beside the rocker. Her antics reminded me of an old western flick, with a disgruntled cowboy in a saloon calling for another round and me as the barmaid. *Yes, Sadie Calloway, a calamity is definitely brewing and your neighbor might as well go ahead and change her name to Jane...Calamity Jane Rumph.*

The thought of living next door to Calamity Jane brought a momentary bright spot to what was rapidly transforming into a dark and dreary morning, both in the proverbial cloud over Miz Eudora's head and the approaching real one, which promised one last snow-fall. I cautiously looked out over the white-blanketed mountainside, still showing signs of the unusual abundance of snow we'd received this season. A glance at my two shamrock plants told me my hope for warmer weather was a bit premature. I prayed my luck with calming my neighbor would be more productive than my weather forecasting, making myself a mental note to carry the plants indoors after her visit.

"What's the problem today?" I asked, wondering whether I really cared to know the current complaint between these two sisters-in-law. It had become part of the daily routine of "Live in Smackass Gap"—as I had come to call the epic saga of the drama that happened each day between them—for one of them to be "outdone" with the other. I'd have figured that, by now, they'd have run out of logical gripes. But then, when it came to those two, nothing was logical. Thus they were now working on compiling quite a hefty list of illogical gripes. That's why I referred to it as "Live" instead of "Life in Smackass Gap." There were days I felt blessed to still be alive at the end of the day. The jury was still out on this day as I apprehensively awaited her answer to my question, which was hampered by the fumes coming from her direction.

"It's not enough that dad-blasted Mabel moved up here and built that chalet of a house on top of Chunky Gal Mountain and then promptly proclaimed herself "Queen of the Hills" of the Queen of the Hills. Now she's gonna mess around and take over the music at the church and Mrs. Azalee will wind up quitting playing the piano and life at church will never be the same. Why, Mrs. Azalee is half the reason people attend church at First Church, Smackass. That welcomin' smile of hers when everyone comes in the door is enough to make a body feel good even without hearin' a romp-stompin' sermon by Preacher Jake. And for them who are too blind to notice her lovely smile, they can't help but feel better when they get a load of her hat every Sunday. A body never knows whether she'll show up in a bird nest, a cornucopia, a field of flowers or the nativity scene. I've heard some of the women in my Sunday School class say they can't wait to get there every week just to see what hat she'll wear that day. She don't hold a candle to that Red Hat Nanny when it comes to makin' hats, but she's the closest second I've ever see'd.

"And you know, she can play anything on that old piano. I reckon it's near as old as she is, if not older. She don't need a lick of music, which is how our choir has been singin' for all these years. Without music, except for the hymnbooks we got not all that long ago…maybe fifty years or so. They just rear back and let it rip. But that Mabel, she's all into gettin' them fancy folders and a mess of music she called something like 'octavos.' Land sakes! That sounds like a disease or some food kin to avocados instead of some "Sunday go-to-meetin' music."

"P'SHAA! Octavos, I reckon! If that Mabel gets her way, we might as well bar the doors. Won't nobody come to church. I'd give the flour sack right off my back if that dandy director we got now wouldn't retire. Maybe I ought to go have a word of prayer with her and inform her that God don't retire, and neither should we, at least when it comes to doin' the Lord's work. Or better yet, maybe I ought to go bend the ear of Mr. Grover Swicegood, who's in charge of the Church Council, and tell him they'll need to be buryin' might nigh all the church if they let Mabel come in and take over that position. We'd do better if my mule Clyde took charge.

"Land sakes! Clyde's hee-hawing is more in tune and pleasant to listen to than that blasted caterwauling of hers. At least I look forward to hearing him every morning. What on earth are we gonna do if she winds up being in charge of the music at First Church, Smackass?"

She paused for a second—which relieved me tremendously for I was amazed she hadn't already hyperventilated from not breathing—before adding, "Maybe we ought to just go ahead and bury Mabel and be done with it." (Now you understand why I feared the only "grave" thing about this day would be Mabel showing up at my doorstep within the next bit.)

Having heard some rumor about the church searching for a new music director, to replace our current one who was retiring effective the last Sunday in February, I asked, "You mean Mabel is trying to get her foot in the door?"

"No, ma'am, I don't mean that a'tall. If all we had to worry about was her foot, it wouldn't be so bad, but she's done gone and got her whole body in the church. Not only in the church, but in the choir. It all started when she went and bought those high-fallutin' choir robes for everybody. I don't know why in the world she had to go and spend all that money. Them robes didn't help them sing one bit better. Especially with her up there singin' with them. And then she got the notion they needed to be more 'up to speed' and 'current' with their music selections, so she went and bought a whole mess of new music, them things she called 'octavos,' which didn't sound nothing like a name for church music. Then she decided they needed something to put the 'octavos' in so they looked 'uniform,' as if them robes didn't already make them look like they wuz in a uniform.

"Land sakes, sounded more like they wuz goin' to be playin' sports or workin' in the hospital than singin' in the choir. Our choir's been doin' a fine job of healin' the sick and savin' souls with their music without uniforms, and Mr. Grover Swicegood ought to tell her so. And that bit about 'up to speed,' she's obviously never sung *I'll Fly Away* with our choir. She'd find out how fast they could go. Not to mention *Keep on the Firing Line.* I'd like to keep her on the firing line! And since when does she know anything about current? I wish she'd just take her 'current' right on down the Tennessee River.

"P'SHAA! 'Up to speed' and 'current,' I reckon!" Miz Eudora's complaining came to a grinding halt. Not because she had no more to say on the subject. She'd simply huffed and puffed so much before she ever got to this point that "the little engine that could" had given out of steam.

"Why don't I get you another round of coffee?" I got no response, which I took to mean she was refueling. When I got back with her filled mug, she'd obviously had enough time to stoke the fire, for she was ready to go again.

"What I mean is she's trying to get her voice in the door." Miz Eudora gave a few more huffs between puffs. "No, I don't mean that either. She's done gone and got her voice up in the choir loft, where she sits on the back row every Sunday staring out over the congregation like a hawk. Then between all them notes she hits in trying to find the right one, I can't tell if she's hootin' like an owl, or warblin' like a turkey buzzard.

"Land sakes! If she winds up gettin' herself in charge of the music, we might as well go ahead and advertise that we have a bird sanctuary instead of a choir!"

She halted her ranting for a minute. "Hey, I've got an idea! Maybe we can convince her to go to Six Flags over Jesus. I'll bet they'd love to have a bird sanctuary to go along with their skate park." Sadly, she wasn't kidding.

Try as I may, I couldn't think of one thing to say to Miz Eudora, or at least one that would make a dent in the "hissy fit" she was in the throes of. I thought of suggesting that since she was so interested in having Mabel in a firing line, she might think about hunting season. I wasn't sure when hunters could go after birds in the mountains, but I was sure there was a time for it. Problem was, I was afraid she'd take me seriously on that matter too. So rather than say anything, I reached for her empty mug and went to retrieve a third cup of coffee for her. I contemplated putting a triple shot in it, but decided even that wouldn't dampen her dither. When I returned to the porch, it was as if I had never left, for she was still lost in her own conversation.

"What I think makes this all the worse is that my dear sweet baby brother, John G., had such a beautiful voice. Ma used to say it was too bad he went to Carolina to be a proctologist 'cause he could have had such a wonderful career as an Irish tenor."

Mulling over her comment, I asked, "But don't

you have to be Irish to be an Irish tenor?"

"You sure do."

Certain that Rumph had to be of Germanic origin, I said, "I would not have considered Jarvis to be an Irish name."

"Jarvis isn't. But my mother's side of the family is where the Irish kicked in. Ma took a heap o' pride in her Irish heritage. Her family came here straight from Ireland. In fact, her father was one of the miners who settled here to carry the corundum out of these hills by mule-drawn wagons. Although I can't prove it, I wouldn't put it past him for being the one to come up with the idea of naming this place Smackass Gap. But I'd surely be mighty proud to know it if he had."

She reared back and gave a huge chortle. "If I ever find out he did, I'd swear he was also a fortune teller."

"Why do you say that?"

"Because he would have known that somewhere down his lineage, John G. was going to marry Mabel and that someone ought to give her a good sm…"

"Excuse me a moment, Miz Eudora," I interrupted, not sure I wanted to hear the rest of her convoluted explanation. "I believe I hear my clothes dryer calling me." *A poor excuse*, I reprimanded myself as I ran through the house, *but it was the fastest one I could come up with.*

As I made my way back to the dryer that wasn't even on, I thought as how the morning had already seen my front porch as the stage for a pit bull, a train and now a disgruntled cowboy—or *cowgirl*, as it was in this case. *So much for the quiet serenity of a tiny hole-in-the-wall place called Smackass Gap,* I mused. My front porch had been privy to more drama in the past forty-five minutes than a Broadway musical, and the star had only made one notable point, albeit it twice, which was that her sister-in-law was a snake in the grass. I felt rather certain that would have made a great musical number.

Suddenly I became amused, and also greatly intrigued, over how ironic it would be if my otherwise sweet little neighbor was a descendent of the real Calamity Jane, either on her German or Irish side. So intrigued, in fact, I decided to investigate the matter. Not knowing much about Western lore, nor the history of Calamity Jane, I decided to pay a visit to Mary Fonda and her knowledgeable staff at the Moss Memorial Library before the day was over. Digging up facts and legends regarding Calamity Jane was about as close to gardening as I was going to come. Researching her family roots was surely safer than me trying to root any other type of flower or vegetable, and would reap more of a reward. Then a thrillingly sinister chill rushed down my spine. *What if the paths of Calamity Jane and the Jarvis or Rumph lines do cross?*

My rambling thoughts came to a grinding halt as Miz Eudora gulped down the last of her remaining coffee, slammed the mug on the small patio table and stood, all in one swift motion. "I'm going home to dig in my flower garden and root some shrubbery and flowers. Digging in the dirt always did tend to give me a bit of peace. Right now, I'm not sure nothing less than a bulldozer could offer me a mite of peace, but I'm goin' home and start shovelin'."

As I watched Miz Eudora tromp back home, her steps a little less forceful than they'd been upon her arrival, I wondered whether all her fuming had taken some of the edge off her frustration. It appeared my only indication of the answer to that question would be whether or not I could still see smoke rolling from inside the Rumph house later in the day. *If you see smoke rolling outside the house, you'll know she went and got herself a bulldozer*, I joked to myself.

My thoughts returned to whether there was even a remote possibility that my neighbor and Calamity Jane shared a bloodline somewhere down the line. It mattered not. Just the idea of our resident "snake in the grass" had brought me to an appealing way to spend my day. Before the sun set, I aimed to find out about a few other snakes in the grass. *And maybe even a few saints!*

TWO

Live in Smackass Gap

BY THIS POINT, I'm sure you understand why I labeled my daily existence with Miz Eudora and Mabel "Live in Smackass Gap." I also decided to suggest to the local *Clay County Progress* that it run that title as a column in their newspaper…right alongside the comics! Reading about the latest run-ins between that pair would certainly begin the day with a laugh.

Perhaps the reason I came up with that idea was because—following her morning rampage, which was worse than usual—I was drawing at straws in an effort to find an alternative on which Miz Eudora could focus her energies, anything besides worrying about Mabel taking over the choir. Since her recent captivation with discovering bloopers in church bulletins had grown to include all sorts of publications, I considered she might like to apply her mounting interest into an expertise at editing. You can imagine my shock when the editor of the *Clay County Progress* showed up on her front door step the afternoon of the "snake in the grass" tizzy. *Divine intervention*, I decided, aware I could no longer take credit for the idea.

Long story short, no pun intended, it was agreed between the two that Miz Eudora would start writing a column for the paper about the current happenings of Smackass Gap. I suspected this was the newspaper staff's way of getting her off their back with calls about anything and everything she'd read in their publication. This way, she'd have enough of her own words to criticize and, in the course, would possibly develop an understanding and appreciation for the timeline involved in reporting the news.

Even though I couldn't take credit for this literary contractual agreement between both parties, I did decide to call the newspaper office and suggest "Live in Smackass Gap" as the title for the column. After all, since that phrase was inspired by surviving the daily drama between Miz Eudora and Mabel's actions, it must have also been divine.

Sadie Callaway, you're beginning to sound like Eudora Rumph with that kind of reasoning! My inner voice, which I often thought of as Leon's rational way of looking out for me, was at it again.

Agreed! I subconsciously replied to the voice and turned my attention toward finding a secondary way for my feisty neighbor to occupy her time. That way, I'd make doubly sure she stayed too busy to worry about Mabel. *Or the music at the church.*

I looked down at my two shamrock plants, one with green leaves and small white blossoms and the other a dark purple plant with lavender blossoms, both now safe from the outside temperatures as they sat perched on a table by my front window. As alert as they were, with their tri-leafed heads raised upward, I feared the luck they held was no match for the wrath of Miz Eudora Rumph or Mabel Toast Jarvis, especially when those two ladies' wrath was directed from one to the other.

My watering can handy, I gave each of them a healthy drink and then poured in a little more for good measure. *I need all the good luck I can get*, I surmised, thinking my words were more like a plea to the Almighty than a note to myself. *In fact,* I added disparagingly, *I'm not sure two pots full of* four-leaf *clovers would be enough luck for today.* I set the watering can down and retreated to my favorite reading chair with a stout mug of triple-shot coffee, stronger even than it had been that morning.

As I picked up the newspaper and began to leaf through the pages to check on the current conditions in Clay County, I was suddenly struck with another horrible fear. What was going to happen between that pair of sisters-in-law when Miz Eudora began to tell the public about "that blamed ole Mabel?" *And worse, Sadie Calloway, what is going to happen to you when you get caught between Miz Eudora and "that blamed ol' Mabel?"*

"Blamed" was a good description of Mabel, for no matter what went wrong in Smackass Gap, Miz Eudora blamed her. But I must be fair. It was a situation that was equally as true "with the shoe on the other foot." No matter which way things went, except how Mabel wanted them to go, it was the fault of Miz Eudora. It was like living next door to a human double-edged sword, and you dared not take sides. That's why I certainly dared not getting caught between them, especially when the pen was considered mightier than the sword and Miz Eudora was now behind the pen.

My mind scrambled to come up with a back-up plan of how to keep Miz Eudora so occupied that she wouldn't have time to antagonize over Mabel and the choir. Sadly, after wrestling with multiple ideas, I had still come up empty-handed. *I'm not sure anything short of a miracle by Saint Patrick could save this day,* I concluded, now heartily praying to the Trinity portrayed in the three petals of my clovers, the same Trinity in the leaves which the patron saint had told the king about all those years ago. Fairly certain I had all the Powers that be—the Father, the Son and the Holy Spirit—in this project of taking care of the two sisters-in-law with me, I jerked my eyes open and stared at the two shamrock plants, aware that St. Anthony must have jumped on board with St. Patrick in the answering of this prayer.

No wonder St. Anthony is known as "the quickest saint." He certainly was quick to help me with this calamity. No wonder people refer to him as "the miracle saint," since he is attributed as helping find lost things. He certainly helped me find a perfect solution to this problem.

I instantly mulled over how I would set about laying out this newly-concocted plan, that had planted itself in my mind during the short prayer, which I felt sure would be the perfect solution to keeping the two women out of each other's way.

Ahem! I heard in the back of my mind. *Yes, Leon, and thanks to you too. After all, this is something you often suggested to troubled individuals. And yes, I know. Why didn't I think of it earlier?* I smiled, thinking how, during the years of our blissful marriage, my dear husband would often gently lead me to finding my own solution to a problem. It seemed he was still doing it.

Now all I had to do was sit back and wait for Miz Eudora to appear on my doorstep for coffee the next morning. Sure she would arrive, still with a heavy step that said she was "loaded for bear"—*or at least for Mabel*—I would be ready for her. "Why don't you check into your family's genealogy, Miz Eudora?" I would suggest, certain the research of her family's background would be of great interest and, following

Leon's lead as a counselor, would therapeutically offer her a positive way to vent her frustrations regarding her sister-in-law.

After all, it was her talking briefly of her relatives and how they were some of the first homesteaders in the area that prompted me to delve into the genealogy of Calamity Jane. In only the few minutes of her visit, she provided me an incredible education about her ancestry and an equally impressive appreciation for this place I now called "home." The more I thought about it, the more convinced I was that I'd come up with just the right thing to distract her, at least for a while, while she chewed on the idea of taking on her genealogy as a hobby. In reality, I was counting on it being more of a peacemaker than a hobby, but that was my own private secret and one I would never share with her.

My ladylike manners vanished as I turned up the mug and downed the coffee in one long swig, reverting back to my own medieval Anglo-Saxon ancestry. All I lacked was an oversized stein. *And maybe a shot of something besides three scoops of coffee.*

As I glanced back at the two shamrock plants, that now seemed to be smiling at me, I surmised that somewhere on the Jarvis farm, maybe even generations back before Miz Eudora's ma and pa were even thought about, there must have been a pretty hearty stand of four-leaf clovers. Either that, or my neighbor had managed to get herself blessed with the "luck o' the Irish" by mistake somewhere along the line. I made a mental note to take a closer look in her garden on my next visit, for there had to be some now spread around the Rumph farm too.

Maybe four-leaf clovers ran between the two farms, I decided, recalling that the Jarvis farm—where Miz Eudora was born and lived her whole life until she married Horace Buchanan Rumph and "took to housekeeping"—joined the Rumph farm. *Four-leaf clovers or not, God certainly blessed this woman I call my dear neighbor.* I thought back to the few details she'd shared with me during my time of residency in this place. Pa Jarvis had done a lot of bartering with his vegetables to make ends meet for his family, and Miz Eudora had learned the art of bartering well. She'd bartered corn for carrots – or carats, as was the case in her illustrious diamond and tanzanite ring – and from the looks of things, had come out on top, especially when you consider the 70-percent discount she got on her end. I dare say Horace never had to offer a discount to sell his "corn."

I laughed, thinking of the idiosyncrasy of her and that "bundle of carats." She had, of course, taken to wearing the ring all the time except while she was working. *When you look at it that way, I guess she doesn't wear it much of the time at all.* But she did at least wear it in public, which I suspected was simply to "get Mabel's goat."

Speaking of that, I decided to add Mabel's genealogy to my list with Calamity Jane to see if somewhere along the line, some of her family had actually tended goats. *Or at least sheep*, I chuckled to myself, *black or otherwise.*

I retired that evening, satisfied with my conclusion. My time at the library "exhuming" facts about Calamity Jane had sparked an interest in my own family's roots, and had provided an alternative to me belaboring the point of Miz Eudora worrying about Mabel and the choir. There was no doubt I could reconvene with Calamity Jane the next day when I hoped to take my neighbor to dig up her own roots.

"Live in Smackass Gap," I uttered softly as I drifted into a deep sleep, now anxious to read the newspaper column's first installment by Miz Eudora. "What could be better?"

THREE

My Wild Irish Rose

WHEN MIZ EUDORA didn't show up on my door-step resembling a train engine the next morning, I figured it was safe to meander over toward her house for our daily coffee ritual. The cloud of the previous day had brought only a dusting of snow, more of a last ditch effort to say farewell until the next winter. It had been a dainty snowfall, more like God was sifting it from the heavens, making sure there was not a single flake left before He turned the sun loose to announce the upcoming arrival of spring. The temperature was warm enough to place my shamrocks back on the front porch. *And hopefully leave them*, I noted as they turned their tri-leaf foliage to greet the sun. It wasn't like I was into warding off bad spirits, but I was taking all the luck I could get, and since St. Patrick had pronounced them a symbol for the Trinity, I wasn't turning down any religious help.

As I ventured my way across the road to Miz Eudora's house, I could have sworn I even heard a bird chirping in anticipation of spring. Either that, or Mabel was "warming up" that singing voice of hers. However, since it sounded like neither an owl nor a turkey buzzard, I stuck with my first inkling of a bird chirping. It wasn't until I reached nearly midway down Miz Eudora's driveway that I realized what I heard was my neighbor singing, something I'd never heard before. I listened intently until I recognized the song as *My Wild Irish Rose*. My steps became purposely slow and labored so I wouldn't disturb her.

"Miz Eudora," I called out when she finished the song, "I had no idea you could sing."

She blushed when she realized I'd caught her. "I can't … not really. I was just mimickin' one of the songs my brother used to sing to Ma before he took off to Carolina." Her blush melted as she gave a melancholic sigh. "Ma was always in such hopes that John G. would find his own beautiful Irish rose when he went off to college. Too bad the closest he ever got was the thorn."

I wasn't quick enough to stop an escaping laugh, but I tried desperately to mask it under my breath before it amassed into a full-blown cackle.

"Sadie, I just don't know how to thank you enough. What you did for me yesterday was about the greatest gift a person could have given me."

"Oh," I replied, thinking back, unable to recall any kind of gift I'd given her the day before. Taking a guess, I continued, "I can't take credit for that coffee. It was a mis…,"

"Not the strong coffee," she interrupted, "although it reminded me of what Pa used when he made his Irish coffee."

"So your father *was* Irish?" I questioned, affirming my hunch about her background.

"No, ma'am, he wasn't," she answered, bursting my bubble. "It's just he liked the Irish coffee that came with marryin' Ma."

"Ah," I nodded, catching her drift and feeling somewhat elated that I'd been partially right in my conclusions.

"Folks 'round here say that's why his 'shine was the best. They say he added that Irish touch to it. He used to wink and tell them that all he did was have Katy stick her finger in each batch."

"Katy," I repeated, realizing I didn't recollect ever hearing the actual names of her mother and father. "Was that your mother's name?"

"No, it was actually Anna Kathleen Peay before she married Pa, at which time she became Anna Kathleen Peay Jarvis. But Pa always called her Katy. He said it suited her spunk and vitality better."

"Ah," I muttered again, now understanding the source of my neighbor's spunk and vitality. Anxious to get from Katy's finger to what Miz Eudora used to keep Mabel at bay, I alluded to our prior topic of conversation. "But what about Horace's special blend?"

"What about it?" she asked while pouring our coffee.

"I thought he was reputed to have the best 'shine in the county. Was it your pa's old family recipe?"

"It was Pa's recipe, minus Ma's finger, which she never did really put in any of the batches. Pa just said that to make people wonder, and to keep them from trying to copy his blend. Horace blended Pa's recipe with a hint of his own pa's German ale recipe."

"I didn't realize you came from such a long line of … of 'brewers,'" I responded, stalling while trying to be as politically correct as possible, but afraid I'd stuck my foot in my mouth. I couldn't help but wonder if that's why she referred to Horace's brew as his "special blend."

Miz Eudora, noticing my discomfort, replied, "That's alright, Sadie. Most of us 'brewers' came from 'Hebrewers.'" She paused until she was content that I'd caught her joke. "In fact, the Jarvis family was largely responsible for the establishment of First Church, Smackass."

That comment prompted a whole slew of questions from me, but I never got a chance to ask them for she never slowed down.

"Now about the handin' down of recipes and

special techniques," she continued, her pronunciations forcing me to pay close attention and "decipher" her unusual expressions. "What's that word I hear all them women in their red hats sayin'? Tweet … tween … no, tweak. That's what they did. Each generation took the recipe of the past generation and tweaked it a little to add its own special touch. That's why Pa said Ma put her finger in all his batches." She laughed outright. "I reckon we did alright to be a clan of 'teetotalers.'"

It took me a second to catch her drift. "You mean you made it, but none of you drank it?"

"None of us 'cept Horace. You know, they say the ones what makes it best don't drink it. The only time my pa ever touched the stuff was in an occasional Irish coffee. Horace … now that was another story. He didn't have no problem samplin' the goods. But Pa said I wuz just gonna have to deal with Horace, 'cause with a last name like Rumph, I wuz gonna be dealin' with a lot." She gave an angelic smile, a hint of a blush returning to her cheeks. "You know, I really never minded Horace a bit. He did alright by me."

Judging from the number of carats in the ring she'd bought the previous year from the money she'd saved—buried in a jar in the back yard—from one of his "bumper crops," I'd say he did do alright by her. "Miz Eudora, do you mind if I ask a rather personal question?"

"Land sakes, Sadie! I don't reckon I do. You're not like that cussed Mabel, 'cause you don't mean no harm by it. Besides, if I do mind, I'll say so and be plenty quick about it."

"That's plenty fair enough," I replied, knowing she meant exactly that. Choosing my words carefully, I prodded on. "If all of you were 'Hebrewers,' as you called it and attended First Church, Smackass, didn't anyone have a problem with … with your clan making moonshine?"

"Is that all you wanted to ask me?" she asked, giving no indication of an answer.

I nodded my head sheepishly.

"Land sakes, child! If that's all you wanted to know, why didn't you just say so?"

I thought that was exactly what I had done, but decided it best to keep my mouth shut, which was a good thing because she went right on.

"If you wanted to feed your family, that's what you did. There weren't any jobs for the most part, and when crops had their bad years, you had to make a livin' somehow. Corn grows good up here in these mountains, so there was usually enough corn to get by. Besides, everybody had to have some 'shine for medicinal purposes. You couldn't always afford the doctor, and even if you could, he couldn't always get 'round in the winter. A man had to do what a man had to do." She paused only briefly and then added a quick afterthought. "A woman, too, if it got too difficult."

I gathered from the "umph" she put in her last sentence that it was all she had to say on that matter. All our talk about "'shinin'" had left me with one last question though. "If the ones who made it never drank it, how did they know whether it was good or not?"

"I reckon 'cause they never had anybody bring any back. All they ever got was empty jars for the next batch. It was cheaper if you brought back the jar."

Although I wasn't totally convinced by her answer, I figured her reasoning made about as much sense as anything else. I also figured we'd "flogged that dead horse" long enough. "How did you get the name Eudora?" I asked, in a quick effort to change the subject toward a conversation on her genealogy, praying she would take the bite. For a number that's supposed to have special significance in the Bible and reputed to be so lucky, the seven words of that question led me to just about more trouble than I could get out of, the result of which was unbeknownst to me at that moment, and of which I still wouldn't realize for a while.

"I don't know hide nor hair about that name," she answered blandly, "except it was a family name somewhere along the line in Pa's family." Miz Eudora took on that winsome gaze that appears when "she gets a mind" about something. "Now it's my turn to ask a question," she said as she entwined the fingers of both hands and began running her thumbs around each other in a circular motion. It was a habit of hers I'd noticed when she was either anxious about some matter or was attempting to pass the time of day.

"Ever since yesterday when you gave me 'bout the greatest gift a body's ever given me, for which I wish to thank you greatly, I've had this hankerin' to learn more about where I come from. Like somethin's drivin' me to find out about all my ma's Irish ancestors and about where my pa come from. I'd even like to see if I can dig up where Horace's clan was before they landed in Smackass Gap."

After recovering from the initial, albeit comical, shock of Miz Eudora's description of the Rumphs landing in Smackass Gap, which she made sound as historically important as the pilgrims landing on Plymouth Rock, I stumbled to pick my jaw up off the floor. "Uh…uh…I, uh…," I struggled in an effort to acknowledge her thanks. My lack of speech, I instantly realized, came more from the fact that not only had she taken the bite, she'd already chewed it up and spit it back at me. It seemed the Good Lord had already beaten me to the punch by planting that seed yesterday by allowing me to be His unknowing catalyst.

Divine intervention, I mused for the second time in two days. *Maybe there really* is *something to this lucky shamrock, or at least its symbolism of the Holy*

Trinity. If that's so, we'll have one last intervention tomorrow. With that, I determined I needed waste no more time conniving how to handle Miz Eudora and the situation of Mabel taking over the choir. The Almighty already had it under control. Thus I decided to sit back and watch this pre-determined scenario play itself out.

"Miz Eudora," I began, my voice back under control, "how would you like to go to the library this morning? They have lots of genealogy records and I have a bit of digging I'm working on there myself. Since you've got this newly-discovered 'hankerin' ' to find your roots, perhaps you can locate the relative for whom you were named." Those were words I later learned I should have left alone, just like the seven-word question regarding her name.

"That's a dandy idea! Would you mind giving me a ride into town when we finish our coffee? I'd like to get started diggin' right away. Why, I can pick up where I left off yesterday in my flower garden and I'll bet this will be a paschal more fun. That Mary and her gals sure know their stuff in that library. Why, with their help, I'll bet I find that relative in no time."

I smiled and nodded. This was the most excited I had seen Miz Eudora since I'd met her. She was even more excited than when she'd first met all those Red Hatters who had become her dearest friends. *No wonder folks get so caught up in all that genealogy stuff,* I mused. *Perhaps I should give it a try myself.* But then I was too afraid of what relatives might come out of the woodwork, ones who were best left where they were. I'd settle with looking into Calamity Jane's past and seeing how far removed it was from Calamity Eudora's. *And for fun, you might check into Mabel's, just to see if she's all she's cracked up to be.* A shudder ran up my spine, causing me to decide I wasn't that equipped to handle calamities.

Miz Eudora's eyes were gazing off into the distance, as if she were somewhere in another world. From the look on her face, it looked to be a pleasant place. "You wanna hear 'bout the sweetest story I ever did hear tell of in Smackass Gap? This one's not so old, 'cause I remember it. In fact, it happened not too long before you moved here. All this talk about roses and families brought it to mind."

"I'd love to hear it, Miz Eudora. You've certainly allowed me to bend your ear 'a-plenty' this morning, so now it's your turn."

A contemplative smile wiped itself across her face. "You know, I ain't much into mush and love stories. Leastways not the kind of mush you don't eat." Her comment brought a smile to my own face. "And I don't know whether this woman was an Irish rose or not, but to Mr. Leland Moffitt, his wife must'a been the sweetest thing that ever was. Poor man, his wife of fifty years had to be put in a home right after their big golden celebration. Now I'll tell you, that really *was* a celebration." Miz Eudora's mind must have been ramblin' back to Horace's passing and "the celebration," as Preacher Jake had termed it, for her next words were, "I still ain't quite figured out why being married fifty years and dying is both a celebration. If that's the case, they might as well go ahead and send you a sympathy card when you get married."

I snickered aloud, thinking how in many cases she was right in her assessment. Leon had dealt with his share of applicable cases in his career as a practicing counselor.

"But back to the story of poor old Leland, it nearly killed him when the family made the decision to place her in 'a home.' Didn't none of them want to, but they had no choice. She couldn't do a thing for herself nor another soul anymore. Everyone felt so sorry for Leland. We felt sorry for her, too, but she didn't know the difference for the most part. Leland's the one what was still in his full capacity and it nearly broke his heart in two to see her like that. He went to the home at supper to see her and feed her every single day. This went on for a few years.

"As time went on, he began to lose his sight and a few of his faculties too. It got to the point that if someone saw him coming down the road in his pickup truck on his way there or back, they'd pull off to the side of the road. You weren't quite sure whether he'd run into you or not. Even Horace had to get out of his way a few times." She shook her head in pity.

"Truth be known, Leland's the reason we got our first stoplight here. He kept pullin' out on Highway 64 right in front of eighteen wheelers, like he'd forgot it wasn't the mountain road it was in our 'bringin' up days.' Everyone was afraid he was going to get himself 'kilt.'

"Too bad, though; it didn't make much difference about the light. He still ran into somebody one day and wrecked his pick-up truck. After that, his kids took his driver's license away and refused to get his truck fixed."

"How sad," I said, figuring that to be the end of the story.

"That ain't the half of it," Miz Eudora continued. "When that happened, he'd hop on his tractor every day at supper to still go visit her and make sure she was fed. That went on for months until it got cold. Poor Leland wrapped a big roll of plastic around his tractor so he could still go to 'the home' in the snow and rain. It was the most pitiful sight we'd ever seen 'round here."

"That truly is heartrendering. What a demonstration of love."

"That still ain't the half of it," she added, not missing a beat. "One day he ran the tractor off the road and into a ditch. His kids took the tractor away."

"Why didn't one of them simply take him to visit his wife?"

"Because they all worked and didn't have time to take him over there every day. And they weren't as dedicated as their pa. I told you this was a story of sweet love. Apparently he got it all and it didn't pass on to his offspring. Not to be outdone, he got himself two canes 'cause he could barely walk anymore. That first wreck in his truck didn't help that matter a'tall. Kinda messed up his good leg. One was already messed up some 'cause of the war. But there he'd go, hobblin' down the street on those two canes. Broke my heart every day when I'd see him pass by my road on Highway 64. There was many a day when I wanted to take him on Horace's tractor to see his wife, but I figured that would take away his pride. One thing you don't want to do to a mountain man is take away his pride," she added. "Horace said the men folk who sat around down at Clay's Corner of a mornin' would talk about how pitiful it was one of them couldn't offer their dear friend Leland a ride. But then that would have been like puttin' him in the home, too, and no one was willing to rob him of that blessing every day. That was the only thing left he could do for others … and himself."

She gave a quiet sigh. "So nobody picked him up, and he hot-footed it down to the home every single day after his wife went there. He did alright, 'cause he managed to take care of her 'til she took her last breath.

Then he died shortly afterwards and his kids put the two canes in the coffin with him."

I sat there spellbound, wishing I had a handful of tissues but afraid to ask for one for I knew all she had was handkerchiefs. "You are absolutely right, Miz Eudora. That truly is about the sweetest thing I've ever heard."

"Too bad my baby brother couldn't have found someone to love like that. Instead he died an early death 'cause of all that misery and pain he felt every time he got stabbed by that thorn."

Not wishing to rehash that, I excused myself to walk home and bring the car back. We still had a trip to the library. In only one day, she had become quite diligent in finding out about her roots and I wanted to make sure she stayed preoccupied so she didn't focus on "the thorn."

"My wild Irish Rose," I sang as I drove my car back to the Rumph house, "the sweetest flow'r that grows …" *I knew Miz Eudora was Irish! Maybe it was that feisty spirit of hers that gave her away.* I wasn't sure about the sweetest, but she was certainly the most colorful rose in Smackass Gap. And the song was right. "You may search everywhere, but none can compare with my wild Irish rose."

FOUR

To a Wild Rose

STORMS IN THE mountains of North Carolina can be a very ominous threat of nature. They can hover over one area one minute and another area the next. They can circle around and land back where they started. They can dart back and forth between two points. Given that, I'll now explain the next day.

The reverberation of thunder, echoing through the hills, valleys and gaps, literally shook the ground under one's foot. Lightning flashes, bouncing like a cat on a hot tin roof, zapped from the ground, trees or other objects in their way, singeing everything in their path. Drops of rain pelted the earth, the leaves and all the surrounding surfaces, like repeated and percussive strikes of a flurry of mallets on a large kettle-drum. All things considered, storms were much like the aura—at any given time—that hovered over the houses of Miz Eudora Rumph and Mabel Toast ("Mrs. John G.," Mabel liked to emphasize) Jarvis.

That's why there was nothing out of the ordinary during our morning coffee on Miz Eudora's front porch the next day when we heard, "AHH-WHOOP, AHH-WHOOP, AHH-WHOOP!" repeatedly, with Mabel's shrill voice blaring through the cloud of dust that accompanied the startling sound. We'd have thought a siren was coming up the driveway had Mabel's classic yelp not been echoing off the mountains like the roar of thunder, signaling it was the storm's turn to be over the Rumph household on this day.

"What in tarnation are you thunderin' about?" Miz Eudora called out as the car came to a screeching halt.

"For your information, I'll have you know I am not thundering!"

"She's right about that," said Theona Rouette, who was one of Miz Eudora's closest friends and whose grandmother had been an Indian princess. "She's crow …," Her words stopped when she caught sight of Hattie Crow, another of Miz Eudora's dearest friends who was known for her extremely dry wit, staring a hole through her with eagle eyes. These two regulars of our coffee group knew the routine between the two sisters-in-law as well as I did.

"I'll tell you what she's doin'," continued Miz Eudora. "She's hootin' like that old owl out in the barn. It isn't bad enough that she warbles like an old turkey buzzard every Sunday up in the choir. Now she's got to also hoot, and she's not doin' such a hot job of that either."

"Good heavens!" retorted Mabel. "Why, you old goat, who do you think your callin' an old hoot? You don't know anything. Anything at all!"

"I know enough to know that even if I was a goat, I'd be a nanny."

Great! I thought to myself. *Our very own hoot'n'nanny right here in Smackass Gap! Wouldn't that be a match in the choir on Sunday?* The idea of their duo caused me to make a quick dash to the kitchen for more coffee, which was nothing more than an excuse. Had I stayed, they'd have both been angry at my uproar of laughter. "Could I bring you a cup of coffee, Mabel?" I at least had the decency to ask before I reached the front door.

"Yes, Sadie, you certainly may," she answered in her "all-high-and-mighty" voice, as Miz Eudora called it. "Eudora got me so flustered I nearly forgot why I came."

"Good!" roared Miz Eudora. "Maybe you'll just go on ahead and leave since you can't remember why you're here."

With that Hattie and Theona hopped out of their rockers and joined me as I went to the kitchen. Seems I wasn't the only one amused by the banter and in need of an excuse to exit the scene.

"Do you think it's possible for the two of them to get through a day without going off at each other?" asked Theona as we hastily sauntered off toward the kitchen before our laughter erupted like a volcano to go along with the storm brewing on the front porch.

"I don't know," answered Hattie, "but those two can change what they're arguing about more often than I change underwear." Her comment brought another group snicker.

"Some mornings I think I come here just to hear what they'll start a fuss about that day," added Theona.

Come to think of it, I'm not so sure that isn't why I show up here every morning. At least on those mornings when she doesn't reach my house first, I said to myself. *But then, those are the mornings when I know we're in for a hefty sample of a "hissy fit," if not a full-blown "tizzy."*

"That's just the free added attraction for me," stated Hattie. "I still come for the coffee. I've never had coffee as good or as stout as what she makes on top of that pot-bellied stove. One cup of that and you're ready for anything that comes at you during the day."

"Anything except Mabel," I concluded quietly as Miz Eudora came busting through the front door to let off some steam.

"I'm gonna *have* to find a way to take that Mabel out of the contest for our musical director," she stated under her breath, but not nearly quiet enough. Had there been time, I'd have informed her this was for the position of Director of Music for First Church, Smackass, not *American Idol* or some such contestant show, so it wasn't really a contest. But I was too late; she plowed on before I had a chance to open my mouth. "There's got to be some way to take her out of the running." At least that part of her reasoning was right, for it was that precise moment her sister-in-law chose to come "running" through the door, just in time to hear Miz Eudora's next comment. "Land sakes! If that Mabel gets her hand in that music program, our church service will wind up being a dog-and-pony show."

"HMMPH!" retaliated Mabel, who happened to walk in at that exact moment. I wouldn't even consider a dog-and-pony show. Of course, I'd expect no better comparison coming from one whose best friend is a mule named Clyde. Anyone with any sense knows that a dog, not a mule, is man's best friend. Goodness gracious, Eudora Rumph, even *you* ought to have enough sense to know I wouldn't be caught dead doing a regular old dog-and-pony show. If I had anything to do with it, it would be a shih tzu-and-shetland show."

"Need I say more?" asked Miz Eudora, looking in my direction as she pursed her lips and rolled her eyes. "And I thought the dog-and-pony show was bad enough!"

I'm not too sure she had any idea of what Mabel

was talking about, but it didn't matter. She knew enough to know that whatever it was, there was a spectacle to be seen, and the spectacle would be Mabel not the dog, pony, shih tzu or the shetland.

Thankfully Mabel had an appointment, for which it was now Miz Eudora's fault that she was late, so she left exactly as she came…minus the trail of "AHH-WHOOP!" following her all the way back out the driveway. As I watched the cloud of dust eventually disappear down Highway 64 and over Lake Chatuge, I reasoned as how Smackass Gap really did have its own hoot'n'nanny and it was on display at church every Sunday when those two showed up for the service.

"I wish we could pack that Mabel up and send her away," Miz Eudora snapped. It was about that time when a flock of Canadian geese flew overhead, honking loudly with each flap of their wings. "See what I mean?" she continued. "Mabel's just like one of them birds. If she got herself named the new choir director, she'd be up there in front of God and ever'body … at least all the bodies in First Church, Smackass … ever' Sunday, flappin' her arms, which in her case does look like big ol' flaps, and every time she'd flap, she'd be a-honkin'."

What a vividly disastrous picture Miz Eudora had painted for all of us. As I watched the last of the geese flying overhead, all I could see was Mabel's face with wings flapping. My neighbor's description of a Sunday service with Mabel at the helm as the choir director was enough to make me stay home from church, and I was usually now the first person there each week to see what would happen on any given Sunday. However, the thought of Mabel "flappin' and honkin'" was a spectacle even I didn't want to behold. Had a vote been held by the members on the front porch at that moment, Mabel would have been unanimously voted out of "the contest" for which she was "running." But it wasn't us Miz Eudora had to worry about. It was all those members of the Staff Parish Committee who did all the "hirin' and firin'." What I wanted to warn them about was if they went to "hirin'" Mabel, there would be plenty of "firin'" to follow … in the form of Miz Eudora's mouth.

"Sadie, reckon how much a one-way ticket to Canada would cost?" Miz Eudora asked a few moments later.

"I'm not sure," I answered, suspicious of where this sudden and unanticipated line of questioning would lead.

"I'd sure like to buy Mabel a ticket there so she could be up there honkin' with the rest of them geese. You know, she really is just like them. They leave a pile everywhere they land. Nobody wants to walk around behind where they've been."

Hattie and Theona both burst into coughing fits,

excusing themselves and leaving me to deal with the rest of Miz Eudora's latest "hissy fit," which I decided to coin "Mizzy fits" in her case. Her fits were so rampant and "off the wall," I concluded they deserved their own name.

Miz Eudora's words, and the graphic depiction that went along with them, stayed in my mind the whole rest of the day. Even though I tried to follow her good example and offer up a bedtime prayer each evening, it sometimes got left out in the grand scheme of things. And believe me, living in Smackass Gap with my neighbor always entailed a grand scheme of things. But there was no doubt the bedtime prayer was at the forefront of my thoughts on this night. I prayed as fervently, *and desperately*, as I knew how that the Good Lord would not let me have dreams about this situation and that it would fall from my consciousness once I went to sleep.

Oh well, I tried to comfort myself as I climbed into bed and closed my eyes, *we wouldn't have just a hoot'n'nanny. We'd have a "honkin'" hoot'n'nanny. We could advertise in the* Clay County Progress *that we had something no other church in the area had, and people might just "flock" to First Church, Smackass.*

In fact, I suspected half seriously, *it might turn into quite an outreach ministry.* All those "outcasts" in the community—the ones our "fishers of men" were always trying to reel in—might jump right in our pro-verbial nets if we advertised our new worship service as "A Haven for Birds, Dogs and Ponies." *That about covers everyone,* I decided with a chuckle.

The more I thought about it, the more it seemed a creative concept for a new way of reaching people and bringing them into the "net." Suddenly, bringing people into "the fold" had lost its appeal. *Why I'll bet they might even "lure" a few new "honkers" for their new "hoot'n'nanny" choir.*

I lay there and meditated for a bit longer, think-ing about what drew Leon and me to this area, when we'd both decided unanimously on this place to settle for our retirement. It was probably much like what brought those first settlers, Irish and otherwise, to this area. The highest places in all of the Eastern United States were found in the Southern Appalachians, mak-ing some of the mountaintops in this region like is-lands of high-elevation habitat. The wild was home to several unique natural communities, and some spe-cies were indigenous only in this particular area and found nowhere else in the world. Other species, like the least weasel, were also found in colder climates far to the north. I suspected, though, there had been plenty of weasels—least and otherwise—who had passed through Clay County's numerous gaps over time, some of whom were surely kin to Miz Eudora. *And maybe even Calamity Jane. Or worse, Mabel.*

On that note of speculation, I offered one last little prayer, pleading that I'd had "enough nightmares for one day" in my request for a restful night's sleep. The last thing I remembered were soothing strains of Edward MacDowell's *To a Wild Rose* playing in my mind. Like in "Woodland Sketches," his piano suite from which that most famous of his compositions came, sketches of all the "creatures" of Clay County were playing in the woodlands of Smackass Gap, the most noted creature being a wild rose that honked.

FIVE

Blue Spruce or Loose Screws, It All Sounds the Same to Me

BETWEEN MIZ EUDORA digging in her garden and digging at the library, and Mabel busy readying things for her take-over of the choir, life was rolling along as peaceably as possible in Smackass Gap. Or, should I say, at least as peaceably as possible where those two were concerned. I feared all of that was about to change since the proverbial wrecking ball was about to come down and start swinging. The only mention of Mabel and the choir—after Miz Eudora took up genealogy and writing for the newspaper—had been two weeks prior to the current choir director's final Sunday, scheduled to be the last Sunday in February. That's when Miz Eudora approached Mr. Grover Swicegood and proclaimed herself the newly self-appointed Watcher of the Director of Music.

"Somebody's gotta keep an eye on her," I over-heard Miz Eudora telling him that day on my way out of the sanctuary. "Nobody's got the gall to take over the choir for fear they'll have the wrath of that woman on them. Since she's determined to be in charge of the music, I'm determined to be in charge of making sure she don't have us singin' some alien stuff like they do down at that church where she went in Myers Park over in Charlotte."

I'm not sure what had surprised me more about her statement to him, what she said or her having any knowledge of aliens. It didn't really matter what she said. No one "had a hankerin'" to ruffle her feathers anymore than they did to ruffle Mabel's. Thus, First Church, Smackass, now had a new choir director and a new watcher of the choir director. The thought made me wonder whether I should get Miz Eudora a little brass badge that said, "Music Police." Being it was still a couple of weeks away before the retiring Direc-tor of Music was to step down, I decided the best thing to do was let sleeping dogs lie. Therefore, not another word about it was mentioned from either party until the day Mabel officially stepped up to the plate, which in this case was the director's podium.

Her first act as the newly self-appointed Direc-tor of Music was to call a special rehearsal on the first Saturday morning after she took over the position. "To-day I'm going to teach you the technique of making beautiful music together," she announced when everyone had taken their respective seats in the choir room.

I need to point out here that since Mabel's arrival in Smackass Gap, the church had acquired their own choir room, complete with a pole running the entire length of one of the walls, where the members' robes hung. Over the pole, a wall-length shelf had been added, and slotted, so above each robe was a cubby that held a black choral folder, filled with octavos, for that robe's owner. We were now "downtown," thanks to Mabel's influence—*or rather, insistence*—and gifts to the music fund to make sure her wishes came to fruition. Oh, and about that comment about us being "downtown." Because of our proximity in the lay of the land in Clay County, it might be more appropriate to say our church was "uptown." But no matter whether it was up or down, it was most definitely out of the ordinary, and certainly different than it had ever been before, now that Miz Eudora's sister-in-law had taken up residence and become involved in the music program. Now that you understand that, you're ready for the rest of the story.

Mabel had the group "warming up" with a whole array of vocal exercises on "ah" before changing to lots of other syllables. She had the singers running syllables up and down the scale, or at least she called it "a scale." Considering Mrs. Azalee didn't know a scale from a fin, and she most certainly did not know how to do chord progressions to work her way up and down the scales, she was unable to play for the choir. She could play anything by ear, but she—like the rest of the choir—had never heard these "vocal exercises" before, so she had no ear for them.

"If Mabel keeps this up, they'll be worn out before they even get to sing their first song," Miz Eudora leaned over and shared with me, and anyone else who cared to hear it, which included Mabel, who sent her the usual condescending glare. Since Miz Eudora had appointed herself as the person to report back to the church council on how things were going in the music department, she insisted that she and I had every right to be there to witness the first rehearsal. I hastily reminded her that I was certain proper rehearsal etiquette included sitting quietly during one in progress. My action, I must admit, was more to ward off a funeral of one of the two women in question than my concern for the choir members.

"Now," said Mabel, changing her glare into a warm smile as she looked out over her assembled "flock," "for our final vocal exercise, we're going to sing a familiar tune, the one you typically sing for the hymn *Blest Be the Tie*, only we're going to use the words 'Blue Spruce' all the way through. Like this." She looked at Mrs. Azalee. "Could you give me a B above Middle C, please?"

After hearing the note, she began to demonstrate the tune, using only a repetition of the two words on the first line of the music. "You get the idea. Now let's do it together."

She picked up her baton from the conductor's black metal stand and pointed it in Mrs. Azalee's direction. When nothing happened, she pointed it again.

Mrs. Azalee gave her usual tender smile and pointed back, using the pencil on the music rack of her piano.

Giving a disconcerted huff, Mabel roared, "Could you give me that same B, please?"

"Why didn't you just say so?" asked Mrs. Azalee, in a polite lyrical tone, as she bobbed her head and flashed her smile in the choir's direction.

"HMMPH!" I heard from Mabel while she beat the baton on the lip of the music stand several times. She lifted the baton in her right hand, raising her left hand at the same time, as she gave the upbeat to bring the choir in. The singers actually came in at the same time and on the same pitch, or at least as close as they were going to get to it. There were two brothers, a tenor and a bass, both of whom were slightly—*no, majorly*—off pitch.

"Poor things," observed Miz Eudora with a shake of her head. "They couldn't find a pitch between them, even if it was floating atop my big black wash pot."

About the time the choir reached the end of the first line, I detected something amiss among the singers. "Oh, that's just Hazeline," Miz Eudora informed me when she saw the troubled expression on my face. "She's the woman who sits in front of us every Sunday and can't ever hear the right words. Our old director wouldn't let her sing, so she decided to give it a whirl 'agin' now that Mabel was takin' over and sendin' out open invitations for all who were interested to join the choir."

A closer listen told me Hazeline was mistakenly singing "Loose screw, loose screw, loose screw" instead of "Blue spruce, blue spruce, blue spruce."

"Seems she's the only one in here who really knows what's goin' on," Miz Eudora added with a relatively big chuckle. "She always has been known to call it as she sees it." That comment, which also didn't go unnoticed by Mabel, received another haughty glare, this one more menacing than the first.

From there, the rehearsal went downhill in a hurry. "We don't even have an anthem ready to sing tomorrow," complained one of the members.

"We could just sing 'Blue Spruce' and tell them we're getting an early start on Christmas," commented another.

"Or we could sing *Just a Little Talk with Jesus*," added one of the basses. "That's one we basses can really sink our teeth into and we do it every time we don't have something ready to sing on Sunday."

"They need more than just a *little* talk with Jesus," blurted out Miz Eudora. "That brother who sings the bass part is so bad, even one of Theona's prayer chains couldn't get him caught up. If he's not on the wrong note, he's on the wrong word. Land sakes! Sometimes he's even on the wrong line." She took a deep breath and kept going, as if the air she'd just taken in had also brought an accompanying fresh thought. "Maybe if he'd sink his teeth in it instead of his voice, it wouldn't be so bad. Why doesn't someone suggest to him to take a bite out of the music instead of singin' it?"

By this time there was an upheaval of laughter in the room. As if Mabel hadn't already lost control of the group, Hazeline, having only understood the bit about taking bites, asked, "What did they say we were eating for lunch on Sunday? I didn't know we were having a meal after church. I'll be glad to make one of my pineapple pound cakes."

"While that brother is busy taking bites," stated Miz Eudora, "Hazeline ought to keep to baking desserts for all our get-togethers. I'm sure the choir can find a job for that brother who sings tenor. Maybe he can park cars or something."

"That's it!" shouted Mabel. "I'll sing a solo tomorrow and we'll prepare a choral piece on Wednesday evening at your regularly scheduled rehearsal to sing for the next Sunday." Her words were lost as everyone placed their black folders in their cubbies above their robes and exited the choir room, each one giving an opinion about what he or she thought the choir should sing the next day.

"I think the idea of a covered dish lunch was a good idea myself," was the last thing I heard as Hazeline got in her car to go home and make her pineapple pound cake.

"Oh well," Miz Eudora said as we climbed in my car. "The choir will enjoy Hazeline's cake. You and I will come early tomorrow morning. You be in charge of making coffee for the choir to go along with the cake, and I'll take care of Mabel."

Those last five words meant only one thing, to which I neither made a comment nor asked a question. I was too busy counting the days until the Ides of March, and contemplating whether like Shakespeare's play, *Julius Caesar*, Smackass Gap needed its own soothsayer standing atop Chunky Gal Mountain warning, "Beware the Ides of March." My only dilemma was whether the warning should be for Miz Eudora, Mabel, myself, First Church or the entire community within earshot of Chunky Gal Mountain. Finally reasoning the latter choice was probably the best, I forced my mind to think of more pleasant things than either Julius Caesar, Miz Eudora or Mabel. *And especially that choir rehearsal!*

I had to admit the choir rehearsal, with all that talk about blue spruces, did put me in the frame of mind to get a head start on my Christmas shopping. After dropping Miz Eudora off, I headed for a peacefully quiet afternoon in Helen, Georgia, with all its beautiful Bavarian shops, while singing intermittent phrases of "Blue Spruce" and "Loose Screw" along the way. I decided to suggest that option to Mabel for the choir's next rehearsal.

Or at least her next attempt at making them sing those vocal exercises!

SIX

Top o' the Mornin'

"TOP O' THE mornin' to you, my dear Sadie!" Miz Eudora announced. There was a noticeable clip to her step as she bounced up my front porch steps on the Monday morning following the infamous choir rehearsal.

"Top o' the mornin' to you," I replied, wondering what had brought about her cheerful disposition, but not brave enough to ask. Although I was extremely grateful for the change in her demeanor from the day before, I began to mentally question whether this was the real Eudora Rumph or if Mabel had kidnapped my neighbor and sent someone else in her stead. *Perhaps the Ides of March came early in Smackass Gap and this is the result!* However, a scrutinizing glance assured me this was indeed the woman I had first met upon my arrival in Smackass Gap, and a reality check told me there could be no other like Eudora Rumph, no matter how badly Mabel might have wished it. Now my concern was what could have possibly happened to make Miz Eudora this ecstatic, especially given the solo by Mabel at yesterday's service following the rehearsal the day before that. *If this is any hint of what's to come on the Ides of March, I'm outta here!* I told myself, remembering it was only two weeks until that noted day. *Even I'm not brave enough to stay around and see the outcome.* I considered excusing myself from her presence and checking the web for local soothsayers to warn the locals to beware, but decided to at least wait out this visit in order to make some sense out of what was going on.

Another glance showed her dancing eyes matched her jovial spirit, hinting that all was going to be well on this day in Smackass Gap. You know the old saying, "If Ma ain't happy, ain't nobody happy." That's exactly how it was with our front porch morning get-togethers. It didn't much matter whether it was my porch or her porch, and the weather made no difference "a-tall." The deciding factor for the day's outlook was whether Miz Eudora was happy or not. From her appearance and words, it looked to be the start of an extraordinarily beautiful day. As the trademarked decals and shirts sold in Rob Tiger's Chinquapin's said, "Life is good."

My face apparently mirrored my confusion, for

she began to explain, "I'm practicin' some of the Irish expressions I still remember hearing from my ma in my growin' up years. She had the most beautiful way of speaking, with the words just rollin' off her tongue. Even her phrases had a rhythm about them, much like the river dances. Ay, how I did love to hear her." She became quiet and I could sense she was in a pleasant daydream of fond memories, in which I let her bask as I went to "fetch" her coffee.

When you consider it was after my suggestion that Miz Eudora take up looking into the genealogy of her family, I reckon what happened next could be deemed my fault. I highly suspect the fact that it had been "one humdinger of a winter," with the coldest temperatures and the most snow Clay County residents had seen in years, was also a deciding factor in my neighbor's need to see green. And I'm not talking just the "green, green grass of home." I'm talking sham-rocks and leprechauns.

"You ever been to Savannah?" she questioned as I returned to the porch and handed her the large mug.

"Savannah, Georgia?" I clarified.

"That's right, where they have the big St. Patrick goings-on."

"Yes, I have," I said with a reflective smile. "It is … was … one of my favorite places to go whenever Leon would get a couple of days off. There is such a rich culture in that city."

"And there's a whoppin' big pile of Irishmen, too, from what I've been learnin' at the library. I'd forgotten the whole of the story about St. Patrick, but thanks to all this genealogy stuff you've given me a hankerin' to discover...,"

There was no need for her to complete the sentence. I knew where this was leading. A trip to Savannah, and I was going to take her. *What have you gotten yourself into, Sadie Callaway? Why didn't you merely suggest she get involved in the prayer shawl ministry or something simple?* I sat there, gazing at her beautiful Irish eyes that were indeed smiling, ablaze with an unruly zest for life. That's when I realized even such a seemingly simple project as a prayer shawl ministry would have sent us on a mission journey to the other side of the country, if not the world, to deliver the finished shawls. Either way, it seemed, I was doomed to an unpredictable adventure with this twosome. That became inevitable the day I moved to Smackass Gap. *No,* I corrected myself, *the day* Mabel *moved to Smackass Gap!* My daydream was interrupted by the question she posed to me with the conclusion of her words.

"... I've learned that Savannah has the second largest St. Patrick's Day parade in the entire United States. Mary showed me this story on her computer yesterday what said they had 300,000 visitors last year for it. You know what that means, don't you?"

The only thing—or at least the most critical thing—it meant to me was that Miz Eudora was "a-mind" to go to Savannah, which also meant one other small thing: I would have to take her. Yet, out of force of habit, I responded with, "What?" I would have given anything could I have retrieved that one word before it hit the air, but as it was, I saw myself now past the point of no return.

"It means if St. Patrick was able to get rid of all those snakes single-handedly, or at least with a little help from God, he can surely get rid of one Mabel."

Like my word, "what," I wished I'd never heard those words hit the air. "Uhhhh," was the only sound I could manage to get to escape my lips, which was okay with Miz Eudora, for she took it as an emphatic, "Ah, yes, I'm right there with you!"

The next thing I know, she was laying out plans of when we'd go and what she would pack for a picnic lunch, complete with goose liver sandwiches. At that point, I was grateful Mabel would be going. I hoped she would bring along her usual appetite so she would also eat my helping of the sandwiches. There was a single simple matter, though, that threatened to blow Miz Eudora's scheme out of the water. You see, it never failed that if Miz Eudora wanted to slip away, Mabel always found out and showed up at the final destination. That's if she didn't manage to arrive on my doorstep and be the first one in the car on the morning of departure. Thus, I ironically deduced it would be just my neighbor's luck to invite her sister-in-law on this "little jaunt" and receive a firm refusal. I don't know why I bothered to have that thought, for I was continually proven wrong when it came to that pair. I guess it was because, in my wildest dreams, I could not even fathom what might conceivably happen when you put those two together.

Such was the case when Mabel arrived a few minutes later to join our coffee circle. I volunteered to get her morning dose of caffeine so I could stand right inside the screen door in case fur started to fly. Rather, as I swiftly took my stance within eavesdropping distance, I heard Miz Eudora politely offer her invitation. "I'm going to Savannah to celebrate my Irish heritage. Would you like to join me?"

The air of grumpiness, which typically followed Mabel up the steps like the trail of dust behind Charles Schultz's famed Pigpen character, dissolved as did her pompous grunt that usually greeted us. "Ah, Savannah!" she softly exclaimed with a wistful sigh. "One of my favorite places. John G. took me there a couple of times for a quiet getaway."

The look of horror that erupted on Miz Eudora's face, along with the sudden loss of her rosy color, caused me to hastily deliver Mabel's coffee and free my hands in case I needed to catch my neighbor on her way to the wooden-slatted porch floor. She took my arm and led me through the front door and to the depths of the kitchen, at the back of the house, where she got right in my face and whispered, "Did you hear that? My baby brother done took her there, more than once even, and tried to get rid of her." She shook her head in disbelief. "I never saw nothin' I didn't think Horace's special blend couldn't cure, and now to think St. Patrick hasn't even been successful yet …," Her words trailed off as she obviously fell deep into thought. "We're gonna have to get a pile of prayers goin' in behind St. Patrick if he's gonna pull this off."

She took off toward her bedroom, like a train engine suddenly lurching forward, and grabbed her purple fopher coat. Following her to the front of the house, where her bedroom stood across from the living room, both of which were just inside the front door, I asked, "Where are you headed off to?"

"I gotta get hold of Preacher Jake right away. I need the biggest prayer chain Smackass Gap has ever see'd." Miz Eudora stopped in her tracks as her right hand hit the front door to push it open. "Better yet, I'd better trek over to Theona's house first. She's got the best prayer connection with the Almighty of anybody I've ever see'd. Between that, and all those things she's got in that ceremonial bag of hers she inherited from her grandmother who was a Cherokee princess, who inherited it from her father the chief, Theona ought to be able to get us some powerful groundwork laid. Can you run me over there, Sadie?"

She didn't wait for an answer as she shoved the screen door open and swiftly made her way past Mabel and down the steps. "Don't go away, Mabel. It's just I forgot one small item of plannin' before I give you the final details of the trip. We'll be back directly and I'll fill you in on all the particulars. There's plenty of coffee on the wood-stove. Help yourself."

Even Mabel, in her "better than everyone else" mode, should have realized something was up if Miz Eudora told her to "Help yourself" with anything concerned with the Rumph household. My neighbor had long before sworn her sister-in-law as off-limits to helping herself, saying, "There's no way in tarnation I'd ever let that cussed Mabel loose on my property. She'd pilfer through ever'thing I got."

I secretly suspected she'd have been more concerned about Mabel finding the last of the stash of Horace's "special blend," since he was no longer around to make more and Miz Eudora had already blown out the back of the oldest barn in Clay County trying to copy his recipe.

None of that mattered on this "top o' the mornin'," as we sped off with Miz Eudora sitting in the front passenger seat, her head bowed, her eyes closed and her hands firmly clasped and flailing wildly. *Oh, well*, I mused, *at least she knows this is one time she's not in charge. I reckon she also expects the Good Lord to also keep Mabel from pilfering.*

It was less than forty-five minutes until we were back in tow with Theona Rouette and Hattie Crow, Miz Eudora's closest confidantes, both of whom she'd first met and picked up in the local Ingle's grocery store like two stray cats. Because our morning promised to be longer than a morning coffee chat, we moved our usual venue of conversation to the living room in front of the dying embers in the fireplace, where Mabel comfortably plopped herself. After we were all settled in with a fresh mug of coffee, Miz Eudora unveiled her plan of taking a trip to Savannah for St. Patrick's Day, minus the real reason of why she was going there.

After she gave us all a remedial lesson on the virtues of the saint, Theona, in reply, asked, "And do you want to know who else is there? Well, he isn't really there, but I hear tell there's a statue of him there." Before giving anyone an opportunity to answer, she burst forth with, "John Wesley!" She said it with such exuberated force that I sensed she could have just as easily been Ed McMahon announcing, "Here's Johnny!" I halfway expected to see Wesley himself, black robe and all, holding a Bible in his hand as he appeared from behind a curtain.

"He's no saint," declared Mabel, in such a thunderous voice that it struck Theona's sweet-voiced comment like an arrow, thrusting it into bits as it fell to the ground.

"No, he's a Methodist," stated Miz Eudora.

My resulting chuckle was unsuccessful in its attempt to stay quiet. Because my deceased husband, Leon, had taught at Emory University—a fine upstanding Methodist institution—in Atlanta, Georgia, I knew a little of the background on Wesley and, therefore unsure which way it was headed, considered it best to nip this conversation promptly in the bud. "John Wesley was no more Methodist than Jesus was Christian." That blunt comment captured the attention of both sisters-in-law as they now stared, bug-eyed, at me. Obviously I had made a bold proclamation which, from their expressions, had never been considered by either of them.

Theona, who was wise not only in her prayer chain capabilities, let her soft voice educate the pair as she informed them that the two men were purely the founders of their respective movements. "John Wesley was actually Anglican and served as the rector at the famed Christ Church in Savannah."

I was grateful she was such a learned woman, and one who was wise in the ways of how to present her knowledge. I, on the other hand, would have probably said it in such a way that both Mabel and Miz Eudora would have clobbered me for sounding so "I told you so."

Theona's brief, but timely, words concluded

with the famous quote by Wesley, "Do all the good you can, by all the means you can, in all the ways you can, in all the places you can, at all the times you can, to all the people you can, as long as ever you can."

I could tell from the look on Miz Eudora's face that Wesley's directive was exactly what she thought she was trying to accomplish by escorting Mabel to Savannah for the St. Patrick's celebration. "St. Patrick might not actually be there, but all the vibes from his persona, not to mention the ones from John Wesley still present and accounted for at Christ Church, must surely be good for something," she later told me in her explanation of why she was so sure her plan would work. I was so "taken aback" by her use of the word "persona," and where she'd learned it, that I never once considered her plan to be without merit.

As I contemplated on her unlikely words—particularly "persona"—that evening as I retired to bed, I said my own prayer of thanks that, in the course of Theona's bold and intelligent explanation of Wesley and the Methodist movement, she never once mentioned Sophia Hopkey. That, I feared, could have started a whole 'nother movement inside the living room of Miz Eudora Rumph.

"Whew!" I ended my prayer, but instead of with the usual "Amen!" I added a quick postscript to include that the next day, and those following, would also begin with a "Top o' the mornin'!"

That caused me to think of my shamrocks and how their leaf formations closed at night. Maybe Miz Eudora would be better off praying that Mabel would be like a shamrock and close up from dusk 'til dawn. Somehow I felt she'd be as likely to have that happen as she would having St. Patrick run her sister-in-law out of Smackass Gap. I decided not to mention that preposterous thought to my neighbor. Otherwise, I was afraid she'd change her prayer request to a permanent solar eclipse to hang over Clay County so it would be dark all the time. With that, I thanked my lucky stars and decided it best to be content with a "Top o' the mornin'!"

Oh, and in case you're wondering, I did find out the reason behind it being such a "top o' the mornin'" for Miz Eudora. It seems the current Director of Music decided to stay on until the 4th of July, following the fiasco of Mabel's first rehearsal. Not to mention the solo she sang on the Sunday following the rehearsal. The solo did, however, go along perfectly with the sermon, which happened to be about Abraham and the offering of Isaac. There was only one slight discrepancy. There was redemption for poor Isaac. There was none for the solo. It was slaughtered all the way to the altar! *Not to mention throughout the rest of the sanctuary. Not one soul present was spared, and all ears were sacrificed for the sake of Mabel's special music, which was indeed blood-curdling.*

There was one other small tidbit regarding the choir director's decision to stay until July 4th. Although it had nothing at all to do with St. Patrick, it had everything to do with green. The "greenbacks" that Miz Eudora gave her to stay on a while longer, that is. Needless to say, I was able to do away with my notion of being on the lookout for a soothsayer, who I feared might appear atop Chunky Gal Mountain warning, "Beware the Ides of March." However that brought about a new worry—"the rocket's red glare" and "the bombs bursting in air," come July 4th.

Forget it, Sadie, I heard from that small inside voice. *Go to sleep before it* is *the "top o' the mornin'!"*

SEVEN

Oh, I Want to Be in That Number

MIZ EUDORA WOUND up making a daily schedule of which cemeteries we were going to visit to learn about those "dear saints who had passed on" from the Peay, Jarvis and Rumph families. It wasn't such a bad way to pass the days, for each excursion included a picnic basket filled with a variety of Miz Eudora's prize-winning culinary specialties. I was happy to trek among the graves in search of her ancestors, just to walk off all the calories she piled on us every day. There was only one problem with our excursions. We learned there were more sinners than saints buried throughout those patches of ground. And I don't mean just your plain old sinners; there were plenty of "outright lyin', cheatin', cussin' scoundrels" from the past. At least that's what Miz Eudora called them.

For some reason, I had it in my head that once a person died, people stood up and told nothing but nice things about them. I guess that only lasted until the eulogy was over, or at least in Miz Eudora's case. She gave me the bottom-line "to the core" history of every person buried in Clay County, "and parts around," whether they were her kin or not. Thus, the days were as colorful as they were delicious. But I will have to say, at the end of each day, she'd always put the dear souls we'd discovered on that excursion back to rest with "Bless their hearts" or "They meant well," which I quickly learned is what one says when he or she can't think of anything nice to say about a person. Likewise, that was Miz Eudora's way, obviously passed down from all those generations of saints and sinners in her family, of redeeming each soul.

All that aside, Miz Eudora found little in her past that she considered to be worthwhile until one morning when she stumbled across something, thanks to Mary's wonderful assistant, while at the library. "Would you look at this?" she called to me as I read through a new magazine. As I approached the computer where she was reading some information, which the library assistant had discovered for her, she read aloud, "Eudora means 'good gift.'" She flashed the biggest smile as she looked at me and proclaimed excitedly, "I'm a good gift, Sadie. That's why my parents named me that. I guess that means they really wanted a child to have named me that." She was so proud that I halfway expected to see tears of joy glisten in her eyes.

I don't know who was more anxious to share that news with Mabel. Miz Eudora was more anxious to share it; I was more anxious to see the look on her sister-in-law's face. I figured together we'd have to catch her when she passed out from hearing that revelation.

"And look at this," she continued, "the last name Peay means one who lived at the sign of the peacock. I wonder if that's how the Peacock Playhouse got its name. Maybe once upon a time one of my ma's ancestors lived where the Peacock Playhouse sign hangs now." Before I had time to ask, she informed me, "My relatives on my pa's side came from Northern Yorkshire, where there was a Cistercian monastery." Given the fact she had a rather difficult time pronouncing the type of monastery it was, I figured she didn't have a clue what that was. But from the way she was sitting—proud as a peacock, no less—it must have sounded important to her.

"Can you read this next part to me, Sadie? There must have been some foreigners in my family tree somewhere 'cause I can't quite make out this next part."

I saw no need to explain to her that, unlike Theona who was part American Indian, most all of us in Smackass Gap had some "foreigners" in our family trees. That was the topic of a deep discussion for another day's "trekin'" through the cemeteries. "'The Jarvis family came from Jervaulx,' which is pronounced Jarvis just like your maiden name. It looks like Jarvis has a compound meaning, meaning there is a meaning for each syllable of the word," I explained. "The first half, 'Jar,' appears to be named for Northern Yorkshire's river Ure, and 'vis' is a derivative of 'vaulx,' which means valley.

"So Jarvis means a river valley, kind of like Lake Chatuge," she concluded with great pleasure, resembling a young child who's just made an important discovery. Then she looked a bit perplexed. "Except Lake Chatuge is man-made," she added, "and it wasn't here when all them people came over from Northern Yorkshire." Her facial expression mirrored the inquisitiveness going on inside her mind. "Oh well, I guess the Tennessee River was close enough to here when they came over to make them think it was like over there." With that, she appeared quite pleased with herself again.

"It goes on to say that 'Jarvis comes from the given name of Gervaise, which is an English form of the German name Gervasius,' which comes from the two words meaning 'spear' and 'vase.'

"Well there you go," she said, with amazing comprehension of what I'd just said, although I wasn't sure I understood. "No wonder I was drawn to that vase the day you took me with Hattie to my first yard sale. It's too bad they didn't have a spear, too, so I could have gone ahead and taken care of Mabel to start with. Then we wouldn't have to be a-goin' through all of this right now and I could be gettin' my fields plowed and ready for plantin'."

I never was sure of her reasoning, but she always managed to come up with a good point, no matter how flawed it first appeared. That was obviously enough information for her to muddle over for one day, for she bid her farewells to Mary and the library staff and walked out the door. I couldn't tell from her reaction whether she was glad to be "in that number" of those in the Peay and Jarvis families who had settled here or not. As I followed her to the car, I quickly assessed that she was anxious to go share the meaning of her name with Mabel. *That ought to be good for a few fireworks,* I mused with a grain of humor, certain that I wanted to be "in that number" who was present when Miz Eudora shared that news.

WHILE THEONA WAS known to be the peacemaker, it was Hattie who was the social secretary of our five-member group. That's why I should not have been at all surprised when the two of them showed up on my doorstep just as Miz Eudora and I were coming home from our morning of "diggin'" at the cemetery. Hattie barely gave us time to unload the picnic basket from the car before she instigated the suggestion, "Why don't we invite Miz Eudora's Red Hatter friends to join us in Savannah? Those ladies are so much fun. They surely do know how to have a good time." My urge, to remind Hattie this was a "mission trip"—the mission being to discourage Mabel from taking over the choir—and not for playing and making merry, did not take root fast enough. Before I had a chance to communicate that bit of trivia, the three of them were already giving enthusiastic nods accompanied by expressions of approval.

"Especially all those Georgia ladies," Theona chimed in.

"And since the place we're going is in Georgia, they're already halfway there," Hattie commented, not taking into account that some points of the state were as far away from Savannah as Smackass Gap. Besides, this was meant to be a "mission trip," the mission being to get Mabel back from whence she came. So for Theona and Hattie, at least for the moment, it seemed they had traded their thinking caps for red hats. They both should have known better than to lead us into such a dangerous predicament. And talk about caps and hats, there was no telling where Miz Eudora's head would be if all those ladies showed up. She'd be so engrossed in having fun with them that she'd forget all about "the snake in the grass we're goin' to have driven out of Smackass Gap." From the looks of the way things were headed, the way Mabel was "goin' to be driven out of Smackass Gap" was in the back seat of my car on the way to Savannah. *The same way she'll be driven back to Smackass Gap,* I feared, given the direction of the ongoing comments.

"It will be int'restin' to see where Carly has her underwear this time and which way she's wearin' her clothes," stated Miz Eudora, indicating that she was already on board with Hattie's idea. "Remember how she had her t-shirt on back'ards that first time she came here? Said she wuz always bass ack'ards!"

Why I didn't open my mouth to object was beyond me. I guess I was too busy thinking how I should have been the one wearing the shirt backwards because "bass ack'ards" was how this day—which was on the heels of the "top o' the mornin'" day—was headed. In merely a matter of minutes, I'd gone from enjoying some of the best food Smackass Gap had to offer to being roped into a scheme that was past the point of no return.

Needless to say, the remainder of the day was spent calling, writing and e-mailing Miz Eudora's ever-increasing list of contacts. The duty of contacting everyone fell to Theona, Hattie and me while Miz Eudora went home to finish making plans, which included how to coax Mabel into going since this wasn't her idea.

Theona wrote notes, Hattie called and I took the chore of e-mailing those with internet addresses.

Before the afternoon was over, we'd already received several phone and online responses, many of the ladies ready to hit the road. Shortly after Theona's notes had time to reach mailboxes, responses from "takers" were coming in daily. It wasn't long before two chartered buses were filled with passengers traveling from seven states. I had to hand it to Miz Eudora. She had a prayer warrior (literally), a social networker, a saint, and God all working in her favor, not to mention nearly a hundred women with raging, out-of-kilter hormones and hot flashes. One of those options, if not a combination of all of them, could surely handle Mabel. After all, all Miz Eudora cared about was sending her back "from whence she came," but at the very least, making sure she didn't take over the music at First Church, Smackass.

How difficult could that be? I asked myself, trying to feel some positive note. *Maybe we'll have time to have fun and make merry with that bunch of ladies after all.* A part of me wanted to jump up and down at the thought of a road trip, but the skeptical side kept my feet on the ground and my thoughts troubled. Troubled to the point I felt I was caught up in the words of *When the Saints Go Marchin' In*.

Even though my husband had been on the staff at Emory University, and had spoken occasionally at religious functions, I had not been much of a church goer in my adult life before getting tied up with Miz Eudora, and "tied up" was exactly how I felt at the moment. Whether I liked it or not, I saw myself caught up in the number of folks who would be marchin' into the streets of Savannah the weekend prior to St. Patrick's Day. However, unlike the song, I was not singing, "O Lord, I want to be in that number." The fact of the matter was, I wanted to be anywhere *but* in that number!

I had, on the other hand, been acquainted with the town of New Orleans, thanks to my love of Dixieland and Jazz. Leon took me there every five years or so to feed my fettish for its food and music. Preservation Hall was among my favorite stops, so I knew all too well about the origin and some of the history of *When the Saints Go Marchin' In* which, contrary to what many of the Saints' fans there think, was not written for their football team's grand entrance to the field. I'm sure, considering they finally got their first Superbowl win, I'd have a hard time convincing some fans of that.

Considered to have been originally written as a funeral march for slaves following the Civil War, I knew *When the Saints* had its roots in Mississippi or Louisiana, depending on whose word you took. I also knew it was played by instruments that could be carried and played, following the coffin. The tradition

was to play it slowly, like the funeral dirge it was written to be, on the way to the cemetery, and to play it
"hot"—as some called it—on the way back from the
cemetery, giving praise and joy that the deceased was
now among "the saints."

Then when the piece became so popular that
jazz musician Louis Armstrong recorded it in 1938, it
grew to be sung in every genre by all types of musicians, to the point that New Orleans' musicians grew
to hate playing it because it was requested so many
times. That tidbit of useless knowledge brought to
mind the fee sign I remembered hanging in Preservation Hall from my first visit there. It read, "$1 for stan-
dard requests, $2 for unusual requests, and $5 for 'The
Saints.'" The price had gone up to $10 the last time I
was there.

*It's a good thing you don't have to pay to hear
it in your mind*, I noted, listening to the verses in my
head. *No matter the cost at this point,* I decided as it
played repeatedly in my mind. *For three reasons.* First,
I was beginning to feel like a slave to Miz Eudora on
this mission. I was not at all in favor of it, although
my inner self was always ready for another jaunt to
Savannah. Second, I loved "hot" jazz and Dixieland
music and never minded paying the fee to hear it, so
hearing it free in my mind was a good thing (although
I was prone to finding a jazz funeral procession on
my ventures to New Orleans' to get the real flavor of

When the Saints). Third, I think it was my subconscious telling me I wanted no part of this number, saints or otherwise.

So there you go, Sadie. Two votes against, one vote for. And you're going why?

I sat alone on my front porch that evening, letting my eyes stare haphazardly across the road and over the Rumph farm. As I looked at the mountain that backed her yard in the distance, I noted a peep of light, peeking through the window of a house seated just below the mountain's peak. That was Mabel's chalet, and there was no doubt in my mind she was seated by that light, busy with two items of agenda: one, looking down on her "lowly sister-in-law," and the other, planning what she would do come July when she would finally secure the coveted position as the new music director. It mattered not that she was the only person who coveted it; it was nonetheless coveted. It was also her way of putting herself in charge, which she liked to be, just like her notion of putting her house in that exact location of John G.'s inherited property so she could look down on Miz Eudora, "in every sense of the word," she was fond of saying.

I allowed my eyes to gaze up into the sky, at the stars raining light down in the darkness of the last of the evenings of a still-winter sky, which is an unbelievably breathtaking sight from the higher Appalachian elevations. I prayed those same stars also rained down some glorious scheme for making Mabel think she was in charge of the upcoming trip. I left my concerns to the One whom I knew was ultimately in charge of this entire saga, with a little help from a prayer warrior, a social networker, a saint and all those women. Figuring that to be enough help for "the Good Lord," I went back to basking in the situation at hand. It wouldn't be long until I would be able to hear the crickets, their voices chirping their "hot" rendition of whatever it was they sang, and imagined Miz Eudora and her Smackass crew along with all the ladies who would show up in red hats, who most certainly would be "hot" even without the instruments. Their flashes were all they needed.

Face it, Sadie. Like it or not, you are goin' to be in that number! I guess when you considered whether you'd rather be among the number laid to rest in the cemetery, or the number of ladies in red and purple going to Savannah, it no longer seemed so bad.

EIGHT

All That (Sparkles Ain't) Jazz

THERE WAS ONLY one last item of agenda to be
handled before we would be ready to head off for a
fun, and hopefully successful, mission trip to Savannah: informing Mabel we were all soon to be off for a
"green" adventure with two busloads of red-and-purple
clad "hot" ladies.

"Eudora Rumph, if you think I'm taking one
step with you inside Savannah, you'd better think
again. Why, you'll be the laughing stock of the whole
city if you go down there dressed in that ridiculous
purple fopher coat of yours, not to mention the rest of
that horrible get-up you wear with it. So if you have
any notion that I'm going to be seen with you, you'd
better get yourself some new clothes."

"What they'll think she is," contradicted Hattie,
"is artistic," but her words were to no avail. They were

lost underneath the heavy cloud of scorn Mabel had just created. Along with the gloom and doom that now hung over the living room of the Rumph house was the heat rising between the two sisters-in-law, making it feel like a blazing inferno. It couldn't have been worse had a fire-breathing dragon come tromping its way down Highway 64.

"Yes," stated Mabel, nodding her head as if to add credibility, "what you need is a whole new wardrobe." She pivoted her body around until she was staring directly into Miz Eudora's face, whose brow was furrowed and lips were pursed.

Mabel, tilting her head down as she raised her eyebrows over her glasses, basked in this moment of putting the "quietus" on her sister-in-law. I must admit, it was a vision to behold for she rarely got the upper hand. *Or more astounding, the last word*, I reminded myself. A quick glance toward Hattie and Theona told me I wasn't the only one who had noticed this rare moment in Smackass Gap history. At first, I toyed with the idea it was out of respect for her baby brother that Miz Eudora sat there speechless. But once I got over the initial shock, I knew exactly what was going on and understood her tactic. There was no way she was going to let Mabel weasel out of going to Savannah. She also understood Mabel was bluffing, for there was no way she'd stay home. Why, a team of Clay County's best mules wouldn't be able to keep her out of my car when it came time to go. I glanced back to Hattie and Theona, both of whom were still dumbfounded by the silence in the air.

"Now, shall I go shopping for you or are you capable of picking out some suitable attire for yourself?" Mabel questioned as she opened the front door, making it known she had no intention of going shopping with Miz Eudora, but that when my car left, Miz Eudora had best be dressed in some new garb.

The slamming of the door behind Mabel caused enough of a vibration to shoot holes in the cloud that had minutes earlier smothered not only the air, but also the life, out of the Rumph house. It wasn't until she was in her car and halfway out the driveway before Miz Eudora let out her trademark cackle.

Theona's eyes bulged out of her head as Hattie asked, "What got into you back there? I can't believe you just sat there and let her talk to you like that. I was ready to call Preacher Jake, right after I called 911, because I was sure you'd quit breathing."

"She had my goat for a minute, but then I did exactly what Pa taught me. 'If you give a body enough rope, they'll hang themselves.' In her case, it's more like if you let her rattle on long enough, she'll run on long enough to show how really stupid she is. And by jiggers, it worked. She rattled, she ran and she showed. Now all she needs is a dunce hat."

"I don't get it, Miz Eudora," said Theona. "She

rattled and ran alright, but what did she show?"

"I'll tell you what she showed," Hattie began to answer. "She showed her ..."

"Hattie!" I screamed. I wasn't sure how vocal she was about to become, but I had a good feeling.

"Well ..." she hem-hawed, "... you know what I mean. I know she's your sis ... I know she married your baby brother, whom you dearly adored, Miz Eudora, but sometimes that Mabel is more of an ... an ... well, you know, than ..."

"Oh," interrupted Theona, thankfully, but almost not fast enough. "I've got it." She gave an embarrassed giggle.

Miz Eudora, glad everyone now had a clear understanding of what had just "gone down" in the Rumph living room, continued. "You all know as well as I do that Mabel isn't about to miss this trip. But just to make sure, Sadie, could you take me shopping down to that nice Goodwill store where you took me that day to find my celebratin' clothes for Horace's service?"

"I surely could," I answered enthusiastically. When I moved there, Miz Eudora informed me right away that people in Smackass Gap either made it or raised it. Besides the quilted outfit she'd made when she won the International Quilting Contest and appeared at the annual Quilt Show in Paducah, Kentucky, she'd not gotten a stitch of new clothing since I'd met her. At least not besides work dresses she'd made from flour sacks that must have been around since she had been a little girl. *And that gosh-awful spandex outfit she had for when she decided to be a part of the liturgical dance team down at Six Flags over Jesus,* I suddenly remembered, trying to dismiss that vision as quickly as it had appeared.

Thus it was decided that the four of us would all meet for coffee an hour early the next morning so we could be gone on our way to all the local thrift stores before Mabel managed to make her way down the mountain from her chalet. I found it difficult to believe Miz Eudora would be able to find anything more outlandish than the outfit she'd found for Horace's service – the one she called so "celebratory." But I was sure game to try. As I went home to get "rested up" for the next day's mission, I could hardly wait to get started with Hattie, who was known to be Queen of the Yard Sales, Theona, the Peacemaker, and my neighbor, who kept life from getting boring. And then I would hardly be able to wait for Mabel's reaction to the shopping spree.

"Live in Smackass Gap," I murmured, snickering ever so softly.

WE HAD BEEN to five stores with no luck. The only purchase anyone had made was a small trinket, which had nothing to do with our upcoming trip, but that Hattie picked up for a quarter. The Queen of the Yard Sales was determined not to go home without at least one bargain.

"We'd have had better luck if we'd gone to Harrah's," said Theona as we walked out of the last of the stores on our list. "And I'd have gotten a kickback with my Cherokee heritage," she reminded us, beaming in such a way that she really did look like the Indian princess she was.

Ignoring the urge to bite my tongue, I threw out a suggestion. "I know there are certain places we're no longer welcome in Hendersonville and Franklin, so why don't we go the other direction. I know several places in Atlanta where we might be able to find something."

Places where you're known, Sadie. Places where you've volunteered, Sadie. Places where you're putting your own shopping privileges in jeopardy, Sadie.

"That's a great idea!" exclaimed Hattie before I had time to listen to the voices of my conscience, all of which were now reprimanding me.

"Yes, we'd planned the whole day for this mission, so we've still got plenty of time," Theona added.

"Hotlanta, here we come!" Miz Eudora announced. "Maybe I'll get to see the Chippendale Show I missed that time the Red Hatters picked me up by mistake on the day of Horace's 'celebration.' I've seen those two cute little chipmunks on television a time or two at friends' houses, and I wouldn't mind seeing more of them."

Letting that comment drop like a hot potato, I didn't bother to tell her she certainly didn't need to see more of them, chipmunks or Chippendales. I put my biggest sunglasses on, determined not to be recognized, and turned the car toward Atlanta, via Helen Mountain. There was no doubt in my mind that the many diverse cultures of my past home would surely provide just what the doctor—*no,* not *Dr. John G.*—I laughed to myself, *but what Mabel ordered.*

I'll have to say one thing for Mabel. When she does get Miz Eudora's attention, she gets it all the way. We didn't have to hit but one Goodwill store when we reached Atlanta before she had about as much color and sparkle as one person could get all by herself. If I thought the dress she had before had been colorful, I had been sadly mistaken. This new "frock" put her other one to shame with it's oversized rose blooms of red and orange-yellow splattered all over a deep purple and red swirled background, which was also accented by random patterns of wild jungle prints in the weirdest color combinations I had ever seen. Not only was Miz Eudora Rumph going to be the most colorful, sparkling woman in Savannah for St. Patrick's Day, she was also going to be the wildest, if those jungle prints were any indication of what was to come. That was a scary thought, especially when I considered she could do all that even without the excessively "jazzy, snazzy" costume, as Theona called it.

"And we all thought Mabel showed herself at your house yesterday," Hattie commented when Miz Eudora appeared from the dressing room to get our opinions.

"There's no doubt you'll out show her," Theona went on to say when she got a look at the shoes Miz Eudora had found to go with the outfit. They were 3-inch heels, bearing bold horizontal stripes containing every single color in the color wheel. In case you missed the shoes, which even a blind person could have seen, the heels were metallic gold, made of a shimmery fabric covering just like the shoes. There was only one good thing I could think to say when I saw her come out of the dressing room. "You'll certainly stand out in a crowd. Not a soul will miss you. I'm sure your outfit will be the talk of the town." That was before she added a bright orange evening bag covered in bangles and beads, with sequined fruit shapes on the front.

But then, when you considered that everyone else in Savannah would be dressed all in green in anticipation of the big day, there was no doubt Miz Eudora would stand out more than anyone else in the whole place. *Mabel will be sorry she didn't leave well enough alone,* I surmised as I stared at my neighbor proudly modeling her new duds. Now I could hardly wait to see Mabel's reaction. *No doubt it will be every bit as good as when she learns the meaning of Eudora's name!*

"And I had thought the jazz style of *When the Saints Go Marchin' In* was 'hot'," I told her. "It ain't nothing compared to you!"

"If you think this is hot, wait 'til I put on my purple fopher coat with all this. I'll really be working up a sweat then."

It was remarks like that one that made me love the simplicity of my neighbor and my life in Smackass Gap. I stood there staring at Miz Eudora, wishing I had half the guts she did as to wear something that bold out in public. But then, to her, it wasn't at all bold. It was loud, it was colorful, and it made a statement. However, she had no care for what it said to the rest of the world. The only statement she was concerned about her outfit making was the one to Mabel, which would be, "How do you like me now?" And of course, you readers know the answer to that the same as all of us caught up in this story.

Miz Eudora looked at herself in the mirror, an act which I knew was totally unaccustomed to her, and seemed to admire her new look and appreciate feeling like "one of the girls." *Sadly,* I thought, *she's never had opportunity to do this before.* But instantly, my thought of pity for her turned to one of appreciation of my own, appreciation for the fact that she'd never gotten caught up in the way the world sees and judges others. *Well, except for Mabel,* I mused, *which is what keeps her living.* I had long come to believe it was their back-and-forth banter that really did make days enjoyable for them. It was the reason each of them got up every morning.

My analytical musings came to an end when she asked, "Sadie, what do you think?" She was now strutting up and down an aisle in the Goodwill store like one of those models on a runway, which was a most comical sight and was getting nearly as much attention as one of those models would have.

I gazed admiringly at her spunk, and the outfit, and answered, "All that sparkles ain't jazz!"

NINE

When Irish Eyes Are Smiling

A KNOCK ON my door after dark that evening caused me to wonder what was wrong. Most people in Smackass Gap are settled at home by nightfall, especially those of us in my small five-person circle. I cautiously opened it, slowly so I could take a peek at who or what was on the other side, to see a flashlight shining in my eyes and blinding me. But not before I caught a glimpse of Miz Eudora standing there with a huge grin plastered all over her face.

"Sadie, what do you think?" she asked with animated excitement.

What I thought, in response to the very same question she'd asked me in the Goodwill store earlier in the day, was, "I can't see a thing except that 'dad-blasted light you're holdin' that's a-shinin' in my eyes!" which is what I told her with a joking smile.

"That sounds like something I'd have said to Mabel," she said, joking back, but then looking a bit concerned. "Don't reckon you've been around me too long, do you?"

"Yes, it does," I replied, "and no, that could never happen." That inner voice of mine was quick to inform me that last half of my answer was a bold-faced lie, for there was rarely a day that went by when I didn't think I'd been around her and Mabel too long.

"I had to come show you my new get-up," she boasted, bursting in the door as she turned off the flashlight I'd given her in case of emergencies. Given this was the first time I'd seen her make use of it, I figured this must be exactly that … an emergency. As it turned out, it was more of any urgency.

"Where did you find those?" I asked, staring at her once she was in the light of my living room and I could see.

"I didn't find them, I made them," she answered, referring to the crop pants she was wearing. "Don't you remember I told you we either raise it or make it?"

All I could do was nod as I stared at the adorably fashionable crop pants she was wearing.

"While we were on the way home from shopping today, I happened to remember when I was a little girl. Pa bought this sack of flour 'cause it had this brightly colored floral rose pirnt on it. 'Course he did have to pay a little more for it, as I recall. I reckon it was some special issue or something, but all of a sudden it struck me today 'cause I remember him comin' in the door with the biggest smile I'd ever see'd on him. He was totin' a big old sack of flour, covered in this rose-print, and said to my ma, 'I got this 'specially for my wild Irish rose.'

"I don't recall ever seein' my ma nor my pa ever beam any more than they did that day," she admitted, with a tear that didn't go unnoticed. Her words made me feel as if I were caught up in a fairy tale, much like the day she told me about Leland and his beautiful wild Irish rose. "When I thought about it today, I remembered my ma put the flour sack back in her cedar chest where she could take it out and see it every day. She was awful proud of it, and there was a gleam in her eye ever' time she took a notion to look at it. After Pa died, she didn't pull it out nearly so often. I think it saddened her 'cause she missed Pa so bad. I reckon after she died, it was 'outta sight, outta mind,' 'cause I never once thought about it again until today on the way home."

The melancholic expression that had reflected from her face as she told the story changed to an exuberant smile. "Anyway, I got to thinkin' as to how this whole trip to Savannah is 'cause of that thorn, so I'll be the wild Irish rose."

She's got that part right! She'll be the wild Irish

rose, with or without the crop pants, not to mention that garb she bought earlier today. I stood there admiring her outfit, with crop pants tailored to the point they could have easily come from some fancy boutique in Atlanta, a white shirt with a beautiful rose painted on it, and red fabric tennis shoes on which she'd painted white roses to match the ones on the pants. She was absolutely darling, which was not an adjective commonly used to describe her. "So you made all of this since this afternoon?"

As she nodded, something rather odd struck me. "Wait a minute! You said these were in the cedar chest."

"That's right."

"The same 'blamed ol' cedar chest' that held your black wool dress you were fretting about wearing to Horace's funeral because you couldn't get to it?"

"Yep!" she said, a note of bragging present in her voice.

"Then how were you able to get to it and get the flour sack out?" I asked in astonishment.

"Land sakes! There wasn't much to it. You know what they say. 'Where there's a will, there's a way.' I reckon when Horace died, I didn't have much will to accept he was gone and I wasn't too excited 'bout draggin' out that chest to find my black dress that was probably eaten half up by the moths anyway. Then when Preacher Jake came over and told me not to worry none 'bout the black dress 'cause it was gonna be a celebration, I didn't see no call to go workin' so hard to pull it out.

"But now this, this was a different matter. This *is* gonna be a celebration! A real celebration 'cause I'm gonna get to celebrate riddin' our gap of Mabel, and I'll get to celebrate my Irish heritage. Why, Sadie, this is gonna be the biggest celebration I ever celebrated in my whole life."

By now, she was literally glowing with enchantment, making me feel even more like I was caught up in a fairy tale. I should have known there was no stopping her once she got a notion in that brain of hers, but now I was sure of it. After suggesting she add this outfit to her line of Smack from the Gap items, I asked her to sit and visit for a short while longer. She was so delighted with herself that she suggested we make the theme of our Savannah trip "My Wild Irish Rose." Her Irish eyes were smiling so vibrantly that I agreed it was a marvelous idea.

"I can contact all those who've replied to let them know to wear something with roses on it. Since they're all into red anyway, that shouldn't be too hard for them." That's when I noticed the cute buttons on the hem of her crop pants. "Where did you find those? Don't tell me they were in the 'blamed ol' cedar chest' too?"

"No, ma'am. I cut these off another flour sack dress that had seen its better days. They were nothing but little white swirls, but it's amazin' what a touch of red and green food coloring and dye can do."

"You really can raise or make anything, can't you, Miz Eudora?" I asked in amazement.

"Purt near," she answered. "I can just about make anything 'cept makin' Mabel leave Smackass Gap, but I'm workin' hard as I can on that!" A devilish glimmer appeared in her eye. "And I'm not too good at making moonshine." She paused a second. "But I'm a purty good hand to blow up barns!"

She sat there, with the innocence of a young child, and a heart more tender than anyone I'd ever known—except when it came to Mabel. She was a trusting soul, and when she smiled her typically endearing smile, even her eyes smiled. All the recent talk of her Irish heritage and Irish roses reminded me of a song I'd heard long ago, and one I was sure she knew. "Miz Eudora, did you ever hear *When Irish Eyes Are Smiling?*"

"Land sakes, child! My pa used to sing that to my ma nearly ev'ry evening after supper. I do declare, I b'lieve that's what prompted my baby brother, John G., to want to sing so bad. And you should have heard Pa and John G. together. Why, my ma used to say that together, their voices had such warmth we didn't ne'er need a fire. Course, she was exaggeratin', you know, but my, oh my, how the two o' them could sing."

I could tell from the expression on her face that in her mind, the two of them were singing now. "Do you remember any of the words? Why don't you sing it to me now?"

"Land sakes! You want me to sing? That'd be worse than Mabel caterwauling up there on the top of Chunky Gal. We'd hear Chunky Gal groaning in pain, 'specially if Mabel was to hear me and join in. We might have our own Mt. St. Helen right here in Smackass Gap." Of course, she was cackling the whole time she was going on with all this rhetoric.

"P'SHAA! Sing, I reckon."

Knowing only a few words of the chorus, I began to sing myself, "When Irish eyes are smiling, sure, 'tis like the morn in Spring…"

As I was hoping, she joined in, so softly that she was barely audible at first, "In the lilt of Irish laughter, you can hear the angels sing. When Irish hearts are happy, all the world seems bright and gay. And when Irish eyes are smiling, sure, they steal your heart away." With each passing phrase, she blossomed— like that beautiful rose she was—until her confidence sent the words soaring throughout my living room, bringing life into my Clay County home as I had never known it before.

There's a tear in your eye, and I'm wondering why,
For it never should be there at all.
With such pow'r in your smile,
Sure a stone you'd beguile,
So there's never a teardrop should fall.
When your sweet lilting laughter's
like some fairy song,
And your eyes twinkle bright as can be;
You should laugh all the while
and all other times smile,
And now, smile a smile for me.

When Irish eyes are smiling,
Sure, 'tis like the morn in Spring.
In the lilt of Irish laughter
You can hear the angels sing.
When Irish hearts are happy,
All the world seems bright and gay.
And when Irish eyes are smiling,
Sure, they steal your heart away.

For your smile is a part of the love in your heart,
And it makes even sunshine more bright.
Like the linnet's sweet song,
crooning all the day long,
Comes your laughter and light.
For the springtime of life is the sweetest of all
There is ne'er a real care or regret;
And while springtime is ours
throughout all of youth's hours,
Let us smile each chance we get.

She sang the chorus once more. Her face, although blank, showed she was in her own little world with her ma and pa, and John G., seated around a fire in the home in which she had grown up. It was a happy time, when she was young and carefree, having no worries in the world … a time even more simple than now. That expression lingered for a few minutes after the last note had ended and she realized I was staring at her in amazement. I wanted to clap, or tell her how beautiful it was, or something, but I knew that would destroy the pure ambience of the moment. She needed to take care of this in her own way, which she rightly did.

"P'SHAA!" Her face was blushing, as if she couldn't believe she had bared that much of herself with anyone. "Sing, I reckon, Sadie. I ain't never won no blue ribbon for singin'."

Through those words, I perceived exactly what she was thinking and why it was so important that the music at First Church, Smackass, stay at the standard to which she was accustomed. Her days of sitting on that back porch—reaping the rewards of her gardening that were shared with much of the community, and the ribbons she then reaped at the fair—were filled with the music she had heard as a child. *Music that filled her home and her days with love.*

She stared at the floor for a brief moment, and when she looked back at me, it was as if the past few minutes had been a dream sequence for both of us. "I'd best be gettin' home now. Tomorrow's another day and I need all the rest I can get to take care of Mabel."

Insisting she allow me to take her in the car, I went to the adjoining room to retrieve my keys. When I returned she was glaring straight at me, just like she had been when she burst in the door. "Sadie, what do you think?" She looked down at the outfit she had whipped up in a matter of hours, as if to joggle my memory. That was probably a good thing; I was so lost in her world that I nearly forgot all about her new creation.

What I wanted to say was, "Miz Eudora, you have the most wonderful childlike spirit of anyone I've ever met, you are the most talented person I've ever met, and you are the most interesting neighbor in the whole world." But instead, I winked and offered a huge smile, big enough to match those Irish eyes of hers that were smiling back at me, and the words, "I think all that sparkles ain't jazz!"

TEN

Dirty, Slick and Overhung

I HAD AN inkling Miz Eudora had given no fore-thought to what would happen once we reached Savannah, at least in regards to "gettin' rid" of Mabel. She was determined if St. Patrick could drive all the snakes out of Ireland, he could easily drive Mabel out of Smackass Gap. I contemplated suggesting she hire a snake charmer as a backup plan, but decided that consideration was best kept private for the moment. *At least until we see how far St. Patrick gets with the job.* So alas, that one hope is all she'd banked our trip on. But as far as to how we would reach that end, I was sure she'd given it no other thought. That thought, or lack of, was a dilemma that troubled me terribly. Especially when it seemed all she'd been concerned with, once the invitations to join her in Savannah had been made, was what she was going to do with all her friends once they arrived to the appointed destination at the appointed hour.

That's why, when we made our last pit stop before reaching Savannah—after informing my crew that this fair town was not known for its public restrooms—I took her aside. "Miz Eudora, do you have a game plan on how to go about getting St. Patrick, or at least his spirit and maybe some help from all those Irish, to get rid of Mabel?"

"Yes, ma'am, that's simple. We'll have to pull a slick one on her."

"Don't you mean a fast one?"

"No, ma'am, I mean a slick one, as we're going to have to figure out which person in Savannah is slick enough to work a transforming spell on Mabel. I've been prayin' God would show me just the right one."

Like I figured, there was nothing planned past checking in the motel, going to eat at Paula Deen's Lady & Sons Restaurant, floundering ourselves at Mrs. Wilkes' Boarding House, and taking the Foody Tour and the Haunted History Tour with two busloads of ladies who would be arriving only a couple of hours after us. The only way I saw any results coming from this effort was if Mabel ate herself into oblivion, between all the different restaurants we'd be sampling, or got the wits scared out of her on the Haunted History Tour. *Then there's always the outside chance one of those spirits might just carry her away.* I laughed aloud. *This is Mabel we're talking about. They'd bring her back!*

My personal deliberation, inspired by the fact that Savannah was home to Johnny Mercer, the famed lyricist who penned *That Old Black Magic*, prompted me to consider suggesting we go to New Orleans and find someone to perform some "old black magic," but then I remembered the story of the woman from *Midnight in the Garden of Good and Evil*, not to mention all the pirates, prisoners and hoodlums who'd originally settled in Savannah. Miz Eudora was in luck. There were plenty of ways and people right here to "take out" Mabel, in case her idea of St. Patrick didn't pan out.

Flustered concern was still obviously written all over my face, though, for Miz Eudora motioned for me to follow her to a tree, draped with Spanish moss—as if that were a shield to keep our conversation private. "Now, now, Sadie, halt your worryin'. Don't you think if the Good Lord put the notion in my head about St. Patrick and the snakes and Mabel, the Good Lord is also gonna put the notion in the person's head who's supposed to be leading our snake, which in this case is Mabel, right to St. Patrick?"

I had to admit she had me. There was no way I could comprehend a reasonable answer because I didn't even comprehend the question. *Which is totally unreasonable!* I fathomed. But as I stood there, the sun shadowing around her face like a lace headdress thanks to the Spanish moss, my devious little neighbor momentarily possessed the pure innocence of one of those Madonna icons with the gold circle outlining her silhouette, a woman to whom God had sent an angel to deliver His secret. I had to trust this same Good Lord she was counting on could surely take care of my insecurities. Thus, we all piled back in my Honda and drove straight toward the City Market, the hub of Savannah's historic district. *After all,* I tried hopelessly to soothe myself, *this is definitely going to be a historical event.*

As I pulled the car to the corner adjacent to the City Market, where the noted four-star hotel—which shall remain nameless to protect the innocent—was situated, I decided to put the matter to rest with one last little thought. *Maybe not historical, but definitely memorable!*

As Miz Eudora's Irish luck—not to mention her Good Lord's influence—would have it, the first person she encountered when we rolled up to the curb in front of the hotel was "Dirty Harry." No joke! I had to rub my eyes and bop my ears a few times, but that was definitely how he introduced himself to us. He looked nothing like Clint Eastwood's character; he was much larger, African-American, had friendly eyes and a smiling face. *Make that a smile. That's enough of a difference to know he's not Eastwood's Dirty Harry.*

"I hear they have regular showers and indoor plumbing in these rooms," Miz Eudora offered in response to his introduction. "I'll be glad to let you come up and use mine. Then you won't have people callin' you dirty anymore." It was one thing that everyone within earshot now knew they were in the presence of "a real character," but not the one made famous by Eastwood. Her comment caused me to fear she had been around the Hinton Rural Center in Smackass Gap and all their mission workers a little too long. Now we were going to be taking in "boarders" at this fine establishment, which happened to be one of the ritziest hotels in all of Savannah.

Dirty Harry's grin was priceless, especially considering he had no clue the woman speaking to him was not pulling his leg. "Thank you, ma'am, for the kind offer, but that's not exactly how I got my name."

There were now two issues at play. First, I didn't bother to share with this most pleasant specimen of a valet that the woman addressing him had no idea who Clint Eastwood was, much less the name of his famed character. Secondly, I didn't dare conjecture why he actually *did* "inherit" that name, although the jovial disposition and innocent face of this man, who had so cordially greeted us, bore no witness to the first things that came to mind. In fact, carrying the enigma of a childlike spirit himself, he looked like the kind of person every parent would want their kid to be, or the kind of adult young male who would take extraordinarily good care of his grandma. But putting all that aside, before I had time to explain to her that Dirty Harry—or at least this one—was the valet who was supposed to be parking our car, or at least I hoped that was the only reason he was standing on the street corner with a name like that, Miz Eudora pulled him over to one side.

"Say, Dirty Harry," she whispered, which I managed to hear as I moved closer to eavesdrop, "I've got this sister-in-law I kind of need to dispose of. Do you think you could help me out?"

His grin burst into a full-fledged bout of laughter, still having no idea she was serious, and not exactly aware of what she meant by "dispose of." From his reaction, I concluded he must stumble upon a lot of families here with a sister-in-law or mother-in-law they wished "disposed of."

"I don't know about helping you dispose of her, but I guess I could slip her a Mickey when she isn't looking." I could barely make out his soft words for his roar of laughter.

"PSHAA!" exclaimed Miz Eudora, making no effort to keep her words secretive. "She don't need any help with a Mickey. Land sakes! Every time I leave her alone for a few minutes, she gets herself hooked up with some Tom, Dick or Harry. Why, when we set out on the Delta Queen for its last Mississippi River cruise a couple of years ago, she managed to get herself caught up in a fake marriage to some old geezer. To this day, we don't know if his name was Tom, Dick *or* Harry. All I know is when his wife caught up to him, I suspect he got a good beatin' with the rollin' pin or the iron skillet. Shoot fire, after what he did, she ought to have clobbered him with both."

By this point, not only was Dirty Harry rolling in laughter. Everyone who had pulled up to the curb for valet service had gotten out and was listening to his run-on with Miz Eudora. When he was able to catch enough of a breath to speak, he gave her a cordial slap on the back and blurted, "You're one live wire, you know that, lady?"

"She's a live wire alright," I answered for her, grabbing her and escorting her toward the front door of the hotel, with instructions for Hattie and Theona to take her inside and keep her out of trouble until I got Dirty Harry back to work with parking my car. "She's such a live wire that I'm going to suggest she change the name of her column in the *Clay County Progress* to "Live *Wire* in Smackass Gap," I said under my breath.

"Where are you ladies from?" Dirty Harry called behind us.

"Go, go, go!" I shouted, pushing Miz Eudora forward and trying to avoid the question.

It was no use. Miz Eudora turned and invitingly

replied, "Smackass Gap, North Carolina."

If I had thought the laughter to be boisterous before, it was nothing like what was coming from the curb now. People had crowded down the sidewalk of both streets lining the hotel and were joining in the amusement. I'd seen people whose eyes were glued to the tight wire performers at the circus, but here in the streets of Savannah, they were privy to "the Live Wire of Smackass." Our local performer, it seemed, had already gotten herself a name for her act! *Which isn't new. It's the same act everywhere she goes!* I surreptitiously said to myself.

"She's kidding, right?" asked a man in the crowd.

"How rude!" exclaimed a woman.

"No and no," I responded boldly. "No, she's not kidding, and no, it most certainly is not rude. That's where we live, and if you have anything derogatory to say about it, I'd say you're the one who's rude!" Suddenly, I felt my cheeks redden with embarrassment that I'd had the nerve to speak that way, much less on the sidewalks of Savannah where we had now gathered an audience. *The "Live Wire" must be rubbing off on others*, I feared, or at least excused for want of having a reason to blame my actions. I should have taken my actions as a clue of what was to come.

"She's for real!" yelled a younger man who held up his cell phone. "I just checked it out." As people began to mill around him, with some checking their own Blackberry or phones, he called out, "And you must be Miz Eudora Rumph."

That was too much for Theona and Hattie to handle, for Miz Eudora broke loose and headed back through the crowd. "Let me see that thing. What kind of person are you? I never told you my name. Do you work for the gov'nment or somethin'?"

"No, ma'am," he answered with a chuckle. "I work for the newspaper. Do you mind if I get a shot?"

"A shot? Land sakes! Mabel's the one we're tryin' to get rid of, not me!"

"Does she always act this way?" asked another woman.

"Only if she's awake," I nearly blurted out, but kindly refrained.

"She's a hoot!" called out some man.

"No, Mabel's the hoot," replied Miz Eudora. "I'm the nanny, except I'm not really. That's just because Mabel didn't know the difference between a billy and a nanny, but I'm not really an old goat anyway, so it don't much matter."

"From the sound of it," said Dirty Harry, with a wink to Miz Eudora, "Mabel doesn't know the difference between Tom, Dick or Harry either."

"Does she appear regularly?" asked a young person in the crowd, holding up a cell phone to take a picture, which I sincerely hoped wouldn't appear on

YouTube by evening.

"Only in Smackass Gap," I had the urge to re-ply, but again remained silent.

"Do you have a card?" asked another woman.

"A card? Well, I do have one, but it's a 'Con-gratulations on Your Move' card and I was intendin' to write 'Good Riddance' on it once we disposed of Mabel."

The newspaper guy had whipped out his cam-era and showed it to Miz Eudora. "Here. This is what I wanted to use to get a shot of you. Do you mind?"

"Oh, I see," nodded Miz Eudora. "You don't work for the gov'nment. You're one o' them paparazzi people."

"She must get this kind of attention everywhere she goes," commented another lady, "if she knows about the paparazzi."

With that, cameras and phones started clicking from every direction. *Forget YouTube. We'll probably end up on* America's Funniest Home Videos. There was suddenly an avalanche of comments and ques-tions, none of which I had a chance to respond to, nor wanted to had I had the opportunity.

One man scooted over beside Miz Eudora and kissed her on the check. "Quick!" he instructed to his wife. "Get my picture with her. The guys at home won't believe this." His friend jumped on the other side and also planted a big kiss on the other cheek, so that they were both in the photo at the same time. It wasn't long before several other guys had followed suit and were standing in line to do the same thing.

"Wow!" exclaimed Miz Eudora with a blush. "I believe I like this place. Maybe we should suggest to Preacher Jake that I put up a kissing booth right here on the street corner as a fund raiser for our youth's next mission trip."

Now both she and the crowd were out of control. I was thankful to see a police officer walking toward our private little party. "You folks getting into the St. Patrick's Day spirits a little too soon?" he asked politely as he walked toward Miz Eudora, rightfully seeing her to be the focus of the crowd.

"No sir," she answered politely. "I did come here because of St. Patrick's Day coming up and all, but just because I wanted to dispose of Mabel and then I met Dirty Harry and asked him if he could help me. And then all these people started to crowd around and take pictures when I told them I was from Smackass Gap."

"Where?" he asked, causing me to dread an upheaval for Round Two.

"Here," offered the newspaper reporter, showing the officer the screen on his Blackberry.

"Well, I'll be. So we have a celebrity in our midst today. What else is new on the streets of Savannah? Especially this time of year." He laughed. "Why doesn't someone take her over to that spot where *Forrest Gump* was filmed? Maybe that Tom Hanks look-a-like is there today. They'd be quite a pair."

He extended his hand to Miz Eudora. "Welcome to Savannah, ma'am." Then he turned to the rest of the crowd. "Now let's see if we can't get this crowd off the street corner so the people checking into the hotel can get through." As he turned to keep walking, he suddenly stopped. "What was that you said about disposing of a body?"

"Oh, that's just my sister-in-law. That's why we came here. I'm hoping to get rid of her, but it may be a big job, so I have two busloads of friends coming to help me."

"Is she always like this?" he asked, genuine concern beginning to fill his eyes.

I couldn't resist a snicker. "Yes," I answered, but getting robbed of a chance to explain.

You see, fortunately, Mabel had been asleep in the back seat ever since an hour outside Savannah; unfortunately, she chose this time to wake up and exit the car, which was still at the curb since Dirty Harry didn't want to miss any of the show.

Mabel, with impeccable timing, said nothing of real importance, yet explained everything. "What's taking all of you so long?" she roared loudly before noticing the crowd *or* the policeman. "Why haven't you checked us in yet? I'm going inside to have a look around in the gift shop. Hurry it up, you ninny, I'm ready to hit the streets of Savannah."

"That's Mabel," Miz Eudora informed the policeman, pulling on his sleeve.

"I see," he nodded with apparent understanding. "You ladies have a good day! And good luck with the disposal." He could barely control his laughter as he headed through the crowd, which was beginning to dissipate. What he didn't say, but was easily readable through his expression was, "You ladies will need the luck of every Irish person here to dispose of *her*."

A few more cameras flashed as I again headed Miz Eudora toward the front door of the hotel to leave her in the not-so-trusty care of Hattie and Theona, who were both all smiles. "We'll try to do better this time," said Theona, with her angelic expression.

"Just don't let her go near the gift shop, whatever you do," I instructed with a chuckle.

"Well, you four do what you need to do," ordered Mabel in her usual condescending manner as she exited the shop. "But while you're burning daylight, I'm hitting the streets until you all get a plan of action. Sadie, you call me from your cell phone when you've planned something worthwhile."

"I'll tell you what's gonna be worthwhile," whispered Miz Eudora, earning nods from both Hattie and Theona. The three of them looked like those little dogs that used to sit in the backs of car windows with their heads bobbing up and down.

I, too, nodded obediently, glad the culprit for the cause of this trip literally *would be* "disposed of" for the moment. Back on the curb, Dirty Harry was retrieving our bags before whisking my car off to some parking deck across the street. I slipped him a hefty tip as he carted the bags in the front door of the hotel, although the best tip I could think of for him at the moment was to stay out of the path of Miz Eudora Rumph. *And Mabel*, I added as a mental footnote.

"I think we're on the right track," Miz Eudora offered. "That Dirty Harry seemed awful nice. And did you hear him? He said if we needed any help with anything, anything a-tall while we're here, he'd be glad to help us."

My only response was a nod. I hadn't even gotten in my hotel room and this woman, much older than myself, had zonked nearly all the energy out of me for one day.

When I finally got us checked in at the front desk, with Mabel in one room and the rest of us sharing a quad room, I turned to see a bellman standing beside our luggage. Another African-American male, this one tall, slender and dressed to the nines in his fancy uniform, he had a smile that was dreadfully contagious and also quite persuasive.

"How are you lovely ladies doing on this fine afternoon?" he asked as he took the room keys from me and opened our door.

They certainly train the guys well around this joint, I thought to myself. *They ought to fare very well with the large crowd of over-fifty-aged women about to crash in on this place. The women will love the attention and the men will love the tips.*

"I'm Willie," the bellman, still all smiles, said as he escorted us to the elevator. "If you need anything, anything at all, during your stay here, you call down to the front desk and ask for me or whoever is on duty at the time. Now if it's anytime between this time of day until five o'clock, I'll be here. Just ask for Slick Willie. That's what they call me. If it's after five, the next person on duty will be glad to help."

"Did you hear that, Sadie? They're lined up here waitin' to help us with disposin' of Mabel. St. Patrick must'a been awful busy these last few days." Then Miz Eudora turned toward him as we exited the elevator and followed him down a hallway. "I'm sorry, mister, but could you say that last part again, about what they call you?"

"Yes, ma'am," he answered with a broad grin that stretched all the way across his whole face. "Slick Willie!" he repeated, this time adding a little punch to each syllable with great energy, as he opened a door and led us into a room. "That's what they call me and that's a fact."

"Did you hear that, Sadie?" Miz Eudora asked,

punching me so hard with her elbow that she nearly bowled me over onto one of the two beds. "I told you we needed to pull a slick one on Mabel. I been praying that the Good Lord would help me pull a slick one on Mabel, and not only did He answer my prayer, we no more than got here and He sent Slick Willie to do it! That's a slick one if I ever heard of it. I told you there was nothing to worry about."

How was I to argue with that?

Slick Willie, who was now listening intently, stood at the door with one hand on the knob, ready to make a mad dash at a moment's notice if necessary. When I first saw him turn on the charm in the hotel's lobby, I figured he could handle anyone who came through that door. I failed to consider he'd have to deal with Miz Eudora. Looking at him now, he was as intimidated by what might come out of her mouth as I was at this point.

"Say there, Mr. Slick Willie," she said, walking toward him, "you look like you could charm the socks off anybody." She stopped talking and gave him a scrutinizing once-over, making me grateful she stopped with naming only socks.

He laughed, still holding onto the doorknob. "That's what my wife says. Says that's what reeled her in, my endearing charm."

"I'm glad to hear that, because I need you to use all the ooze you got to help me dispose of my sister-in-law."

"Say what?" he asked, frantically opening the door and putting one foot out into the hallway.

"Have you got a sister-in-law you wish you didn't have?" she asked, seriousness written all over her face.

"I sure do, and more than one. But I don't want to dispose of either one of them, and if I did, it would be with an Uzi and certainly not my ooze of charm."

"Obviously your sisters-in-law don't treat people like Mabel. Honestly, that woman! I don't know where she gets off thinkin' she can just move in and start tellin' everybody on the place what to do and how to act. She's worse than them dad-burned half-backs. We might as well go ahead and call her a full-back."

"Have you ever thought about sending this Mabel off to a football team?" he asked with a laugh, not understanding the mountain folks' jargon for people who'd gone from the north to Florida and had settled back halfway between, landing them in or around Smackass Gap.

"No, we're awfully proud of our Yellow Jackets back home, so I'd never put something like her off on them." Without missing a beat, she continued, "But I'll tell you what I have done to her." Miz Eudora went on to tell him about how horribly Mabel sang, and how she'd ruined the Christmas pageant and now how she had a mind to take over the music program at First Church, Smackass.

"Where'd you say?" he asked, sounding like she had when she asked about his name. That's when he noticed my Smackass Gap t-shirt. "Hey, I'd like to have one of them for my wife."

"What size is she?" asked Miz Eudora.

"Probably about your size," he answered.

"Well, I'll tell you what. You help me dispose of Mabel and you can have mine."

"I don't know," he replied hesitantly, "I don't know about knocking anybody off. Besides, if I was into that kind of stuff, it would take way more than some t-shirt to pay me, even if it did say Smackass Gap."

"What she means ...," I began to explain as I pulled him back into the room and away from her ear-shot. After I gave him a few more details in plain English, Slick Willie turned back to face Miz Eudora.

"Well, why didn't you just say so?" he asked, his face beaming with a smile so broad that all his teeth shone, making him more charming than ever. "You had me goin' there for a minute."

"I saw you goin' out the door. That's why I had to grab a-holt of your sleeve and pull you back in. I knowed you wuz a gift from God and I couldn't let you get away. Unlike Mabel, I'm not in the habit of grabbin' onto men I don't know."

"You mean I'm going to have to go through all this again with her?"

"No sir, you've got nothing to worry about. I brought along enough of Horace's special blend to take care of that. I just need you to help me come up with a plan, 'create a diversion' I think I heard someone call it, so I can make sure she goes back to her own home in Charlotte instead of mine when we leave here. Shoot fire, she can go to anybody's home as long as it isn't mine. All I want is for someone to drive her out of Smackass Gap like St. Patrick did all those snakes out of Ireland."

"I got'cha," he replied, making me relieved one of us could decipher her dialect. "You say she likes music and thinks she can sing?" He watched, with great interest and deep in thought, as Miz Eudora nodded. "And she thinks she's all high and mighty?" He received another nod. "Then I know exactly how to handle her."

Whipping a card from inside his jacket pocket, he continued. "You see, they don't call me Slick Willie for nothing. I actually own a shoe shine business. I have all the business at the airport. That's how I got my name. I can shine your shoes slicker than a baby's bottom. Why, I can have your shoes so shiny they'll put the sun to shame. Tell you what I'll do."

Miz Eudora was all ears as she leaned her head toward him. Before the next five minutes were over,

he'd already arranged for Mabel to have a private concert in one of the hotel's conference rooms, where his
best employee from his shoeshine business would
"crash the party, charm her socks off, make her feel
all pampered and whisk her away, giving her such a
night on the town she'll never want to leave."

"You're sure that's gonna work?"

"I've not seen this guy lose one yet. He doesn't
miss a single customer passing through at the airport,
but when it comes to the ladies, he's even more of a
sure shot. They say he's got more charm than Georgia's
got peanuts!"

"Wait a minute! We *do* want her to leave. That's
the whole scheme. I want her back in Charlotte with
them dad-burned beady-eyed critters she wears around
her neck. I don't ever want her to come back to
Smackass Gap. I'll be more'n happy to send all her
things to her. Lord knows we don't want to keep none
of that stuff in Clay County!"

"Don't you go worrying about nothing. She'll
be swept off her feet better than if he'd have used a
vacuum cleaner."

"What do you say now, Sadie? I knew St. Patrick
was the answer for getting rid of our snake." Apparently satisfied, she headed for the suitcase I'd let her
borrow. "Alright, Slick Willie, here's your t-shirt. I
hope your wife enjoys it."

"Thank you," Slick Willie replied as he held

the shirt up and inspected it with a grin. "I'm gonna have some fun with this tonight," he joked, giving Miz Eudora another wink. "Say," he said, pausing outside the door for a moment, "if that special blend's as good as you say it is, you could make yourself a small mint down here on St. Patrick's Day." He gave her a playful wink. "You might need a helper though and I'd be just the man for the job."

Slick Willie's entrepreneurial skills were keen, exhibiting why he was a master at what he did. Now I fully understood the reason behind his name. He was obviously slick when it came to making a dollar, and did it in an "almost" honest and respectable manner.

"I'm not about to turn any of that stuff loose down here for St. Patrick's Day. I pulled that stunt on the Delta Queen when I had to deal with Mabel, and nearly got myself in more trouble than we could get out of all together. I'll not try that again. Besides, I don't drink, so I don't need any of those mint juleps I keep readin' 'bout down here. I might wake up and find myself in an even more compromising position than Mabel found herself in on that riverboat."

With that, Slick Willie gave Miz Eudora a big laugh and a handshake and told her he'd see her at the ballroom later to clue her in on the final details. In the meanwhile, she was to alert all her lady friends to be at Ballroom A at nine o'clock that evening for "the disposal." Although, both he and I suggested she didn't call it that as she went about extending the invitation. "A night of fun to long be remembered" is what we finally agreed she should invite them to attend.

Before he'd had time to reach the elevator, Miz Eudora was now busily making plans. "We'd best get going if we're gonna meet those two busloads of women when they get to the Inn at Ellis Square. I want to make sure they all get their invitation for tonight. We need to stop off in the gift shop to get Hattie and Theona. They can help us and we'll be done in no time. But first, I want to check out the beautiful view that nice lady at the front desk told you about. Wonder if it's as beautiful as the view out of my house over Lake Chatuge?"

She went straight for the window and whisked the curtain panels open. "Land sakes!" she screamed, as if she'd seen a ghost. "Would you look at the size of that belly?"

I did as she said and immediately wished I hadn't.

"If that lady at the front desk calls this beautiful," she continued, "I'd hate to see what she calls Mabel." Miz Eudora squinted as she put her face right up next to the glass and stared out in disbelief.

As I glanced at a man's hairy chest and belly, so rotund it looked like his midriff would hit the bottom of the pool if he floated on his stomach, I had to agree with her. Had I not known better, and had this way-too-exposed specimen before my eyes not had a beard, I'd have sworn that Mabel was trying out a new bikini. Then a horrible thought crossed my mind. *She is one of triplets and one of the other three is male. Surely this isn't Milton T. Surely she didn't suggest he join her here for the weekend.* Then another unsightly thought, one more unsightly than the vision outside our window, crossed my mind as I moved closer to the window and closely surveyed the entire pool area. *What if Melba and Milton T. Toast are both here?*

"Why don't we close the curtain back?" I suggested. "Maybe we can try a view of the pool later." I'd never thought of it before, and wished I hadn't then, but suddenly a vision of Miz Eudora and Mabel sitting by the pool, both dressed in little more than the man out the window, splattered itself across my brain. "Better yet, why don't we take a walk down along the riverfront? I'll bet that would be a fantastic view." *Anything to get my mind off this vision of those two at the pool*, I told myself.

"I b'lieve I'd like that," she replied. "Do you think we might be able to get that nice Slick Willie and Dirty Harry to go along with us and point out all the things to look for?"

"That's not quite in their job description," I informed her. "A valet takes care of your vehicle during your stay and the bellman takes care of getting your luggage to and from your room while you're here."

"And disposin' of Mabel," she offered with a mischievous grin. "But then, who's gonna show us the ropes?"

"I think the right phrase is 'show us the town,' and that would be a tour guide. Why don't we go meet your ladies, help them get checked in and give them the itinerary for the evening? Then we'll find a tour guide to make sure you see the town."

I wanted to further explain that I thought we'd seen enough for one afternoon. *Dirty Harry, Slick Willie and ... well, whoever he was, he was certainly overhung!*

ELEVEN

The Grapes of Wrath

MIZ EUDORA WAS determined she could find the Inn at Ellis Square on her own and make sure the ladies joining us had no problems checking in (she had them staying there so they wouldn't be "overexposed" to Mabel) while I found us a tour guide. "That way we won't miss any shopping time," she insisted.

Even though her destination was only two blocks away, the sight of her tearing off across the street unnerved me. Since she'd never before been to Savannah, I slowly trailed her, wanting to make sure she didn't get lost. *Sadie, how do you expect a woman in a get-up like hers to get lost?* There went that internal voice again, making me feel totally foolish, as usual.

Nevertheless, I watched Miz Eudora—from several yards behind—as she paused for a moment at each business to stare in the storefront windows. Then, on sudden impulse, she pushed a door open with great vigor and pranced into one of the stores with un- abashed enthusiasm. By the time she reached the front counter, I caught up with her and gently pulled her away from the counter to the back corner for a mo- ment of privacy.

"Miz Eudora, what are you doing in a wine shoppe?" I asked. "I didn't know you drank."

"May I help you ladies with something?" came a cordial voice from behind the counter.

"To answer both your questions," Miz Eudora spoke up, "I don't partake of the stuff," she announced firmly in my direction. Then turning to the woman behind the counter, whose clothing, accessories and jewelry hinted she was definitely of the upper crust, she stated, "I need a few pointers on the art of fermentin' and I thought your store might be just the place to give them to me.

"You see, I had the sad misfortune of blowin' the back out of my barn last year when I tried to make a batch of …" She leaned over the top of the glass counter and whispered, "'sparklin' water' for my sis- ter-in-law Mabel."

"Wasn't that sweet?" asked the lady behind the counter, politely.

"Nah, it wasn't too sweet," Miz Eudora has- tened to reply. "It was so stout Mr. Grover Swicegood said it wasn't fit for nothin', not even castor oil for my mule, Clyde."

The lady pretended to cough as a way to politely disguise her snicker. "No, I meant wasn't the thought and your effort in making the champagne a sweet one?"

"I wouldn't go that far, either," admitted Miz Eudora. "I was simply tryin' to save our little congregation the expense of havin' to buy earplugs for all its members."

"Well, I've certainly heard of corks coming out with enough force to reverberate throughout a small dining room, but I've never heard of one causing the need for earplugs."

Miz Eudora gave the most innocent little chuckle, something I was not accustomed to hearing from her. Had one not known better, they'd have gotten the idea—from her demeanor and genuinely sincere voice and pleasant mood—that she was the sweetest little old lady to ever come out of Clay County, North Carolina. "It isn't the cork shootin' out that causes the problem, it's that dad-burned caterwauling of my sister-in-law, Mabel Toast Jarvis."

From there, the two women broke into a friendly conversation that ranged from Mabel's inability to sing to the "special blend," to the aftermath of the blown up barn. Within five minutes, one would have suspected they were long-time acquaintances.

"You don't have a Georgia peach voice," noted Miz Eudora a few minutes into the conversation.

"That's because I'm from Kentucky," admitted the woman behind the counter.

"What part? I was just up there."

"I'm sure you've never heard of this place, it's so tiny. It's called Possum Trot."

Miz Eudora's eyes lit up. "As in the other side of Paducah from Monkey's Eyebrow?"

"That would be the one," answered the woman. "How did you know that? Very few people in the world know about Possum Trot, much less Monkey's Eyebrow. Heck, most of them don't even know about Paducah."

Miz Eudora whipped out her blue ribbon from her purse and proudly showed it to the woman. "I won this at least year's quilt show. I'm already working on another prize quilt to see if I can't win again."

The woman, who now introduced herself as Stephanie, began to share mountain stories of her own background and how she got from Possum Trot to such a completely opposite place as Savannah. Before long, the two women not only knew each other's names, but their background and current states in life.

"You've got six children?" questioned Miz Eudora. "How in the world do you have time to be making wine if you have six children?"

Miz Eudora's comment made me laugh aloud

as I recalled the day she asked Preacher Jake how Johann Sebastian Bach had the time to write a cantata for every Sunday when he had so many children. He was taken aback, but not nearly as much as when she uttered, "They must not have had stops on the organs back then. Mr. Bach apparently didn't spend time on the registrations like that dandy organist over in Asheville that Sadie took me to hear."

I prayed she wouldn't come out with something like that now, making me want to crawl in the wood-work. But it was obviously my lucky day. The two woman delved deeper into the subjects of their differences, all held together by one string called Possum Trot, Kentucky.

"Eudora Rumph!" we heard from the familiar, but more condescending than usual, voice as it came roaring across the room from the door to the counter, more viciously than had it been on the waves of a brutal storm. The three of us, even though I was merely an innocent bystander, had been so caught up in the enjoyable company of each other that no one had even heard the door's bell forewarning us that a storm was brewing at the high seas—even though these "high seas" were only the waters of the Savannah River rippling by a couple of blocks away. "What on earth are you doing in this shop? You have no more clue about the fine quality of wine than I do about farming with that cussed mule of yours."

"Hello there," offered Stephanie, whose voice was oozing with more sugar than a whole vat of smashed grapes, "you must be Mabel Toast Jarvis." Her voice, combined with her body language as she extended her hand for a genteel Southern-belle lady-like handshake, represented the fine quality of upbringing she'd experienced from growing up in the Kentucky Derby state. "I've heard so much about you."

"Why yes," Mabel responded, her voice suddenly warm enough to melt butter, "I must admit that my reputation typically does precede me." She returned the handshake, turning her head ever so slightly, but exactly enough to visually say to Miz Eudora that she could now take a back seat, or better yet, make her exit.

Mabel's preceded reputation served as the cause for the next chain of events. Stephanie explained to her about the free wine tasting offered at the shop, which was a source of great interest of Mabel. However, instead of those thimble-sized cups generally used for sampling, Stephanie filled up regular-sized wine glasses. It wasn't long before the three of us were back in conversation, with Mabel stumbling out the front door while warbling through continued choruses of *How Dry I Am*, as loudly and boisterously as she could, after telling Stephanie she much preferred the drier varieties.

"I'll take a whole case of wine," stated Miz

Eudora enthusiastically, "the driest one you've got. Better than that, could you possibly take me to your winery and teach me how to make it?"

Before I knew what had happened, Miz Eudora had obtained a private invitation to the Shannon Winery in Sylvania, about an hour northwest of Savannah. She'd been given a history of the winery, whose owner had moved to Georgia from western North Carolina. I could tell, even though the two had not yet met, she liked "the homeboy" already and was anxious to learn all she could from him. Within a short span of time, I'd quickly surmised three other important points about Miz Eudora Rumph and the discovery of this wine shop ... besides all the health values of red wine. First, with a name like Shannon, there had to be some Irish background connected to that winery. Second, I concluded there was more wrath in these grapes, at least in Miz Eudora's way of thinking, than in John Steinbeck's Pulitzer Prize winning novel, *The Grapes of Wrath*. Lastly, I also suspected that somewhere, hidden back on the Rumph farm near where the infamous still once stood, and where certain sections of it still laid partially buried, a vineyard of muscadine grapes was going to appear, complete with the two halves of a huge wooden keg in which to stomp the grapes. Somehow I pictured what would have otherwise been a chore as a delightful honor to Miz Eudora, who would immensely enjoy every stomp.

Seems these grapes of wrath are going to be a great stress-reliever. Maybe she can make a business out of letting others around the mountainside come and stomp out their angers—or "wraths" *as the case may be!* That's when I decided the oaken bucket halves might need to be traded in for several oblong feeding troughs like the one she had for Clyde. *On second thought, she could invite all these friends of her to join in the fun. I was certain there was a lot of fun to be had with muscadine grapes on the Rumph farm, regardless of whether they "took care of Mabel." At least she'd be good and healthy with all the servings of muscadines.* I contemplated on tossing out the consideration of those good and healthy values of muscadine grapes keeping Mabel around longer, but concluded it would be more entertaining to sit back and watch what happened.

There was one other point accomplished by Miz Eudora's spontaneous visit to the Shannon Winery Shop. On our next visit to the library, I was going to have Mary locate a copy of Steinbeck's book for me that I hadn't read since high school. I figured it might point me to a few more insights about this woman I called my neighbor. *And the wrath between the two sisters-in-law.*

TWELVE

Fanning the Flame

"WHAT IN HEAVEN'S name do you think you're doing with that fan, Mabel?" Miz Eudora inquired, loudly enough for everyone on the entire floor to hear, when we returned to our hotel from meeting the ladies on the buses and discovered Mabel. We'd stumbled upon a nice little unexpected surprise, thanks to my neighbor running into the store manager of Paula Deen's gift shop, which was across the street from the wine shop, and Miz Eudora now wanting to "freshen up," a detail she'd overheard from one of the ladies on one of the buses.

"I'm practicing."

"Practicin' for what? You look like a peacock what's got his tail feathers caught in an electric fence."

"HMMPH! Don't you understand anything, Eudora Rumph?" Mabel gave a disgusted grunt. "Well, I guess I couldn't expect some uncouth ninny like you to understand anything about romance. Here, let me give you a few pointers." She cupped both hands, with her fingers pointed up, and closed the fan from both sides. Then, in a sweeping motion, which for Mabel was a pretty hefty sweep, she cupped her left hand beneath her right elbow, which was bent in an upward position as she held the closed fan clasped in her right hand. She had the appearance of one of those flamenco dancers who does the motion of holding up one hand and forearm, and then switches the stance to hold up the opposite hand and forearm. I was amazed at the level of grace with which she held that position. It could have been quite a stunning sight, but because of the "flaps" on her arm, it resembled a pelican holding a fish in its mouth more than anything else.

"Now pay attention," she ordered, "I don't have time to do this but once. I have bigger fish to fry." Her comment served to further substantiate my visual image of the pelican with the fish.

"How do you expect to fry fish after what you did with the possum last year at Thanksgiving?" Miz Eudora asked, befuddled.

"It's a manner of speaking," I politely explained before Mabel had a chance to tear into her. "She isn't really going to fry anything, and she doesn't really mean fish. She's simply going to try to lure someone in with her ..." I decided best to stop and leave well enough alone while I still could. "It's simply a phrase, like some of the things you say from time to time."

"I got it," Miz Eudora said. "Like 'when the cat's away, the mice will play.'"

"Then you'd better get this," Mabel shot at her, "because you're cutting into my practice time. Now watch this," she said, holding the fan closed, but high in her left hand as she strutted around the hotel room. "This means I would like to make your acquaintance."

"Why do you want to make my acquaintance? You already know me."

"Not you, you ninny! It is to be directed toward a man whom you would like to meet."

"I told you, it's a nanny, not a ninny. And why do you want to meet some man? You already had the best man there was and you did him in."

"Hush, and pay attention. I want to make sure I have all the moves down pat before we head out to dinner this evening." She opened the fan. "This is a signal to alert the person in whose direction you are looking to wait outside for you." Closing the fan, she added, "This tells the man I want to speak to him." Mabel went through several other positions with the fan, informing Miz Eudora how to say, "Yes," "No," "Follow me," and "We are being watched."

"What's the man supposed to do?" asked Miz Eudora, now with great curiosity. "Take out his handkerchief and send you return signals?"

"No!" Mabel huffed. "He simply follows my

lead. Good heavens, Eudora. You are impossible, absolutely impossible. Leave me be so I can make sure my motions are naturally graceful. Why did you come to bother me anyway?"

"Bother you? This is our room. Yours is on the next floor up."

Surely Mabel's confusion has nothing to do with the five glasses of wine she just consumed! I concluded.

"But since you're here," Miz Eudora continued, "I was goin' to tell you we're all leavin' for Paula Deen's gift shop next to her restaurant in ten minutes. We'll be eatin' supper there at six, but one of her sons is going to be there now to personally meet all of us ladies and have his picture made with us. After that, we're all goin' out on the town for a couple of hours before it's time to go back there to eat. But never mind, it appears you're too busy. Go practice in your own room."

"One of her sons?" Mabel repeated, her interest now greatly piqued. "Which one? Oh, never mind, they're both rather cute." She gave some floozy fan motion, for which I doubted she knew the meaning, and that I was certain I didn't want to know. "And we're going to have our photograph made with him?"

Miz Eudora then turned to me with a loud whisper, "I hope that Mrs. Paula's son knows the signal for 'Run the other direction.'" She gave a mischievous grin. "And he better know the one for 'Fast!'"

Mabel rushed out the door. "Hush up and leave me be! I need to learn all the motions to make sure I'm capable of fanning the flame before I go over there."

"Fannin' the flame?" Miz Eudora asked as we fluffed her curls. "Land sakes! She'd do better catchin' a man if she'd learn the way to his heart is his stomach. She needs to learn to cook instead of fannin' the flame and leavin' him to cookin' for himself.

"P'SHAA! Fannin' the flame, I reckon!"

After a few minutes of silence, during which I could tell Miz Eudora was deep in thought as we walked from the hotel to Paula's gift shop, she piped up with, "It's a good thing she's plannin' on fannin' instead of honkin'! Land sakes, that honkin' of hers is enough to run even St. Patrick out of Savannah! At least she won't be honkin' here no more after Slick Willie's friend hauls her, I mean sweeps her, outta here after tonight." She thought a couple of more seconds and added, "At least that son of Mrs. Paula's knows how to cook lestin' she starts fannin' too ferociously in his direction. His stomach'll be taken care of.

"P'SHAA! Fannin', I reckon!"

Two "P'SHAAs" in less than five minutes? That means Miz Eudora's dander is really up. I didn't get an opportunity to soothe her by telling her to put that worry out of her mind. By the time we reached the corner leading to the restaurant's gift shop, there was a long line of ladies dressed in their Smackass Gap t-shirts waiting to meet one of Paula Deen's charming sons. Had I not known better, I'd have guessed there was a feather convention in town. While Miz Eudora managed to strike up a conversation with nearly every one of the women in the line, I saw most all of them were already licking their chops, though I wasn't sure whether it was due to the food they'd be eating later or the chance to meet a handsome young man. Either way, excitement was in the air.

And a photographer's around the corner, I noted, spotting a man with professional-looking camera equipment approach Miz Eudora. *He must be here to take pictures and charge the tourists.* Wanting to make sure Miz Eudora didn't get herself lured into an expensive scam, I moved closer to hear the man's words.

"Excuse me, ma'am," he said courteously and with a big smile. Since the smile looked sincere and not like what Miz Eudora called "a mule eatin' briars" smile, I decided to at least hear him out before shooing him on his way. "My current assignment is to do an entire photo spread on the colorful characters who visit Savannah for the St. Patrick's Day festivities. Since those officially begin this evening, I just arrived. Seeing you must be the ringleader of all these women, do you mind if I hang out around here and snap a few shots of you ladies?" He, noticing my skeptical eye, handed a business card to each of us. It bore his photo and his credentials, helping me feel more at ease.

"I don't mind a bit," she answered, "long as you stay back outta the way once Mrs. Deen's son, Bobby, comes out in a few minutes. These ladies are lined up like flies on …"

Suddenly the door opened—none too soon for me, nor the rest of her words—and out walked Bobby, Paula's younger son. It was unbelievable to see the way some of them swooned when he came out in his white t-shirt and jeans, flashing a smile that lit up the entire sidewalk. All eyes were on his as cameras flashed.

Not to mention the professional photographer's clicking finger was "goin' to town." *He found the mother lode*, I observed, watching him work his magic with the lens as each woman stepped up beside Bobby. *He'll have to work some magic to make some of these women look good,* I joked, thinking of Miz Eudora and Mabel. *Oh well,* I concluded, a*fter spotting Miz Eudora, he needs look no further.*

My attention returned to watching the women with Bobby, or rather, him with them. I'd never seen a more polite young man as he greeted each woman by name—thanks to their nametags—and paused for a photo with each of them. It was quite a sight to be-hold. *And I had thought their hormones were raging* before *we got here,* I mused, taking in the entire scene.

Some of them had aprons, cookbooks, t-shirts or other items from the gift shop, which he considerately took time to autograph.

"AHH-WHOOP!"

I spun around just in time to see Mabel round the corner and spot Bobby surrounded by all Miz Eudora's friends. Her hands were digging in her purse and shortly came out with her fan and a ladies linen handkerchief. She began fanning wildly with one hand while blotting the perspiration off her face with the other, all the while shoving her way to the front of the line.

"Not so fast, Mabel," yelled Miz Eudora when she saw what was happening.

She should have saved her breath. I learned one thing from Mabel's bold and tactless effort. Don't mess with a woman wearing a hat, especially when there's a good-looking man involved. She'll fight you tooth and nail to keep you out of her territory. I didn't see any teeth biting into Mabel, but I did see several fingernails poking into her as women pushed her right back to the end of the line.

"HMMPH!" huffed Mabel indignantly. "Eudora Rumph, this is all your doings. You need to take care of these women immediately. There's no way I'm standing in line like a common housewife. After all, I'm *the* Mrs. John G. Jarvis and I'm sure Bobby would rather hold my hand and sign my fan than waste his time on all these floozies that rode a hot bus down here. He has no interest in them."

"If that's the way you really feel," retaliated Miz Eudora, "then I'm sure you'll understand that the best should be saved for last and since you think you're better than everyone else, you're right where you need to be." What happened next went so fast I missed most of it, but hat feathers were blowing and the personal feathers of both the sisters-in-law were ruffled.

When it appeared eminent Mabel was on the losing end of this battle, she became aggressively more defensive. "HMMPH!" This time her response sounded more like a desperate bark. "I should go and leave you here in your squalor with all these crazy old bats."

"Just go ahead and go! I ain't sendin' out no personalized invitations!" Miz Eudora's rising ire was causing me to debate whether I should take cover and suggest for all the other "crazy old bats" to join me. But then she laughed that distinctive cackle, which at the moment more appropriately resembled a witch at Halloween. "We might be crazy old bats, but we sure do know how to have fun in all our hats!"

"If you want to go through the rest of your life with a bunch of ladies who like to play dress up, that's fine with me, but for me, I intend to find me a man who can take care of me the way a real queen should be treated."

"P'SHAA!" was the only response Mabel received, which surprised even me. *For once, maybe Mabel's stumped her*, I ventured, although I found that hard to believe. When I later mentioned the fact that I was surprised she'd given no more of a reaction, my sly—or *"slick"*—neighbor informed me that she was going to let Mabel "trip on her own fan." I started to tell her I thought the word was "feet," but halted, deciding this was another of her own phrases, which I termed "Eudoraisms," only this one was coined solely for Mabel.

Her exit meant plenty more fun for all the rest of us. It also meant Miz Eudora gawked at Bobby enough for both she and Mabel. I had a hunch he would get at least a line or two in the next edition of *Live in Smackass Gap.*

Once she'd made sure all the women had spoken to Bobby and been photographed with him, she set out and did exactly what she'd told Mabel: had an afternoon on the town. *With her own personal photographer in tow.* As appealing as an afternoon nap sounded, this was an opportunity of a lifetime I wasn't about to miss. Thus, she kept me hopping as I tried to keep up with her. She was worse than a kid in a candy store, several of which we took in, and a bull in a china shop, in one of which she found herself a new teapot for when her red-hatted friends "come a-callin'."

I seriously doubt there was one square or area

of Savannah that didn't glimpse my neighbor as she took in every sight she could, or that didn't glimpse her, thanks to the cameraman. From posing with tattooed men to striking a similar pose to that of John Wesley, she was captured in more precarious positions than I knew any one individual could achieve. People even stopped her and had her pose with their dogs, with some pet owners offering to tip her. She made a point of trying to match the face on each dog, but accepted no money. "Too bad Mabel isn't here, they could get two dogs in the picture for the price of one!" she'd howl with each of the dog photos. There was only one incident, when a dog apparently mistook all the red on her for the fire hydrant.

Not one shop was left unturned as she visited each one she came to, buying little but enjoying much. From the looks of it, customers and shop owners benefited as much from her presence as she did theirs. People followed her into stores simply to get a better look at her and wound up being paying customers.

One of the shops bore one of those signs that read, "Your husband called. He said to buy anything you want." Miz Eudora immediately rushed to the store's clerk. "Did Horace say where he was?" Receiving only a stunned glare, she continued. "Did he tell you where he hid the rest of the bumper crops so I could buy what I want?"

I drug her out and onto the sidewalk, halting

any further explanation of that matter, but not before she purchased a wooden butterfly painted purple with red dots. It was not just any purple butterfly; it would balance on anything. She became so enamored with it that she was standing outside the row of shops balancing the butterfly on not only her fingers, but also on her toes. At one point, she was even in the fountain balancing it on her tongue. I was afraid the storeowners would call the cops, but she was creating so much inquisitive attention that the butterflies, dragonflies, and every other balancing creature they had were selling faster than clerks could take money. The bad thing is she encouraged all the other ladies, most of whom now had their own balancing creature, to do the same.

I'd never thought of Miz Eudora as the problem child at school, but seeing her in this light—or fountain, as it was—made me wonder. Fearing what she might do next, and knowing I didn't want to be caught in the picture with her, I headed for a shop down the street. The last time I saw her with the butterfly, she had it on her thumb, which was out in the street thumbing for a ride. I later heard the butterfly got a ride; she did not.

By the end of her shopping spree, she could have been a poster child—with the photographer in tow, there was still that chance—for the popular saying, "Shop 'til you drop" and for one of the soda companies, since she was holding onto her soda for dear life and looking as if she might be taking her last breath. I caught up with her outside the Cotton Exchange where, quite bedraggled, she was dragging her shopping bags with one hand and carrying her soda in the other. She took a seat, more aptly in a reclined position, on the steps of the former Cotton Exchange, which for a while after its heyday had been a freemason's hall.

A kind man on his jog paused to offer a playful tease, trying to instill a burst of energy. "Is this where the ladies hang out that are for sale?" He was unprepared for exactly how much energy his question would stir.

"No, sir," she answered, sitting aright and instantly bubbling with gusto, "but if you'll wait here a few minutes, I've got a lady I'll be glad to sell you." She started to take off running, but whipped back around. "In fact, I'll be glad to give her to you."

I quickly explained the man was joking with her and pretty soon the three of us were caught up in an enjoyable dialogue, with him offering a detailed report of much of the local history of this exact spot.

"What happened over there?" Miz Eudora asked, pointing toward what was left of a circular brick construction in front of the Cotton Exchange.

"Well, it was one Saturday morning early and a car came speeding up Drayton Street. The driver didn't even slow down at the stop sign and came crashing through the wrought iron fence there and hit the edge of the fountain. That sent the car airborne and it crashed right through the historic Griffin statue and fountain that used to be perched there, and then landed right here on the steps of the Cotton Exchange where you're standing." He stopped as Miz Eudora looked down at her feet and then back out toward where the former Griffin had sat.

"I was out for my daily walk that morning and happened to see the whole thing," the man continued. "They had to rescue the driver with the Jaws of Life, but thankfully there were no life-threatening injuries. I thought it was some Hollywood stunt at first, but it was for real."

"That sounds almost like Mabel during last year's Christmas pageant. She came crashing down the mountain in my motorized outhouse and crashed right through the middle of the live nativity. She took out some of the shepherds, wisemen and the Angel of the Lord. Thankfully, none of them had life-threatening injuries either. They didn't have to use the Jaws of Life on Mabel, but she sure got plenty of my jaw when the Christmas pageant was all said and done."

Their friendly chat was interrupted by some of the ladies who spotted Miz Eudora and begged her to join them for more shopping along Factors Walk, which the man had just explained to us was where the factors—cotton merchants—once conducted their business. Some of them shared photos they'd tagged of her, bringing a source of delight to the informative man, who had become nearly as enamored with her in her purple fopher coat and red hat as she had with the purple butterfly with the red dots.

"I make no excuses for her," was my only response when they showed me the photos. "She is her own person." I couldn't help but laugh as I thought of suggesting that both the town council and the church council write a disclaimer and send it with her wherever she went. I also couldn't help but laugh at some of their images of her. If theirs were this hilarious, I could hardly wait to see the ones captured by her photographer, following her every move.

You'd have thought Miz Eudora didn't know the difference between historic Savannah and the Rumph farm. Had Mabel seen the pictures, her words would have most assuredly been, "You can take Eudora out of the mountains, but you can't take the mountains out of her." You see, what the photos showed was if she took a notion she was tired, she also took a notion to "rest a spell," no matter whether it was on a garden's ledge, with her leg atop the railing at the river, against a statue, leaning on a pole, or sitting on one of the massive branches draped with Spanish moss. There were so many pictures of her that one would have easily suspected she was one of the city's famous statues, given her statuesque poses in many of the shots.

One of my personal favorites was when she was

caught on camera welcoming all the passengers who'd arrived on the riverboat that had just docked on the Savannah River. I was surprised they didn't "tuck tail and run" when they got a glimpse of her, especially if they also got a glimpse of all her friends wandering the streets. Had I been them, I'd have been afraid the place had been invaded. But from the looks captured on their faces, they quite enjoyed the welcoming committee of one.

On the other hand, I was mortified when I saw the shot one had gotten of her coming out of a men's restroom. I guess my warning regarding the lack of restrooms wasn't taken seriously enough. My embarrassment lightened "a mite" when I saw the man waiting outside the door was a minister friend of hers who'd once lived near Smackass Gap. He had ridden one of the buses with his wife, who was to be honored during the course of the "special concert" since her birthday officially signified she would go from wearing pink to wearing red.

I'm sure he thought nothing of her coming out of the men's restroom. In fact, since he knew about Miz Eudora's restroom at home—her outhouse—I'm sure he wouldn't have been shocked at her next action either. After looking at all the photos and bidding good-bye to the kind gentleman who'd given her a second wind, she "took a notion" to check out the Royal Restrooms she spotted in the small parking area in front of Factor's Walk.

"Would you look at this?" she yelled, her words trailing behind her like an echo. "This must be the Cadillac version of my motorized outhouse. It's even got a ramp up to the stalls." She stopped to read the print on the back of the facility: "A Regal Portable Restroom Experience." The print went on to say the traveling restrooms were available for weddings, special events and festivals.

"I reckon they knew all these ladies comin' down here was a special event, 'specially with so many of them being queens. Wasn't it nice of them to want to give all our royal ladies a regal experience?" Of course, she had to try it out to see what a regal bathroom experience was like. "So I'll know how to treat the ladies when they come to Smackass Gap," she said. "You know in that fancy hotel where we stayed in New Orleans, Sadie, they had the toilet paper done up with a little gold seal ever' time we went in the bathroom. Maybe they even wipe here."

I cowered my head and walked to a bench far enough away that I hoped people would not think we were together. Even that didn't keep me from being in the line of fire of her recurring actions, one right after the other.

The next unplanned activity was the kick-line she got going right on the sidewalk. Several of the ladies, while struggling to hold each other up, posed as another passing red hatter took their picture. Car horns on the street began to blow as passersby waved, which caused the women to not only lose their concentration, but also their balance. Half of them fell into the fountain beside them as the others tumbled over the bench behind them.

"I didn't know Savannah had its very own Rockettes," said a lady walking by what could best be described as a circus act.

"Oh, we're not the Rockettes," Miz Eudora hastened to explain as she pulled her purple fopher coat back over her knees and repositioned her hat. "We're the Smackettes."

"Excuse me, Miz Eudora," I interrupted as I rushed from the bench where I'd been trying to hide. "I think it's nearly time for dinner. We'd better go back to the room and freshen up." Hopefully I saved her from being noted as "the freshest lady in Savannah."

BEFORE WE KNEW it, it was time to reassemble at Lady and Sons Restaurant for dinner. We were all escorted by a polite—*and quite handsome, I might add*—young man to the lower level that was reserved exclusively for us. The buffet line was filled with all those dishes for which Paula Deen is noted. Women took their places at the circular tables and anxiously waited their table's number to be called. Not only had they long awaited this experience, the day's travels and an afternoon on the town had significantly heightened their appetites. I wasn't sure how much food a hundred hungry women could chow down, but I was about to find out.

"Where's Mabel?" asked one of the Red Hatters. "I thought she was having dinner with us. She told some of us she was planning a special surprise for us by singing some dinner music for us while we ate."

"Land sakes!" exclaimed Miz Eudora. "Dinner music? I don't want none of you ladies gettin' sick while you're a-eatin'. I'd better go head her off before she gets here. Any of you ladies got an idea where she is?"

"The last time I saw her," answered another of the Red Hatters, "she was headed toward the corner of Jefferson Street and Williamson Street. Said she was going to try out her fanning technique and see what she came up with."

Suffering a sudden gut-wrenching feeling, I hastily instructed Miz Eudora to stay with the others while I went to find Mabel. My instruction worked as well as the one when you tell someone, "Don't look," and the first thing they do is look, because my neighbor tore in right behind me in my quest to hopefully search and rescue Mabel. I didn't bother to inform her we were now on a *real* mission. Somehow I think she intercepted that point from my facial expression and body language.

"P'SHAA! Dinner music, I reckon!" Miz Eudora huffed as she ran out the door behind me. "But don't you ladies worry none," she called back. "There will be a concert tonight back at the hotel after our Haunted History Tour and you won't want to miss it. I promise it'll be a doozey. I have it on Sli … good authority."

What else I didn't share with Miz Eudora, and a fact I was sure she wouldn't have interpreted, was I immediately recognized the corner for which Mabel was headed as Club One, the "home" establishment where Lady Chablis, of the famed *Midnight in the Garden of Good and Evil*, still frequented once a month to do shows. *Too bad Slick Willie and Dirty Harry didn't give us the tour*, I mused as I approached the famed corner. *They'd have made sure Mabel understood what kind of bar this was before she burst into it with what, I'm sure, was a grand entrance.* I couldn't help but wonder whether Mabel had yet encountered "The Grand Empress of Savannah," and if so, whether her Myers Park background would have allowed her to even recognize this city's distinguished "most colorful" character, who starred in the same role in Eastwood's renowned movie. For both characters, I prayed this wasn't Lady Chablis' night.

From a city tour Leon and I had once taken here,

I had heard there was a dance floor on the main floor, and on certain nights, there was karaoke. As we reached the front door, I also quickly prayed this was not one of those nights, with an addendum to the prayer that no one saw me entering the notorious nightclub.

Miz Eudora took a quick glance at the man seated on one side of Mabel, but then turned and literally gawked at the woman, who was actually a man dressed in drag, seated on the other side of Mabel. I was right about her understanding the art of body language. She saw instantly what was going on and decided to take things—*well, some things*—into her own hands, first of which was Mabel's fan. "What on earth do you think you're a-doin'?" she shot at Mabel, loudly enough for everyone in the establishment to hear.

"I'm trying out my fanning techniques on this man," Mabel answered secretively while trying to shoo her sister-in-law away and regain ownership of the the fan, using unobtrusive moves that would not be misconstrued by the man.

Ignoring the fan, Miz Eudora swerved the stool on which Mabel was sitting so that she, too, saw the "woman" on her other side. "Well, this one's flamin' alright, and it don't look to me like he ... needs any fannin'. If you ask me, he needs a bucket of water thrown on him to put out the fire."

Mabel opened her mouth to offer a "spirited" retaliation, but then suddenly got a good look at the "woman" seated beside her. It wasn't until that moment when she understood. A quick perusal around the room cued her into the fact that she was "out of her element," to say the least. Miz Eudora and I each took one of her elbows, which up until now, had been used for strategic fanning techniques. Only now they were both quite limp, as well as the rest of her, as we led her out of the nightclub and back toward the establishment of the lady we were actually supposed to be visiting. I simply breathed a sigh of relief that this was indeed not the evening for Lady Chablis' appearance as we exited the building, all eyes now on us. They'd had enough of a show for one night. Once again I found myself praying, this time that no one on the outside saw us leaving the building. *With Mabel,* or *any excess baggage*, I uttered silently, baffled over the current whereabouts of the fan.

Miz Eudora hit the street with that loud cackle of hers and declared, "Land sakes! I never in my life thought I'd see something like that, much less walk right into the midst of it! Thank St. Patrick, my poor baby brother, John G., wasn't around to witness the kind of places his widow is hanging out in." Her choice of words prompted a grin from me. "Well, I'll say one thing for you, Mabel. You certainly got a few 'pointers' all right." She gave another boisterous cackle.

"P'SHAA! Fannin' the flame, I reckon!"

"HMMPH!" huffed Mabel, in a more subdued

tone than usual, while forcefully crushing her fan into her purse before any other "flame" had an opportunity to appreciate her artistic way of using it. *At least I know where the fan is now*, I noted with another sigh of relief. I'd been terrified that she was so proud of it, she had perhaps had it engraved with her name and address, and further terrified the finder might decide to return it to its rightful keeper.

As did many others of the phrases which Miz Eudora threw out, "fannin' the flame" had taken on a whole new meaning for me, one I was sure would ne'er be forgotten.

THIRTEEN

Kissing the Blarney Stone

WE HAD BEEN instructed by the tour bus company to wait outside the entrance of Lady & Sons following our meal. They were to pick us up for a Haunted History Tour before our "special concert." Everyone else had finished eating by the time Miz Eudora and I got back with Mabel, which was probably a good thing. It meant Mabel got to eat everything that was left on the buffet. The ladies didn't seem to mind. They all were happy to have a few extra minutes to look around in the gift shop upstairs. Mabel's "episode" taught me one more lesson. Women in a cookbook store are like kids in a toy store.

When Mabel was sufficiently full and we were able to rejoin our crew, I tried to opt out of the tour, using the excuse I'd already been haunted enough for one evening. I wasn't joking. Neither was Miz Eudora when she convinced me I needed to personally supervise Mabel or we might have another repeat haunting.

Hence, after Mabel's last bite, the hundred women, *and me*, gathered on the sidewalk to catch the bus. Unfortunately, there was a slight miscommunication. There was no bus; there were hundreds of runners—*over 1,700 to be exact*. The tour guide forgot Shamrock Run, a 5K run and fitness walk that's a tradition every year at 6:00 on the Friday evening prior to St. Patrick's Day. It's the official kick-off of the St. Patrick's Day festivities. *If you ask me, that was a miscommunication too. It should be the run-off, not the kick-off.*

"Guess they needed to run off their dinner too," Miz Eudora stated, reminding me she'd never had to stop to allow runners or bicyclists to get past before she could go on her way. I'm not sure she even knew what a marathon was, and to her, a fitness walk was what she did everyday in taking care of the farm.

The tour guide eventually walked to where we were and informed us that we'd simply have to wait until after the race. He'd walked nearly a mile to get to us and most of the women were incapable of walking back to the bus. Especially given they'd just eaten a buffet at Lady & Sons, where most of them had needed a crane just to get up from the table. So we waited ... at least some did; Miz Eudora collected kisses. Even the tour guide was in her line before it was all over. *Probably for lack of anything better to do while waiting for the race to end*, I mused.

For lack of anything better to do, I slipped back into Paula Deen's gift shop. At least, until I heard a loud commotion, which in itself was a feat since it was already so loud with all those women laughing and chattering, not to mention the college students and all the others who'd joined the group. I should have known the commotion involved my neighbor, but I guess it was a matter of wishful thinking I didn't consider that until after I walked back outside and saw her in action.

Miz Eudora was in the middle of the street running alongside all the participants. With her purple fopher coat flapping behind her, and her dress-tail clinging around her knees, she was literally "hauling buggy," as one of the ladies said. People were cheering her on, holding their hands out for high-fives, taking pictures, rushing out into the street to kiss her, anything to boost her so she'd make it to the finish line.

Not only did she finish, she came in inches behind the winner. But then, she didn't start until almost within sight of the finish line so she naturally had an unfair advantage over most of the runners. That didn't stop her from doubling back to our crowd and doing it all over again. She must have crossed that finish line a dozen times, a few of which she was joined by some of our other women. I even caught sight of her doing an Irish jig out in the street to entertain the runners. Most people would have had to "have a few" to do that, but not Miz Eudora and our ladies. She was in her right mind. *Which shows you exactly how right her mind was ... or wasn't!*

"Why are all those men kissing Miz Eudora?" asked one of the women in our entourage, causing me to look down the sidewalk to see men, and some women with babies, now lined up to be photographed kissing my neighbor. The woman had apparently missed the similar display on the sidewalk minutes earlier. "Do they think this is a race to see who can cross the finish line first and then run kiss her?"

"Either that, or they think she's the blarney stone," teased another one of our ladies.

"Well, she's certainly old and moldy enough to pass for it," Mabel replied without missing a beat.

"And considerin' your hankerin' to gab so much, Mabel," Miz Eudora retaliated from down the sidewalk, "you've obviously kissed the real blarney stone on a number of occasions."

Personally, I didn't understand all the fascination with her. Some of the runners and walkers were much more ornate than she was, at least in my eyes, but people weren't rushing to kiss them.

While the two sisters-in-law were going at it as usual, a group of college guys passed, not runners but merely well into the start of a weekend of partying. "What's all this stuff with the red hats?" one of them asked, noticing most of the action on the street centered in our midst.

Do-It-All Deb, one of Miz Eudora's two Vice-Queens of the Sparklin' Shiners, piped up without missing a beat and informed him, "Oh, we're just a bunch of retired hookers." Oddly enough, her comment received not one raised eyebrow, but plenty of snapshots. Following that response, Miz Eudora—as well as the rest of the ladies in red—could have all made a mint with her kissing booth.

Oh well, at least now there's a reason *for us to get so much attention!* I groaned.

By the time the tour bus reached us, the tour company could have easily sold tickets for another entire busload of passengers. People were enthralled by all "the retired hookers," the hats, and not to be outdone, Miz Eudora's long line of pucker-ups.

There was so much laughter, and such a mass of people, a police car finally stopped in front of our growing assembly in an effort to thin out the crowd. "What's going on here?" he asked. That's when he spotted Miz Eudora. "Oh, it's you."

"Hey there, officer!" she yelled, also recognizing him. "This sure is a friendly town you got here. I wish some of these people could come back with me to Smackass Gap to show all them 'halfbacks' how to get along with others."

"Where'd she say?" asked one of the college students.

The police officer threw up his hands. He knew he'd already lost this battle and chalked it up to St. Patrick's Day getting an early start. "You ladies have a good time and be careful. The rest of you stand somewhere besides in the middle of the street. She said, 'Smackass Gap,' and yes, it's a real place. Trust me!"

After such a display, the tour of the Pirates' House and the cemeteries seemed extremely tame, especially after none of the spirits dared take on either Mabel or Miz Eudora. All in all, it was a calm excursion. *The calm before the storm*, I reminded myself, thinking of the concert yet to come. *With everything these women will have to talk about when they get home, people will suspect they've all kissed the blarney stone!*

FOURTEEN

Birth of the Twins

SLICK WILLIE'S PLAN worked great…all except
for one thing. He had the hotel's ballroom all set up
with chairs and a piano so that it had taken on the
appearance of a regular auditorium. The women from
the two buses began to drift in after returning from
dinner at Lady & Sons Restaurant, followed by a
Haunted History Tour. That is, the ones who weren't
too tired from all the day's excitement, or who were
still brave enough to try something else with Miz
Eudora after the haunted tour. As I suspected, not one
single spirit from the tour took off with Mabel. In fact,
we didn't even catch any sightings. Truth be known, I
think the spirits were all too afraid of sighting Mabel,
for she was really feeling her oats at being somewhere
outside the small parameters of Clay County's night
life.

That would probably explain the one thing that didn't go as planned, the one thing Slick Willie didn't take into account. Everyone was present, in their seats and ready for the private concert … everyone except Mabel. The women were beginning to get restless, the man who was to "sweep Mabel off her feet" was there with his "broom" and threatening to be off the clock shortly, and Miz Eudora was pacing the floor.

"Wait a minute," Slick Willie said, pulling Miz Eudora over to the corner. "Didn't you say Mabel likes to sing?"

"Yes, sir. That's the whole reason we're down here."

"Then why doesn't someone get the music going and it will probably lure her in here?" he suggested.

"That's a great idea!" agreed Miz Eudora as she scampered off to the front of the room. "Ladies and gentleman," she said, turning in the direction of the one male, "we're ready to begin."

Slick Willie joined her with a wireless microphone. "I've never seen this act, but from what I'm told, you are in for an unforgettable night of entertainment."

Having shared that much of the story with you, allow me to rephrase myself. There were *two* points that didn't go quite according to Hoyle. Slick Willie had made all the provisions for acquiring the room, setting it up and getting the piano moved into it. The only problem was he had no one to play it. There was a moment's silence until Miz Eudora looked at him and discreetly asked, "Who's gonna play this thing?"

"I figured you had someone to play."

"Well, Mrs. Azalee usually plays at church, but I didn't invite her here. I was afraid it would knock the hat right off'a her head."

Suddenly it was like one of those moments when a person passes out and someone yells, "Is there a doctor in the house?" Slick Willie turned to the audience and asked, "Is there a piano player in the house?"

Thinking that was about the most absurd thing I'd ever seen or heard, I was more than amazed when a whole row of women yelled back, "Carly can play it!"

I had met Carly twice in my adventures with Miz Eudora. The first time was when she was wearing a red undergarment made into a hat on her head. The second time was when we strolled into a restaurant somewhere in Georgia, not having any clue where we were thanks to Mabel's GPS named Wilhelmina, and ran into this same group of women who sat together on this row. "The Traveling Queens," they called themselves, took us to Bethlehem—Georgia, that is—following that lunch so Mabel could have her Christmas cards postmarked from there. I was beginning to think this group of eight women (who now included my neighbor since they'd invited her to be a part of them) could take care of anything, and perhaps Miz Eudora should consider assigning the job of "disposing of" Mabel off to them.

Miz Eudora ran back to the row where they sat. "Hey there, Carly, where's that cute little hat of yours? You know, the one made out of ... well, you know?"

"It's back in the room," Carly answered with a huge smile. "Do you want me to go get it?"

"Nah, you can save that for later. For right now, could you play something on the piano? We're trying to get Mabel in here because ... well, it's a long story, but could you just play?"

"What would you like me to play?" asked Carly, walking toward the piano.

"Anything you want," answered Miz Eudora.

"How about *Georgia on My Mind*," suggested one of the women in Carly's group, "since we're in Georgia?"

Carly's fingers began to glide across "the old 88s" like a master's. Pretty soon she had the entire room caught up in the sultry mood she had created from the soothing notes coming from the instrument.

"Wow!" exclaimed Miz Eudora. "That was real nice. Made me kind of homesick for my own state." With that, she sat down on the bench beside Carly and began to whip out the notes of *Carolina in the Morning*, astounding everyone in the room..

"Where did you learn to play like that?" Carly

asked, joined by others in the room, before I got the chance to pose the same question.

"Oh, I just picked it up when I had nothing better to do," explained Miz Eudora, after she played the last note and was getting up from the bench, "and in Smackass Gap, that was a lot of the time. When Ma used to tell John G. he could be an Irish tenor, she said I should accompany him. That would have sure been a sight better than what we're doing here now, waitin' for that old thorn of his to get herself in here and sing so this nice man and Slick Willie can get rid of her."

She gasped as she realized she'd "let the cat out of the bag," and sat back down at the piano bench in an effort to gloss over her words. "Here, Slick Willie, this one's for you." Her fingers ripped across the keys with *Chattanoogie Shoe Shine Boy.*

After that, she relinquished the piano back to Carly. "What else can you play? We need something rousin' enough to get Mabel out from wherever she is and in here."

As if the Shoe Shine Boy *wasn't rousing enough!* I thought to myself.

"She can play anything," came the unison answer from Carly's row of cheerers.

"Why don't you two try something together?" suggested one of the ladies in the room.

"Yeah," seconded Slick Willie. "Get some rhythm going in here. That ought to bring that old snake out of the grass." Although most of the women cringed at his mention of a snake, or had shivers running down their spines, Miz Eudora nodded with a huge grin.

"You start and I'll catch up," she instructed Carly.

They started with *Mack the Knife* and went into *Chattanooga Choo Choo*. By the time they reached the last train whistle, which Miz Eudora did on the treble end of the piano, Mabel waltzed into the room, to which the duo went straight into *Tennessee Waltz*. I suspected that was in honor of the river for which Miz Eudora wanted her sister-in-law to go down, complete with her "current," but I kept that notion to myself. The duo came to an abrupt ending of that slow piece and instantly went into the intro of *In the Mood*.

"All this music puts me in the singing mood," Mabel informed the crowd as she marched herself right up to the piano.

"I told you that rousing music would get her in here," boasted Slick Willie. "You played *In the Mood* and she's in the mood."

"Yeah, but now we gotta quickly get her outta the mood and outta here," Miz Eudora shot back.

"I've got just the perfect song," said Carly. She began the first notes of *Fly Me to the Moon*, which Miz Eudora listened to and caught on quickly before adding some rhythm and blues in the background.

"Now we're cookin'," observed Slick Willie as Mabel began to hum along with the music until she could think of some of the words. The ones she didn't know, she butchered her way through with words she made up, but no one noticed because the notes were so bad.

"Play *My Way*," requested Mabel. "That's one of my favorites."

"Gladly," replied Miz Eudora, as she leaned over to Carly and quietly added, "I'll get my way when she gets on out of here."

"Can I ask a dumb question?" asked Carly.

"Sure. Mabel does it all the time and she don't even have the courtesy to ask."

"Why did you go to all this trouble to get Mabel in here if all you're wanting to do is get her right back out?"

"Give me a second and I'll give you the answer to your question. It might take a while though. In the meantime, you keep playing. I gotta take care of something real quick." There was no question in my mind as to where she was going when she headed out the door with her purse. A couple of minutes later, Miz Eudora returned with a glass of water and handed it to Mabel. "She'll be ready to go real soon," she said in a whisper as she passed Slick Willie. "Tell your man to get ready." I saw her slip him an extra bill as she added, "This is 'cause he had to wait so long."

"Hey, Mabel, sing that *My Way* song again," Miz Eudora requested, her voice dripping with sweetness, which I immediately noticed was artificial. "But take you a good swig of water so your throat won't be so dry and you can hold out all those long notes and phrases. You know how much gusto that ending takes, so give it the blend … I mean juice."

Mabel, looking quite satisfied with herself, turned to face her sister-in-law. "Why, Eudora Rumph, I knew you'd eventually see things my way and realize what a wonderfully gifted singer I am. I don't, for the life of me, know what took you so long, but at least you finally came to your senses. I guess that's all that matters."

She began to sing as the two women played along behind her. A few bars into the piece, you could hear Mabel's voice changing gears, or at least vocal quality. The rough edges of her voice smoothed out to match the gentle technique of the piano's accompaniment. The words, which were now becoming a bit slurred, were still better than when she'd butchered them so. All in all, she reached a pleasant plateau with "her way."

So much so, she never suspected anything out of the ordinary when a tall, very distinguished-looking man approached her. A good fifteen years her junior, but with hair graying around the edges, he began to sing, "Hello, my baby, hello, my honey, hello, my ragtime gal," with which Carly and Miz Eudora quickly picked up his key and played along. At the conclusion of the song, he announced, "Ma'am, I know this town has been waiting for years to see something like you come along. Emma Kelly left a big void when she left us."

"And she's going to leave an even bigger void when people hear Mabel!" Carly responded in shock, making sure Miz Eudora, and those of us on the front row, were the only ones to hear her comment.

"He's ever' bit as good as Slick Willie told me he was," Miz Eudora whispered back to her, watching the hired "hit man"—or more correctly, "sweep man"—in action. But when he began to sing Could I Have This Dance for the Rest of My Life, the color flushed from her face.

"What's the matter?" asked Carly, noticing the change in her piano partner.

"I'm not sure how that water's gonna work with dancing. It does a fine job for singing, but I've never tried it for anything besides that." Her face took on an even more sickly appearance. "Last time I left her on a dance floor with this stuff …,"

She winced. "Oh, I'm not sure that even Slick Willie's guy can handle this," she said sadly as Mabel strolled out of the room dancing, which looked more like lumbering, from side to side with her escort. "Oh well," she concluded as she started to play Goodnight,

Irene, "as long as she doesn't come back, it's no longer my problem. I've done what I came here to do." As she watched the man sachet Mabel right out of the room, Miz Eudora stood and announced the show was over.

"You two can't quit now," called someone from the audience. "You've just gotten started."

"Are you sure you two haven't played the piano together before?" someone asked loudly from the back of the room.

"Yeah! Maybe they just tried to pull one over on us and that was part of the show," yelled someone else.

"Who cares?" asked another. "It surely was a great treat, rehearsed or not!"

The rest of the comments were requests for more songs, all of which were answered. Slick Willie soon disappeared without a word, for which I didn't blame him. His work was done, and I was sure he was anxious to get home and deliver that Smackass Gap t-shirt to his wife. But I was wrong. He and another guy soon came back, rolling another piano into the room and placing it next to the first one. Cheers came from the crowd as people from the hotel's bar, and guests hearing the strains of music on the way to their rooms, ventured into the ballroom that was soon filled to over-flowing. Carly excused herself for a moment to make a quick phone call, but Miz Eudora jumped full speed into a jitterbug-paced rag, to which a few of the women got up and danced. By the time she finished, Carly was back and people were calling out tunes so fast, the duo could only play through each one once before going into another.

It seemed only minutes when a tall, slender unassuming guy appeared at the back door. Carly lost no time in running back to grab his arm and pull him to the front of the room where the two pianos were. "Here, you take this one," she said to him. "I'll play along with my friend." She gave the opening bars of *Kansas City*, to which he immediately joined in. It was only a couple of seconds until Miz Eudora was right in there behind them. This pattern went on for several rounds, with each one taking a turn at leading off. They also took turns switching off on the pianos, so that all three got a chance to share a piano with both the other two.

"Those ladies are good. They need a stage name for themselves," someone announced loudly, receiving several loud affirmative cheers, many of which came from The Traveling Queens.

As people in the room started throwing out names for the duo, a man asked jokingly, "What is that woman? A savant?" His eyes were glued to Miz Eudora who, after a few measures of any song, would jump in with the right key and notes.

Miz Eudora, who missed neither a beat nor a

note on the piano, replied in his direction, "No, sir, but that's the nicest compliment I ever did receive. I've been called an idiot on many occasions, although usually by Mabel, but never a savant. Thank you very kindly. I can't wait to get home and tell Preacher Jake and the rest of the people in Smackass Gap!" Her comment brought an even more robust round of laughter, especially by those who had just heard the name of her home for the first time.

"That's it!" chimed several people at the same time. "They can be the Savant Sisters." Loud applause broke loose throughout the room as people showed their approval of the joint decision on what the two women on the pianos should be called. To show their agreement, Carly and Miz Eudora went immediately into *Crazy* which, although written by Willie Nelson, was made popular by Patsy Cline. One of the Georgia women went flying to the microphone and did her best imitation of the country music legend.

"But what about this nice man?" asked Miz Eudora, bringing to mind no one had any idea who the third pianist was. "Who is he and what's he gonna be?"

"He's my forever friend," answered Carly. "Sorry I didn't introduce him earlier, but we were kind of busy right then. We used to occasionally play gigs together. As for what he does, he's a psychiatrist here in Savannah."

"Sure 'nuff?" Miz Eudora replied, turning to the psychiatrist with a smile. "My brother was a doctor too. He was a proctologist. I guess you both did a lot of probing in your professions." Then, after a few moments of hesitation, she daringly turned to Carly and asked, "Hey, how come you got a nice, handsome man for a forever friend and all I got was Mabel?"

Laughter abounded throughout the room. "Not only can they play, they're funny," observed another man who'd come in with his wife to hear the nightly entertainment, not realizing this was no act, it was simply Miz Eudora. *On second thought, she* is *a comedy act, no script needed.*

Even so, that was the only cue the pair needed to take their "act" on to a new dimension. "That's because Mama always liked you best," Carly answered with a playful laugh. "I had to have something I was best at too."

"Yeah, I guess," Miz Eudora mused, as the pair vamped on the piano during their conversation going on in front of the entire crowd. "Besides, I've still got Smokin' Barb and Do-It-All Deb. Seems I've known them just about forever." The forlorn expression on her face, brought on by the thought that all she had was Mabel, turned to one of glee as she stared out at all the people gathered in the room. "And look back there at those Georgia women with Lady Roadrunner, and at all the rest of these ladies. I couldn't have any better friends than them."

"Amen!" came a chorus of replies.

"Hey, I've got an even better idea," shouted one of the Traveling Queens. "Put those three together and we've got MANIA!" The ladies—and all those who had haphazardly become a part of this audience of an unplanned—*not to mention unprecedented*, I might add—live concert began to whoop, cheer and holler. The whole roomful of people went wild with applause as if they had just been the initiating audience of a hit new group.

With that, the Savant Sisters lit into *When the Saints Go Marchin' In*, joined by Carly's "forever friend," and it was definitely hot. I couldn't help but think how much the mood was akin to that for which the piece was originally written. Once the "dearly departed" had gone on, the music turned into one big celebration. We didn't have a "dearly departed," but we certainly had a "disposed of" who made up for it. And from the looks of things, she was now long gone, which was enough of a reason for Miz Eudora to celebrate on this night.

Mission accomplished, I concluded, watching the entire scenario with a smile.

The women who had arrived in the two buses formed a human train as they lined up behind each other, marched around the room singing a few of the choruses, and then headed out the door and toward their rooms, led by the steam rolling off the fingers of "the little engine that could" and her new soul mate— *no, excuse me*—Savant Sister.

"What a day!" I proclaimed when I finally got Miz Eudora back to our room, leaving Hattie and Theona to fend for themselves. I'd driven nearly seven hours to meet Dirty Harry, Slick Willie, and the owner of some belly I hoped to never again see, eaten at Paula Deen's and gone on a haunted history tour with a hundred women, and seen Mabel literally swept off her feet by some man who, in who knows what way (and one I'm sure I don't care to know) loaded her on a bus back to Charlotte with a one-way ticket.

And I'd heard of the *Birth of the Blues*, but now I'd seen the "Birth of the Twins." I never thought I'd live to see the day I would have said this, but I went to sleep literally yearning for "Live in Smackass Gap." *And for the next time I'll hear the Savant Sisters, and hopefully the "forever friend" perform again!*

FIFTEEN

Life Is Like a Bowl of Chocolate Gravy

AS IF THE women hadn't eaten enough the evening before, Miz Eudora got up extra early the next morning, trotted down to the hotel's kitchen and whipped up a "whoppin' big potful" of her special recipe of chocolate gravy. I'd long since decided whereas Horace was known for his "special blend," she was known for her "special recipe." The folks around Smackass Gap told me a long time back that no one could beat her when it came to making chocolate gravy.

"But we're going on the Foody Tour this morning," I told her, trying to prevent her feelings from being hurt in case she'd have no takers when the ladies boarded the buses.

"That nice young tour director told us not to eat anything because we'd be gettin' breakfast at our first stop. Surely they'll have some biscuits for the gravy.

Miz Eudora & Saints Go Marchin' In

Miz Eudora should have had her head examined before she headed to Savannah with two busloads of ladies with red hats. With Miz Eudora leading the pack, misadventures were sure to happen, especially when Mabel was around trying to run the tour "the proper Myers Park Way."

Always with an eye open for a good man, even in innapproprite places, Miz Eudora managed to find two prospects during her trip.

Ladies who shopped with Miz Eudora learned her eye for the best finds in town.

Miz Eudora found all kinds of things shopping. She even found a little critter that would stay put anywhere you stick it. And, she found some unusual places to stick it!

From lyricist Johnny Mercer to founder of Methodism, John Wesley, Miz Eudora got "plumb tuckered out" chasing her saints all over Savannah.

Obviously, Mabel was not among that illustrious number of "saints" marchin' in!

L̶o and behold, Miz Eudora and her saints bumped into Forrest Gump while he was waiting for a bus. She got so excited she knocked her hat off and had to chase it down the street as the wind blew it away. Mr. Gump was not impressed, nor the drivers she "mooned" in the process.

When Miz Eudora happened upon a 5K marathon, those old red orthopedic shoes thrust her into the race where she danced a jig all the way to the finish line.

And who could forget the Ghost Hunt. Looks like Miz Eudora either saw one or had too much of the "special blend." But, the most frightening haunt of the night was Mabel who scared even the resident spirits!

There's nothing better than good ol' Southern cookin'. Naturally, Paula Deen tops the list of best cooks around. But when it comes to good looks, Paula can't hold a candle to her son, Bobby, who just fell head over heels for Miz Eudora.

Good eatin' was one of the main activities on Miz Eudora's tour. And, no trip to Savannah is complete without a tasty meal at Paula Deen's Lady and Sons.

Miz Eudora had to explain to some of the women that a ho cake was not a dessert that was often served at a "lady-in-red's" birthday party!

From chocolate to barbeque to sloppy 'mater sandwiches to shrimp 'n grits, it was all "finger-lickin' good."

Going...

  Going...

    Gone...

A heavenly experience!

Movin' and groovin'
Rockin' and rollin'
Reelin' and jiggin'
Shakin' and bakin' (in the **hot** Georgia sun)

Miz Eudora had the time of her life swapping dance steps with the city's best dancers.

And, fun was had by all, especially by Miz Eudora's "personal" photographer. He did a fine job making sure Mabel didn't get in and ruin any of the pictures.

Miz Eudora's Savannah tour group.
(Next Page)

After all, Sadie, we *are* in the South." I let the matter drop, just as I did her insistence that we ride the buses with the ladies, meaning Hattie and Theona hopped on one, and Miz Eudora and I hopped aboard the other.

My neighbor changed her tune about southern food at our first stop. "Don't they have bacon here?" she asked when the waitresses brought out plates of shrimp n' grits for all of us. Here we were at Mom and Nikki's, whose signature recipe had just been featured on the Food Channel. Needless to say, their popularity for their soul food was increasing immensely, so I felt honored to be eating one of my favorite southern coastal dishes prepared especially for us by Mom and Nikki themselves. Needless to also say, I felt like going through the floor when, to make matters worse, Miz Eudora went on to ask, "Where's the biscuits?"

Looking back, I have no clue why I was so concerned. All of our ladies were eating a famous signature dish, made from Nikki's own special recipe, and we had brought her lots of business. Miz Eudora and the ladies were not only holding all the babies that belonged to the women of the soul food kitchen, they were trying hats on the babies. From the adorable grins on the babies, I came to realize "hattin'" is fun no matter what age you are.

Once all the hats were back on the heads of their rightful owners, we loaded the bus for Polk's Fresh Market, a locally-owned business that had been in

Savannah for generations. We were welcomed with homegrown tomato sandwiches as we entered the front door. There were all kinds of foods to taste, all from fresh ingredients. Miz Eudora was always served the first bite. I guess everyone took one look at her and figured if the food killed her, no one would care.

After we left Polk's, and all our stomachs were full, the tour guide took us around the historic district, pointing out all the important places and scenes of famous incidents. Not only was Miz Eudora taking in all the sights, she was taking in ways to entertain her friends back in Smackass Gap. "When all my friends come to visit, we can have horse-drawn carriages just like these," she noted as she admired the carriage tours. "Clyde could pull the carriages. I'll bet we could make a lot of money for missions giving tours during the Festival on the Square every July. I think I'll mention that when I get home."

And between that and the kissing booth, the members of the town council will all be on a mission to evacuate you from Clay County that second weekend in July, I reasoned. *They'd have better luck with Mabel selling fans on the sidewalk.* She did, however, stand a chance with doing something like this Foody Tour, where she could serve small samplings of all her best dishes.

Interspersed with tidbits of history and interesting stories, our tour allowed the food from one place to digest before we reached the next one. It helped that we got off the buses and walked for several blocks to our next two stops, which were a pastry shop and a BBQ hut.

It didn't help that traffic kept bottlenecking because drivers were slowing down to take pictures of all the pink and red plumed hats and colorful costumes. I tried to persuade my conscience this was only because the women were dressed in colors other than green for the upcoming festivities. To help that argument with my conscience, I was pleased Miz Eudora wasn't the only one catching the cameras; I somehow didn't feel quite as responsible.

Until ... I suddenly noticed Miz Eudora's hat fly off her head, moving with the same fluidity of motion as the famed feather when it left the tall white steeple at the beginning of *Forrest Gump*. Unlike Forrest, who sat perfectly still and recited the story during all that movement, my neighbor, with her curls blowing wildly in the wind, chased the hat until it landed half a block away, right in the middle of the street. I guess there's no point explaining to you that traffic was now at a dead standstill. You've probably already figured that out.

As if that wasn't bad enough, she then bent over and mooned the people traveling in one direction. When horns started blowing from all directions, she managed to twist herself around so as to politely wave and say "Excuse me" until she had fairly mooned everyone, no matter which direction they were traveling. There was quite a jam when the police officer from the day before appeared—rushing from out of nowhere, it seemed—picked up the hat and handed it to her as he escorted her from the middle of the street.

"And you're here for how long?" he attempted to ask politely while gritting his teeth. I assured him we were leaving his fair city the minute the tour ended. My instinct told me I should simply ask him to follow us so he wouldn't have to find us on his own. Instead, I quietly walked back to the buses with the rest of the passengers.

It was no accident our next stop was at Wright Square Café, a fine chocolatier in the historic district. The women in their hats, known for their love of chocolate, went wild—as if they hadn't already—when they hit the front door and received free samples.

"Did you know they can cover anything in chocolate?" I overheard from one of the women who'd gotten her sample and was eyeing the glass counters of all their delicious offerings.

"With the Easter season approaching, chocolate bunnies are flying off the shelf," said one of the store assistants from another corner.

"I never knew bunnies had wings," Miz Eudora commented. "I know they're good for one thing, but I didn't know it was flying." She shrugged as several pairs of eyes shot in her direction. "Oh well, I guess if there's flying squirrels, there can be flying rabbits."

While the women bought chocolates, Miz Eudora whipped out a small ladle of chocolate gravy for the shop's owner. He went gaga over her concoction, demanding to know where she got it. I could hardly wait for him to learn she made it all by herself, with no fancy equipment. *Only her wood-burning stove and one "pot" that was saved solely for making chocolate gravy.*

I watched them, deep in conversation while comparing notes on the processes of making chocolates and chocolate gravy. With a renewed appreciation, I realized my neighbor truly was a master in the eyes of some the greatest food masters in the South, if not the country. *Another vote for why she needs to try a Foody Tour instead of a kissing booth!*

Once we left the chocolatier and headed for Chippewa Square, I understood a second reason the stop at Wright Square was no accident. We were on our way toward Hull Street, where Tom Hanks—portraying Forrest Gump—sat on the famous bench. The moment the buses stopped, Miz Eudora jumped off and assumed the role of the tour guide. She walked to the exact spot where the bench had sat, and positioned herself so that she looked like she were seated on an invisible bench. The tour guide, in awe, stood back and let her continue her portrayal of the character.

Following Miz Eudora around was like being on a constant mystery adventure. You never knew what would come out of her mouth, or who would show up "out of the woodwork." On this particular day, the character showed up alright, but not out of the wood-work. He literally appeared, from seemingly out of nowhere, right behind Miz Eudora Rumph as she stood explaining to all the ladies exactly where the bench was where Forrest Gump sat to narrate his incredible story in the legendary movie.

You see, none of us saw it—*or rather, him*—coming. It was like one minute he wasn't there and the next minute he was. I wasn't the only one rubbing my eyes when, in mid-sentence, Miz Eudora was joined by a man who looked "more like Tom Hanks than Tom Hanks," one of the women later said. He had on the same red cap, the same blue-and-white plaid shirt and the same box of chocolates, which he opened and offered one to my neighbor.

The policeman had been right; the two of them together were quite a sight. They moved to the near-est bench, where Miz Eudora served him a helping of her chocolate gravy, right out of the pot. I guess you could say it was the Smackass Gap version of fondue. There were no long forks or pieces of bread for dip-ping. They simply each swiped their pointer finger into the large slop jar and brought it back out with a healthy dose of liquid chocolate. Neither of them said a word; the expression on their faces said it all. They were in a world of their own.

Watching the pair go on like they'd been "forever friends," I was reminded of the cop who'd suggested we introduce Miz Eudora to the Tom Hanks look-alike. *Seems their soothsayers come with a badge*, I concluded, recalling that the day's date was the fêted ides of March.

Whoever said, "If you can dream it, it will happen," wasn't kidding! I said to myself. For all the shame and embarrassment I'd felt minutes earlier, I was now beaming because this woman was a part of my life. Thanks to her, I now understood that the church from where the feather came was not even in the same square as the bench. All the other tidbits I'd always wondered about from that movie were now no longer questions. We'd received special consideration from not one, but two, characters.

In the meanwhile, the photographer Miz Eudora had picked up, like one of her "stray cats" at the Ingle's, was doing better than well as he captured her every move. "Looks like he struck it rich," stated one of the women from West Virginia, who knew about mining. "He may never have to work again."

"Yes," I replied, watching as he finished snapping photos of Miz Eudora and the Tom Hanks look-alike. It appeared he'd earned his week's keep at one shooting. *Enough to buy several boxes of chocolates!*

"Okay, ladies!" he yelled. "Let's get one with all of you." That was an easy assignment. All the ladies rushed to be in the picture. After a couple of shots, he announced, "All through here." The ladies said good-bye to "Mr. Gump" as other tourists crowded around the famed character and we boarded the buses.

I'd never considered myself a connoisseur of chocolates, but I did pride myself on being an acceptable connoisseur of movies. Now that the Forrest Gump character had shown his face, I wondered whether we might happen upon Jim Williams, probably Savannah's most notoriously famous character who lived a real-life drama. *If nothing else, maybe we'll spot Kevin Spacey who played Williams in* Midnight in the Garden of Good and Evil. I'd already decided one thing. If we chanced to see Clint Eastwood, I was stopping the bus and getting off.

There was something that bothered me about the whole situation regarding Miz Eudora and the bench, but I couldn't put my finger on it until well after we'd left Chippewa Square for another historic landmark, which in fact did turn out to be the Mercer House, Jim Williams' home that was made incredibly famous in the movie of his story.

While the other ladies jumped off the bus for a better view of the house, and hopefully a peek into the room where all the infamous action of the movie occurred, I cornered my neighbor. "Miz Eudora," I began, anxious for an answer to my question, "how did you know about *Forrest Gump?* You've not watched any movies in decades."

"I hadn't until last week. When I told Mary at the library I was comin' to Savannah, she insisted I watch the movie. She played it for me on one of the televisions at the library, and then she told me all about the feather and the bench scenes being shot right here. I do believe it was better in real life, and I can't wait to tell her so."

Another adventure for Live in Smackass Gap, I told myself, hoping I could be present when Miz Eudora shared this experience with Mary and her library friends.

By the noon hour, the buses were back on their way to the parking lot where I'd left my car. Miz Eudora had served her own special recipe to most of Savannah's finest, including the policeman—whom I was certain was a soothsayer in disguise—who had shown up at every turn. He now even owned his own Smackass Gap t-shirt. Miz Eudora gave him one after he rescued her hat.

From shrimp n' grits, to chocolate, to BBQ, and everything in between, no one went hungry. And if they had, there was always that big pot of chocolate gravy. But by the end of the noon hour, that had all been devoured too. It seemed our trip had come to "a tastefully delightful" close, and I must say we took more out of Savannah than we had come in with. Every person who'd made the trip had to have gained at least five pounds. Each one of them had also left a part of herself in Savannah, for the photographer had snapped nearly a thousand photos.

After retrieving my car, I followed the buses to one last stop before their return to their respective homes, at the request of the photographer. Watching the ladies, their laughter and frivolity evident even from aboard the buses, and thinking about all the places and situations they'd come from, I realized what a valuable lesson I'd learned that day. Whether it's served in a bowl or a box, it's life. *And what a great life it is*, I mumbled to myself as I took a bite of the chocolate "Mr. Gump" had secretly given me.

SIXTEEN

Movin', Groovin', Reelin', and Jiggin'

IT WELL MAY have been Mabel Toast Jarvis who was earlier combing the streets of Savannah while trying out her artistic style of fanning, but it was Eudora Rumph who now took to trying out her moves in the city parks of Savannah. In Miz Eudora's defense though, it was the fault of the photographer who had chosen to use her as the subject of his spread on colorful characters. He got the bright idea she would be a perfect centerfold. Let me go back and rephrase that so you don't get the wrong idea.

Since the paparazzi was nothing new to Miz Eudora, and she'd become so accustomed to people snapping her picture, she had no qualms about agreeing to his request. Therefore, the final item of business on our last afternoon in Savannah with all her friends from the two buses was a group photo. The famed Forsyth Park was selected as the location and the ladies were all arranged in front of its distinguished fountain, which was already flowing with green water in anticipation of St. Patrick's Day. The ladies were all too happy to be a part of the group shot, since a quick survey determined none of them had ever been a centerfold before. They could hardly wait to go home to their seven states and share the news.

The photographer lined up all the ladies, making sure none of their faces were hidden by hats. That was an astronomical task in itself, but then when he tried to get a hundred women all smiling at the same time, my hat was off to him—pun intended.

Conditions could not have been more perfect, as far as the weather was concerned. The temperature was perfect for the ladies to be in their t-shirt sleeves, and the sun was shining brightly, although its afternoon position made it difficult for the photographer to capture all the faces as he wanted. Thus the group shot turned into several. He instructed Miz Eudora to keep changing her expression and pose with each one, making it most entertaining to see the faces and positions she came up with to make the shot appear "unposed." Needless to say, there was none of Miz Eudora's personality that wasn't exposed during his many snaps of the camera. You had to give her credit, she certainly gave him an array of choices to work with in laying out his spread, especially the centerfold.

In the course of picture taking, loud music began drifting from another section of the park, causing the ladies to juke and jive slightly which, in turn, made the photographer's task even more complicated. Seeing he was losing their attention to the rhythm in the air, he quickly finished his work and bid them all a courteous farewell.

As we walked back toward the buses and my car, I could tell the music was getting closer. More precisely, we were getting closer to it. We rounded a tall hedge of flowering shrubs and immediately saw the whereabouts of the music. A group of five young men, all African-American and ranging in age from their late teens to early twenties, were working on a choreographed piece. Another African-American male, obviously the instructor was moving from demonstrating the moves in front of them to walking around behind them to make sure they were all precisely together. They were amazing, demanding the attention of all the ladies as we stopped to admire their work and talent.

The next thing I knew, Miz Eudora handed me her "new used red leather pocketbook" with the words, "Hold this!" and was out in that hot afternoon sun, purple fopher coat and all, moving right along with them while swinging parts of her body I didn't know existed, and if I ever had known, I'd forgotten by now. Within minutes, she was teaching those young black males some moves of her own. I'm not really sure where she came up with those particular moves, but when one comes from a place called Smackass Gap, I highly suspect there's a whole lot of things they have hidden up their sleeves.

And lots of other places, I decided, watching her "go to town" out there on the grass of Forsyth Park in Savannah, Georgia.

Before it was all said and done, the director of the dance troupe was sporting Miz Eudora's red hat and the dancers were holding her in the air for another shot by the photographer, who'd come running back when he spied her movin' and groovin' with a team of black males.

Soon other spectators were stopping to admire, appreciate and comically ogle the activity going on "behind the bushes," as it was later quoted in *Live in Smackass Gap*. Suddenly, the repercussions of the centerfold were much farther-reaching than a simple group picture.

All the ladies seemed content observing this exhibition, which surprised me, for I figured they'd have been right out there with her. *Must be where the ladies in hats draw the line*, I decided, figuring they were either too embarrassed or shy to be a part of this. *Or too busy taking their own snapshots*, I soon realized. But they surely had loads of fun watching her in action.

"Bust a move out there, Miz Eudora!" called one of the Georgia ladies.

My response, which I was sure would have also been Mabel's had she been there, was, "Keep that up, Eudora Rumph, and you're going to bust more than a move!" Respectfully, I kept my response to myself.

It seemed I, along with Mabel in absentia, was the only one to share that opinion as everyone around us, including and besides all the ladies in our group, was cheering her own. I had to admit my elderly neighbor was displaying moves that were new to me. Some of them looked like disco, some resembled steps from an Irish reel or jig, some came straight out of the 50's rock-n-roll era, and the others I'm not sure about. Whatever they were and wherever they came from, they were most definitely unique. Even the experienced black dancers found themselves unable to keep up with her ever-changing motions. Nonetheless, there she was, in the middle of Forsyth Park, holding her own beside this group of dancers.

When the rap music finally ended, she came over to me and retrieved her "new used red leather pocketbook." I halfway expected her to pass out by the time she reached me, but as she took the purse, I realized she hadn't even broken a sweat. She simply walked back down the concrete path back toward the bus as if nothing were out of the ordinary.

One of the dancers came rushing up behind me

and—in a voice and a way that reminded me of the old "Lone Ranger" episodes from my younger days— admirably asked, "Who was that old woman?"

I watched his amazed gaze following her stride toward the bus and proudly answered, "She's my neighbor."

"Does she have a name?" asked one of the other dancers who had also come up behind me.

"She certainly does!" replied one of the other ladies of our group. "Miz Eudora Rumph!"

"Miz Eudora Rumph," repeated yet another dancer who had reached me, mimicking exactly the emphatic "ph" sound at the end of Rumph. "Now that's a mouthful! Where's this Miz Eudora Rumph from?"

"Smackass Gap," called the hat-clad women in unison as they raced to catch up with Miz Eudora.

I couldn't help but snicker as I wondered what those guys were going to tell their friends when they left the park. I'd have loved being a fly on the wall to hear their description of the strange old woman they'd met. I suspected they'd all be accused of trying some illegal substance rather than practicing dance routines.

What I'd anticipated being a five-minute snapshot turned into a spectacular grand finale of our weekend in Savannah, capped off by Miz Eudora and Carly, arm in arm, doing a Huckleberry Finn-type kick-step on their way toward the buses and my car. Even the photographer, who was the cause of the afternoon's merriment, got in on their action when someone placed Miz Eudora's hat on his head.

Watching all of this, and reflecting on the events of the past three days and how St. Patrick was responsible for much of what had transpired, I speculated on how God might judge me in terms of my afterlife. From much of what I knew, it was all about grace. John Wesley had declared it had nothing to do with good works, even though those were quite commendable as per the words of his well-known quote. *It's a shame about those good works,* I decided, reaching down to pick a lone four-leaf clover that I spotted staring up at me. *Otherwise, I'd be in the waiting line for sainthood.* With that, I gave a simple kick-step of my own as I caught up with the one who caused most of those good works.

I'M GETTING AHEAD of myself here, but it's important you know the rest of the story, which didn't come to a close until over a couple of weeks later, following our return home from Savannah.

I never gave Miz Eudora's so-called "moves" another thought as life returned to normal, or at least as normal as it ever is, in Smackass Gap. That was, until one evening when I received a strange call. The phone rang shortly after I sat down to read after washing dishes, two simple activities that together had come to be a relaxing therapy for me. I actually think it was more realistically a way to take up time in the evenings, of keeping my mind off the lonely nights without Leon. Either way, this particular evening's therapy session was interrupted by the unexpected ringing of my telephone.

"Excuse me," began the pleasant male voice on the other end of the phone after I answered. "I hope I'm not intruding, but I did a bit of research online and found your address fell in an area known as Smackass Gap."

"Yes?" I hesitantly replied.

"I'm hoping you might be able to help me. You see, I met a woman named Miz Eudora Rumph a couple of weeks ago at Forsyth Park in Savannah, Georgia."

I immediately recognized the voice from the way he pronounced Miz Eudora's last name. The emphasis he gave the "ph" at the end was the same as the young dancer who had repeated her name in the park. "Yes," I said again, this time as a statement rather than a question, but still inquisitive about where this conversation was heading. I gave him no further answer or information.

"I'm the choreographer for a dance troupe in Savannah. We're auditioning for a national competition next month. I was hoping you might know how to get hold of this woman as we'd like to invite her to join us in the competition."

I stood silent while pinching myself hard several times, making sure I hadn't dozed off in my swivel rocker and was dreaming. When I was convinced I was standing on my feet and indeed having this exchange with this young man, I had to muster up all the composure I had not to laugh aloud. Somehow the thought of Miz Eudora "bustin' all those moves" in front of a panel of judges, and possibly national television, was more than I could sanely comprehend. I took his name and number, and assured him I would get the information to her. From there, he was on his own with her. That's where my good works stopped.

Oh, and about that business regarding the women being a centerfold. You'll notice, if you haven't already, that each and every one of them truly *did* become a centerfold, right there along with Miz Eudora. And if you look closely, you might even catch my neighbor movin', groovin', reelin' or jiggin'. From where I stood during all that dancing, she seemed to be doing all four, plus a few more, at the same time. You see, although each of those dances is set to a different meter, Miz Eudora's body parts apparently didn't all move in the same meter. That's why it appeared she was doing so many moves at the same time, depending on which body part you were watching.

And about rephrasing things so you wouldn't get the wrong idea, I don't know why I bothered. Miz

Eudora took care of the wrong idea. She gave it to everyone; there was no defense, as had been when this whole thing started. The next week's column of *Live in Smackass Gap* was all about her being a centerfold in an entire photo spread, and "showin' her stuff" behind the bushes. It did go on to mention that "while I was movin', groovin', shakin', rattlin', rockin', rollin', reelin' and jiggin', Mabel, on the other hand, was simply jigglin'."

When I confronted Miz Eudora to remind her that Mabel wasn't even there at that point, she replied defiantly, "I know that!" But then, her Irish eyes began dancing as she added, "It doesn't matter where she was at that point. If she was breathin', she was jigglin'!"

"And probably with a fan," I considered mentioning, but decided it best to leave that alone. I felt certain that would be the focus of the next week's column. "Movin', groovin', reelin', and jiggin', *combined with jigglin'*, were enough for one week.

SEVENTEEN

Play It Again, Sam

WITH MABEL OUT of the way, Miz Eudora immediately transformed into a different person. She was suddenly footloose and fancy free...*and green*...from head to toe. The minute all the entourage of visiting women boarded the buses and left to return to their respective seven states, she took off with Carly and Peggy, the newly-installed manager—and glutton for punishment—of the Savant Sisters. The threesome had decided to stay over a couple of days to celebrate St. Patrick's Day in true fashion in Savannah. And true *fashion* it was! I'm not sure their outfits would have made it outside the streets of Savannah, with the exception of maybe New York City or Boston, but on this day, that trio made a fashion statement that was seen the world over. At least by those who looked on the web for interesting individuals who showed up for Savannah's annual St. Patrick's Day celebration.

Oh, and there's one thing I failed to mention here. Although Hattie and Theona decided to take the bus back to Smackass Gap and enjoy the days without the hullabaloo of the dueling sisters-in-law, I was voted to stay back and be the designated driver for whenever Miz Eudora took a notion to go back home. You'll note I was not invited to be a fourth party in the trio's shenanigans, for which I was most grateful. It was much more fun to sit or stand on the outskirts and watch the clamor of those three. All in all, I think it simply brought me one step closer to affirming the belief that my otherwise sweet little neighbor truly *was* kin to Calamity Jane, only she now had two accomplices.

Now back to a description of that widely-publicized fashion statement. As it turned out, Miz Eudora had become so caught up in the Irish spirit by the time St. Patrick's Day arrived, she traded her rose-print flour sack and colorful, sparkling attire for an all-green wardrobe, from her head to her toes. That's right, she trotted over to Gina's, a small beauty supply shop on Savannah's Broughton Street—which immediately became her favorite store—with their selection of colorful wigs, hats, shoes and jewelry. She bought herself a kelly-green pageboy wig, which she topped off with a green sequined cap that she stuffed with newspaper to make it stand up like an engineer's cap. A couple of stores down, she stepped into a classy men's store where she spotted a pair of shamrock-shaped shades on a mannequin right inside the door. Somewhere along the streets, she found a long-sleeved knit shirt of the same vibrant color as her hat, and managed to get herself green beads galore by the time the parade started up. As if she weren't enough of a spectacle by herself, her twin—the other Savant Sister—and their manager each also got the same exact outfit.

Needless to say, as we checked out of our hotel that morning and I watched her trot off in front of me toward the elevator, I was certain I was caught up in some dream and had been dumped in "the Emerald City" with Dorothy. *Even Dirty Harry and Slick Willie wouldn't recognize her like this!* I prayed the dream didn't turn into a nightmare, or rather a "daymare," as it was in this case.

Miz Eudora exited the hotel and before I could turn in the keys and catch up with her, she was outside on the street corner having her photograph made with a group of firemen from New York City. Not just any firemen, mind you, but ones who, because of 9/11, were now world heroes. Time, place and circumstances had brought them to stardom; time, place and Mabel had brought them to Miz Eudora. They were all making a great to-do over her outfit. When they saw the other two women, dressed exactly like her, who exited the building with me, cameras began to flash all over again as bystanders flocked to get photos of the trio together.

It was hard to tell them apart since all three were wearing the same identical clothes. Not only were they wearing the same clothes, but they had the same green hair, the same way-overstuffed sequined caps, the same long-sleeved kelly-green colored jersey covered by a t-shirt of the same shade of green. Carly had even gone to the extreme of purchasing the same shade of lipstick for all of them, which—*luckily,* I noted—wasn't green. Basically if you saw one of them, you saw all of them.

I looked toward the cobblestone street nearby to make sure it had not turned yellow, and that there were no munchkins hanging around. *Who needs sunglasses to make everything look green? All one needs to do it take a good look at these three. They'll be seeing* nothing but *green for a few minutes!*

Thank goodness, Peggy—the manager—took her job seriously and shoved the other two toward East Harris Street and the cathedral. Prior to the legendary parade, there was always a celebration of Mass at the Cathedral of St. John the Baptist on East Harris. Miz Eudora had never set foot in a catholic church before, much less a cathedral, but she was determined not to miss a single thing about this day. I wondered whether the service would be in Latin or English, wishing I could catch the look on her face were she unable to understand it. But then I suspected she'd be so awed by the interior of the cathedral that she wouldn't even hear the words. *There's no telling what she'll be wanting to add to First Church, Smackass when she gets out of this place!* I reasoned, already feeling pity for Preacher Jake, Mr. Grover Swicegood and the church council.

Not wanting to get too close to the trio, I chose to lollygag around outside, though it was difficult not to peek in the back door from time to time to see how—*or what*—she was doing. At the conclusion of the service, Miz Eudora fled the building so hastily that she nearly toppled me down the steps. Not a word was mentioned regarding the beauty inside, nor what was spoken. Her mind was on one thing solely.

"I wonder how Mabel's doin' about now?" she asked.

Wondering whether something in the service had prompted her to feel genuine concern for her sister-in-law, I decided to make a fairly general insight regarding the situation, thus not to insult her. "The sight of Mabel in her present condition, or at least the condition she was in when she left here, ought to get the attention of a few of her socialite friends from Myers Park. They may never allow her to set foot in their country club again."

Her nose twisted as she chewed on my reply. Her reverse psychology obviously had not taken that consequence into account. "If nothing else, I'll bet they don't see her as the social butterfly or social bumble-bee, or whatever it was Mabel said John G. referred to her as in that obituary she wrote about him. You won't ever make me believe my baby brother called her that.

"Land sakes! John G. might have gone off to college to get an education, but he got enough of an education while he was still in Smackass Gap to know the difference between kudzu and a bumblebee. Shoot fire, they're not even the same color!"

She paused a minute to let the steam escape and then started again. "Besides, there's no way she could have been a butterfly 'cause they're beautiful crea-tures. She would have definitely been a bumblebee if anything, 'cause they sting you, just like the thorn on a wild rose.

"P'SHAA! Social bumblebee, I reckon!"

So much for the service having a lasting mean-ing, I rationalized.

The firemen, the same ones we'd met earlier and who were now lining up for the parade, heard Miz Eudora's ranting. So did the crowd who'd gathered around to speak to the firemen and take photos, which meant a whole new round of cameras flashing to catch this woman causing all the commotion.

"Reckon one of you firemen can put her out?" I asked them quietly.

The only response I got was an animated group

laugh, and a reply by one of the younger ones who ventured to say, "I doubt there's a fire hydrant in all of Savannah large enough for that!"

I had to agree. Some things are the same no matter where you are, at least where Miz Eudora is concerned, and assuredly if Mabel is involved. During this time, I noted "the manager" was intelligent enough to keep herself and the other "savant" out of the line of fire.

But aside from that little discharge, the day turned out to be most memorable. Not only for Miz Eudora and her two new best friends, but for all of Savannah, and anyone at points beyond, who subscribed to the online edition of Savannah's newspaper. You see, there were thirty-six photos of people who caught the attention of staff photographers positioned throughout the city. Miz Eudora and her trusty scalawags were in nine of them.

It probably helped that they were right in view of all the television crews and media. Seeing as how Carly seemed to have an "in,"—or was either very persistent—the three of them happened to get seats right on the front row of the bleachers straight across the street from the cathedral. That meant the minute mass was over, they scooted out of the cathedral, scurried across the street and got in position to enjoy the parade. *And be photographed and caught on camera during the entirety of the event.*

From the moment the parade started, Miz Eudora was like a kid at the circus. She cheered and applauded with every passing vehicle, float, band or group of walkers. Watching her made me wonder whether she'd ever been to a circus, which I greatly doubted. I didn't have time to dwell on that, and whatever else she might have missed by growing up in Smackass Gap, because I suddenly realized she was up and out of her seat, and in the middle of the street.

Apparently her welcome to Savannah, with so many men kissing her on the cheek, was interpreted as habit or simply the thing to do in that fair city. Although she didn't start it, she wasted no time in following suit as she dashed out in the street and plastered red lips on the cheeks of soldiers, heroes, prominent Irish men or babies, and basically anyone who couldn't outrun her. I'm not sure how much those bleacher seats right there in front of the Cathedral of St. John the Baptist were, but I'm sure even as expensive as they were, the parade participants would have gladly paid more for that one seat to have kept her at home.

Then there was one other slight predicament. If I had thought the lack of public restrooms was a problem in Savannah previously, I had not taken into consideration what it might be like on St. Patrick's Day with such an overflowing horde, some of whom had already helped themselves to several servings of green beer. After sitting on bleachers—in which half their time was spent standing up and cheering, or running out in the street to bestow kisses and green beads on any characters they deemed worthy—there was a "multitudinal urge," as Miz Eudora appropriately termed it. Not only did she coin the phrase for it, she had a solution for it, which was quickly shot down by the manager.

"What do you mean you don't think I could have entered the outhouse in the parade? If they can have green goats and green spotted horses, they can surely have a motorized outhouse. Especially if we had covered it in kudzu."

I started to suggest they simply have Mabel sprawl across the front of the outhouse since she had been compared to that particular kind of greenery on more than one occasion. But since she'd thus far managed to stay out of the conversation since Mass, I saw no reason to bring her back into it now. However, I did mention we decorate the contraption with shamrocks and fill Miz Eudora's black wash pot with fake gold coins and put it on the front where the moonshine jug usually sat. In fact, she could leave the jug there too, but simply rename it Irish whiskey since supposedly it was her Irish ma's finger 'what made it so good.'"

It was this lack of private quarters, rather than the outlandish green get-up, that captured everyone's attention in the long run. Otherwise, the three happy-go-lucky green individuals would have been out combing the streets like every other Irish person in the city on that day. But like everyone else, after sitting—or rather, standing and dashing into the streets—until the end of the nearly four-hour parade, nature called while they were on their way to find some lunch. Suddenly the need for a restroom became much greater than the need for a restaurant.

"No one told me I should have brought my slop jar," Miz Eudora shared with the other two as they rushed from their vantage-point seats, near the beginning of the parade route, toward River Street to beat the crowd for lunch. Their game plan was to eat lunch immediately after the parade and then go their separate ways. That plan was preempted as they scouted diligently for a ladies' room at every business along the riverfront … to no avail, it turned out. Out of desperation, they finally took an alleyway that appeared to go up to the Bay Street level, where Carly was sure they could find a restroom open to the public.

A policewoman met them a few feet into the alleyway. "Looking for something?" she asked.

"A restaurant," answered Carly.

"Then you won't get there from here. This leads to the kitchens, so only staff persons can access a restaurant from this point. All the front entrances are up another whole level."

A quick survey told them there was no access, at least not one available to them, to the street level. After a round of desperate "aah"s that did no good in drawing sympathy from the officer, the three moaned and groaned their way back to River Street. Finally, they spotted an elevator that ran up to the street level of a restaurant where they were sure they could relieve themselves.

"Are you eating lunch with us?" asked a woman when the elevator door opened at the upper level.

Not to be outdone, Carly immediately answered, "Yes!" None of the three even knew what restaurant they were in. It didn't matter. All that mattered was "a facility." Smiles lit their faces as the hostess led them toward a table, after which they could rush to the restroom.

Suddenly "the need" took a momentary—*a very tiny momentary*—backseat as Miz Eudora punched Carly and said, "Listen! It's a grand piano. In that room next door, there's a grand piano."

The three women stopped dead still, as the hostess kept walking toward a vacant table.

"She's right! There is a piano," stated Carly.

"This place must have a piano bar. You sure know how to pick 'em," joked Peggy as Miz Eudora rushed to the door between the two rooms and peeked in the adjoining room.

"Right there it is," Miz Eudora hailed proudly,

"and there's a man playing it."

"Excuse me, ma'am, but could we get a table on this side?" asked Carly, pointing toward the piano.

"No problem," she answered, changing directions. "Would you like a window seat?"

My desire to say "yes" was vetoed by the other three, who took the table directly at the end of the piano. Just as Miz Eudora predicted, there was a shiny ebony baby grand hidden in a corner, but with a nice view of the restaurant's back door, and the river beyond, for the one playing it. We were met by a waitress the moment we sat, who warned us it might get loud and crazy in that exact spot before the day was over.

What else is new? I wanted to respond. There was no need; she'd already picked up on that.

"I guess when there's three of you like that, you've already had a loud and crazy time," the waitress commented.

"You got that right!" replied Peggy. "You may be the ones who need the warning." Then the manager turned her attention to my unassuming neighbor. "Miz Eudora, how did you know that was a grand piano without seeing it?"

"Because it was the grandest sound I ever heard. It didn't sound a bit like that old thing I tinker on at church every once in a while, or that was in my house when I was growing up."

See what I mean about her vocabulary? Her definition of a "grand piano" was right on target in her mind, but not what the average person thought of as they envisioned a curved bow in the elongated back of a beautiful instrument.

It was that same vocabulary that didn't recognize anything on the menu, so I ordered something for Miz Eudora while she took off for the real reason of our stop here. While the three of them were momentarily gone and I had the opportunity to survey our find, I couldn't help but wonder whether St. Patrick really did have a hand in us landing in such a fortuitous spot. We were in Vic's on the River, one of the finest establishments on the waterfront. I wasn't sure reservations could have been made for this day in this place. From the time it took for the place to be filled, which was basically how much time it took for the three ladies to return, I determined there was more than just a little bit of luck in our finding this place. *Or it finding us!*

While we waited for our food, Peggy took it upon herself to approach the pianist, a man who appeared to be close to the age of Carly and her. "Do you mind if my friend plays a number? She used to play here in Johnny Harris'."

No wonder she can play the hound out of a piano, I instantly assessed. *This is old hat for her*, I joked as I glimpsed at the three of them in their new hats.

"I'm getting ready to take a smoke break," he replied and looked in our direction. "Why don't you play one or two while I'm outside?" Since the other two seated with me were dressed just like Peggy, he aimed his question at both of them. "Do the three of you always dress alike? What are you, triplets or something?"

"No, sir," Miz Eudora rightly answered. "One of the triplets is the reason we're here. You see ..." I jabbed her in the side before she got a chance to totally confuse the man and have them calling the nearest mental facility to make sure we hadn't escaped. I wanted to stay at least long enough to get our food, which I remembered as being excellent in this place.

Carly got up to play when he finished his next number. After playing *Georgia on My Mind*, and receiving an applause, she told Miz Eudora to join her. The two of them did a couple of fun numbers together, dazzling the people who were patronizing the place with more than their clothes. By the time the man's smoke break was over, the duo had made quite an impression.

"Don't stop now," begged one of the waiters, whose request was seconded by others who heard it.

"We'll play a few more when we finish eating, and he takes another smoke break," replied Carly.

That time never came. Well, at least part of it didn't. They never finished eating, and the pianist got lots of smoke breaks that day. Oh, and the Savant Sisters played way more than a few.

"Where did you learn to play like that, Miz Eudora?" asked Peggy, when the duo later took a sweet tea break. It was the same question that had been posed the night before when Mabel was "swept" away.

"What do you think we did at home when I was growin' up? We didn't have television sets back then. Land sakes! It wouldn't have done any good if we had. All we could'a seen would have been snow 'cause there wasn't no reception up there in the high mountains. None of us wanted to watch snow 'cause we saw enough of that in the winter in Smackass Gap."

As usual, her comment held a bit of humor, but sadly, was also true. There was one thing for certain about being around Miz Eudora. She took you back nearly a hundred years, for even though she wasn't that old herself, her ways were every bit that and more. At the same time, though, about the time you became accustomed to her simple ways, she'd come out with some zinger or punch line that would blow you right out of the water of your comfort zone with her.

There was something most serendipitous about being in this setting with my neighbor and these two women, whom I was sure would now be her forever friends. People gathered around them, spoke to them about their music and commented on their attire. It was a whole other world from the one in Clay County, where Miz Eudora's outrageous attire got plenty of attention but no comments. The only one who had the nerve to comment on it was ... *She's not here, we're not going to talk about her*, I told myself.

That serendipitous world was about to take a nosedive, much as it did in Smackass Gap right after Horace passed. The two had no more sat back at the piano and started into their first handful of notes when I noticed Miz Eudora's face drop. (The only way I could tell it was her and not Carly, because of the matching outfits, was that I recognized her expression of dismay far too well, wigs, hats and green clothing notwithstanding.) "Carly ... look!"

I whipped around barely in time to see Mabel plop down in one of the seats at the bar. With due cause, I feared Miz Eudora was going to light into one of her tizzies right there on the piano bench. To cause my fear further consternation, I happened to notice Mabel take out her fan. I also saw her position the little card that contained the language of the fan. *I guess it never occurred to her that the available men in this place might not know that language. She may need a translator.*

I didn't have to worry about that predicament for long. By the time she had listened to The Savant Sisters play a couple of numbers, "the bug to sing was itchin' her pretty good,"which was one of Miz Eudora's "Eudoraisms." My blood pressure was soaring at the thoughts of all that could happen in this particular situation, given a few of the noted miscreants now gathered inside Vic's. I was sure this fine, upscale establishment was nowhere nearly prepared for what could and was about to happen. *Not to mention Savannah's "finest," whom I'm sure are out in full force today.*

Miz Eudora motioned for me to come over to the piano. *Surely she doesn't mean me,* I thought with a shudder, troubled that, unlike these other three, I was not in masquerade. Grabbing the napkin from the table and holding it in front of my face, which I kept lowered, I approached the bench, imaging what I felt at the moment was closely akin to what a "found guilty" criminal feels when approaching a judge's bench. "I didn't do it!" I wanted to yell. That's when I visualized all those criminals on television news holding their heads down and trying to hide their faces. *Yep, I look like one too,* I noted, half jokingly.

"Well, there's one good thing about this," Miz Eudora said, making me wonder what could possibly be good about this, but figuring she was speaking of her costume hiding her real identity. "At least I won't have to waste Mary's time at the library looking up Mabel's ancestry. She's definitely a purebred, blue blood Australian."

"How do you know that?" I inquired, now completely puzzled.

"'Cause she's like one of them boomerangs they

have over there. It don't matter how far nor how many times you throw them out, they always come back." She let out a laugh that I was certain would expose all of us, but thankfully, Mabel was too caught up in looking up a specific fan motion on the little card to pay us any mind. Luckily, Peggy and Carly were able to mask their laughter so we didn't cause too much of a ruckus.

And luckily for the man Mabel was vying for with her fan, he chose that moment to leave for greener pastures. Her attention turned back to her "itchin'" apparently, for she made a straight beeline for the piano, which set off my own bout of laughter as I recalled Miz Eudora's earlier words about her being a social bumblebee. I sat there, the napkin still partially pulled over my face, as I waited for "the sting." It didn't help matters when Carly started playing *Maple Leaf Rag* that, though composed by Scott Joplin, was best known from the movie, *The Sting*.

"How about playing something I can sing?" requested Mabel.

I fully expected Miz Eudora to loudly exclaim there was nothing she could sing, but a glance in my direction stopped her dead in her tracks. *Or rather, words*. Carly must have shared my suspicion, for she quickly asked, "What would you like to sing, madam?"

"Oh, anything you play will be fine."

Miz Eudora's next thought, which was that anything was fine because Mabel would make up any words she didn't know and butcher the song anyway. "How about this one?"

Carly started the intro for Kansas City, to which Mabel began singing. It mattered not that she truly did miss over half the words, all of which she butchered along with the notes. All Miz Eudora heard was the part about "going to Kansas City," which prompted her to ask Mabel how soon she was leaving.

"Maybe you can board the train with this one," suggested Carly as they lit into *Chattanooga Choo-Choo*. She, as well as I, knew something had to be done and soon.

Peggy, who was still stunned, was coming up empty-handed with a plan of how to manage this unfortunate chain of events. She must have had a good connection with St. Patrick or was either extremely lucky, for one of the restaurant's patrons managed it for her.

"Honey, I'll buy you whatever you want to drink if you'll come over here," a man called from the end of the bar.

Mabel stopped her crowing—or warbling, or honking, or whatever it was—and moved to the man's side to take him up on his offer. I don't think she caught even the slightest hint of the underlying meaning of his comment. She was too focused on the way he had prefaced it with the word, "Honey." My favorite part of this amusing scene was how she picked up her purse from the piano bench—where she'd unwittingly set it beside Miz Eudora—and began to "stroll" toward him, one hand on her hip, which was swaying wildly from one side to the other, with her purse hooked at her elbow, and the other hand holding the fan in one of those silly positions as she batted her eyes at him.

And I thought Miz Eudora was bad with Dr. Betz when Mabel had the knee replacement surgery! I would have gagged, but it would have meant that I'd have missed Mabel's next move at attempting to be flirtatious, a move I was sure would be notable. I didn't know who was putting on the bigger show, The Savant Sisters or Mabel. I wasn't too sure about the rest of the patrons inside Vic's, but I would have paid admission to see either one of these acts, and double for both!

My droll thoughts were interrupted when another man called out, "And I'll buy you as much of it as you want if you'll stay over there with him instead of at the piano." He got a wink and the fan being brushed forward by Mabel, which I took to mean he had himself a deal. I wondered if I should clue him in on how much she could down, but I figured he'd gotten himself into this bargain, he could get himself out. Besides, Mabel had no idea he was serious.

To make the episode even more priceless, Miz Eudora broke into a rousing rendition of *Ain't She Sweet* the minute her sister-in-law left the curve of the piano.

"You're playing that for Mabel?" Carly asked in shock.

"Yeah, get a-playin'! She'll never suspect it's me back here if she hears this comin' from the piano." Her reasoning made me question whether she hadn't taken a course somewhere along her schooling at Burnt Schoolhouse—which wasn't burnt at the time she attended it—in reverse psychology. For someone who'd never been outside Clay County, to speak of, before I met her, she certainly knew a lot about it.

Everything went fine for a good while as more and more people meandered into the restaurant after making their way there from the parade, having stopped at what few shops were open along the way. What one has to realize about Savannah is that St. Patrick's Day is like Christmas in the rest of the world. Not much is open besides the restaurants and bars, and Vic's is one of the more upscale places along the riverfront to view the small ships spraying green water at each other, now that the city is no longer allowed to turn the river green. All in all, it was a great establishment in which to spend the afternoon.

That was until Mabel got the bright idea to sing again. You have to understand this was a cultured scale of clientele, so I wasn't concerned about a barroom brawl or anything like that. What I was concerned about was the fear of the two sisters-in-law giving more of a show than this crowd was ready for, green beer, Irish whiskey and all. "Ladies, can you play *My Wild Irish Rose*? I'd like to sing it to the memory of my dearly departed Dr. John G. Jarvis, who came from good Irish stock. Well, at least some of them were decent Irish stock. That sister of his should have been left under the cabbage leaf where they found her. Why, she wouldn't have been good stock even if she'd have been cooked in Corned Beef and Cabbage. But enough about her. Let's get on to the song I'm sure you're all dying to hear me sing."

I saw Miz Eudora turn to Carly and mutter, "I'd rather die than hear her sing it!"

Mabel turned to duo. "Hit it, ladies!"

"I'll hit it, alright," huffed Miz Eudora, rising from the bench.

Carly, who was giving the intro with her left hand caught Miz Eudora's shirttail with her right hand and pulled her back down to the stool. "Let her go. She'll do herself in."

"She'll do more than herself in," Miz Eudora replied curtly, striking a handful of keys with both hands. "When she said these people were dying to hear her sing, she wasn't lying. They'll be dying for sure if they have to listen to her sing for long."

"Don't worry," joked Carly. "I know how to play *The Funeral March*."

That comment was exactly what Miz Eudora

needed to get her mind off her sister-in-law and back on her sister-on-ivories. Mabel had gotten halfway through the chorus when I saw a look I wasn't sure I liked in my neighbor's eye. It was the glimmer that often appeared when her mind was in gear; it usually meant trouble. It also usually meant Mabel was involved. I leaned closer to hear what she was whispering in Carly's ear.

"Do you know how to change keys?"

Carly gave her a questioning glare. "Yes. Do I want to know why?"

"Probably not, but I think she needs to try a little variety."

"I get it." The twinkle that appeared in Carly's eye was almost as mischievous as the one in Miz Eudora's. "What key do you want?"

"About two black keys up ought to be good. Just enough to throw her off." Her cackle interrupted her words. "Not that she's not already off."

Miz Eudora had a point. In fact, Mabel was *so* off-key that I wasn't sure anyone, especially herself, would notice a sudden change in keys. I was wrong. Everyone noticed. Everyone except Mabel, that is. She kept giving it the gas, in more ways than one—which was nothing out of the ordinary for her—until she'd nearly reached the third phrase of the verse. That's when she turned to look at The Savant Sisters who each flashed her a giant smile and waved politely. It must have struck Mabel that she'd messed up, so she turned back around and attempted to reach the notes she was hearing from the piano's opened top.

"Can someone please buy that woman another beer?" asked a man seated near enough to the piano to hear that things were quite amiss.

"Forget buying her a beer. Here's one on the house," offered the barmaid.

"My dear madam," said an obviously well-groomed gentleman seated at the bar. "There isn't enough green beer in Savannah today to make that woman sound good!"

It was at that precise moment Mabel accidently emitted another puff of air, which taking into account her size, was a rather large and powerful odious puff. It was also at that precise moment when a short little man dressed in a green suit and derby, who'd been seated atop a giant pot of gold on one of the parade floats, passed by her on his way to the bar. He instantaneously fell to the floor, shouting, "Don't shoot, lady! I'm just the leprechaun!"

Roaring laughter abounded as it slowly became apparent what had happened. As if Mabel's luck was not already going badly enough, the television crew was canvassing the crowds and chose that exact moment to visit Vic's on the River, catching the entire episode on film. While Mabel's face turned completely red, the rest of the faces around the bar were turning an odd shade of green, matching their attire for the camera.

"That's our cue!" Miz Eudora told Carly excitedly. "Take 'er back to where she was." This time there was no opportunity for words or exchanged glances between the pair, both of whom were holding their breath. Right in the middle of a word, they jacked the piece back down five half steps. "You keep on a-going, I have to take care of something." She went for her purse.

I didn't have to guess too hard about what was coming next. She'd even sewn in a special side pocket the week before just to hold "Mabel's potion" for emergency situations. Miz Eudora whipped out the blend and poured a healthy dose in a water glass and handed it to her sister-in-law. Mabel took a big gulp, which was followed by a few more big gulps, and before she reached the last note of the song, she was singing herself right out the door and onto Bay Street, water glass in one hand and her fan in the other, with her purse dangling from one of her elbows. *And the television cameraman following along right behind her,* I noticed.

With Mabel out of the way, people began to call out requests faster than The Savant Sisters could finish each one. The brandy snifter on the side of the piano was filling up quickly with green, and I don't mean beer. It was their manager who finally had to call it quits.

"You can't quit yet," begged one elderly man. He looked pleadingly at Miz Eudora, who was "the sister" closest to his age. "I'll buy you a Scotch if you'll play just one more song for me."

"I don't drink Scotch," Miz Eudora replied.

"Then I'll buy you a glass of milk."

Miz Eudora peered at him over the top of her green shamrock glasses. "Besides, isn't this the day for Irish Whiskey?"

"Not if you're from Scotland!"

"I'll drink to that!" called out another patron. His comment reminded me of the morning Miz Eudora stomped on my porch and first informed me of Mabel's decision to take over the choir, making her a snake in the grass and causing this whole escapade. Again, I had the odd feeling of being caught up in a wild-west bar with someone buying rounds for all, and I knew we'd better "hit the trail" before the "bad guy"—who in this instance was Mabel—showed back up again for another round.

"Play it again, Sam!" shouted one of the nearby waiters, followed by a chorus of others.

Miz Eudora scooted over, making room for the piano player, who'd had the longest cigarette break of his life. "C'mon, Sam!' she called.

Guess she's never heard that expression before. She obviously thinks they're all talking to the regular piano player, and now she thinks his name is Sam. Thinking it too late to open that can of worms, I joined the applause and the crowd, who was now chanting, "Play it again, Sam!"

"You've got yourself a big bunch o' fans here, Sam," Miz Eudora told him as the trio began the opening bars of *Goodnight, Irene.*

EIGHTEEN

O Danny Boy
(or maybe not!)

"OKAY, YOU TWO," ordered Peggy, "you need to wind it down while we can still worm our way through this crowd and get out of the city." By this time, everyone who'd attended the parade, not to mention all the party-goers who'd come to experience the annual night life of this noted event, was swarming into the streets and restaurants along the riverfront.

"Then let's make this one count," said Carly. "We can't get out of here without playing *Londonderry Air* at least one time through." The duo had played the heartrendering piece, literally painting an image of the Irish countryside on the open back wall behind the piano through their tender and dramatic portrayal of the piece on the keyboard, and were about to come to a close when a lyrical voice came from the front door.

Eyes of the crowd followed the sound while I did a double-take to make sure I'd not unknowingly stumbled into the "special blend." But I was not imagining things. Neither was Miz Eudora when she turned toward the direction of what could have been described as an angel in song.

"O Danny Boy," Mabel began, her voice a beautiful mellow tone that perfectly matched the words of the song. People stood breathlessly still and listened. Tears flowed from some people's eyes, while those who had heard her butchering their favorite Irish songs earlier stood in awed amazement. For the next few minutes, the only sound you could hear inside the establishment, that seconds before had been a din of boisterous merriment, was the singer and the subtle accent of piano keys in the background. Even Carly had cut out because she thought it such a momentous visual and aural occurrence to finally see the two sisters-in-law in perfect harmony. *Not to mention pitch*, I noted as I glimpsed at the pair, sure this was not real.

When the sound of the last note had faded into the air, the crowd was again a cacophony of gibber as thunderous applause broke throughout the building. Those who had heard Mabel earlier in the afternoon were suddenly crammed around the bar wanting "some of what she had." The man, with whom Mabel had earlier done everything but come to blows, stared admiringly in her eyes. He held out his arm, which she accepted as she linked her elbow inside his, and the pair strolled out onto the sidewalk and down Bay Street, the two of them still singing the ballad in harmonious tones. I couldn't help but notice Mabel's other hand demurely cupped around the illustrious fan she'd bought, as she waved it gently back and forth in front of her face.

I guess she learned the proper way to use it for hot flashes, I surmised.

"What about that!" shouted one of the men who had earlier heard Mabel.

"Can you believe it?" asked another, holding up his glass to toast with his wife. "Seems this is a day to celebrate more than just our good old patron saint chasing the snakes out of Ireland."

"I'll drink to that!" called out a deep voice from the back of the crowd. Glasses clinked, toasts were made and everyone took a drink to Mabel's honor.

Miz Eudora, still caught up in the man's question, stood from the piano and blurted out, "No, I can't believe it. She actually knew the name of the man she left with this time. Did you hear that, Carly? She called him Danny. But then she did call him a boy instead of a man. Wonder how on earth she knew his name?"

The crowd returned to their raucous laughter. "His name was Ira," yelled a woman who had been standing beside him earlier.

My neighbor peered in my direction. "So she

sang *Danny Boy* to a man named Ira? Oh well, at least she's gone." She turned to me and quietly mouthed, "So I guess we *can* officially celebrate getting rid of the snakes in Smackass Gap too!"

Sporting an empty tea glass, I raised it in her direction. "Or at least one of them!"

"I really don't think he cared what she called him after that last drink," offered a gentleman standing by the bar.

"Seems the spirit of St. Patrick took care of her," said a man who had heard Mabel when she first started to sing.

"And Ira too," a woman yelled.

Miz Eudora walked to where I was sitting. "St. Patrick didn't have a thing to do with running this snake off." She patted her purse. "It was Horace's special blend." After heaving a hefty sigh, she added, "Again!" Then she gave an even bigger sigh. "Well, at least St. Pat took care of one person. Maybe Ira was a snake in the grass to his brother-in-law." A few snickers followed her comment. "The only problem is she went away alright, but she went away with the man who offered to buy me a glass of milk. Now I reckon I'll have to buy my own."

"Here, lassie," came the sound of a man's voice. "I'll buy you anything you want to drink after that lovely rendition of *Londonderry Air*. That tune is enchanting enough by itself, but when it is paired with

those words, you can't help but see the lush countryside of Ireland with a young couple pledging their love
to each other. Aye, it is truly a picture of a beautiful
song, and it captures the heart of Ireland and love in
the springtime like no other piece of music can. It takes
me back to me homeland every time I hear it." You
could hear his voice begin to crack with emotion. "And
when it gets to that final phrase, 'I'll simply sleep in
peace until you come to me,' I can see a couple …"
His voice trailed off and he was quiet for a second
until he regained his composure. He then turned to
the woman behind the bar. "Give her a tall glass of
green milk. It's on me."

Carly tapped Miz Eudora on the shoulder.
"Don't you think maybe we should get back to rat-
tling the keys?"

"Yeah!" called out a large group of the patrons
in unison.

"Play it again, Sam!" yelled the man with the
deep voice from the back of the room.

Miz Eudora followed Carly back to the piano,
took her seat at the treble end of the shiny baby grand
piano—now that Mabel was out of the way *again*—
and forgot all about beating the crowd as the duo
played *My Wild Irish Rose*. Whilst her fingers glided
masterfully over the keys, the look on her face showed
she was lost in her childhood memories of John G.
singing in the front room of the Jarvis home. After

they finished, a peaceful glow had replaced all the exasperation and determination that had been written on her face during this entire trip.

At least in one way, this endeavor had been a huge success. She turned to Carly, and said loudly enough that I was able to hear, "Well, if Mabel can call Ira Danny, I reckon it's okay if that man calls us Sam. At least he got the first two letters right." A tender smile, which grew into a huge grin, appeared as the pair continued to play requests until well into the evening.

I moved to an empty table near the back of the restaurant, away from the piano but overlooking the water, where I could enjoy the serene respite from Mabel and, for the moment, Miz Eudora Rumph, who was totally consumed by sharing her passion of music with a sister pianist, who too could rip off anything on the ivories. Mabel was in her zone, though no one knew where it was, I was in my zone of recalling blissful memories of sitting along this same riverfront with Leon, and Miz Eudora was contentedly submerged in her zone.

By the time the night lingered on to the closing hours, there were more than just Irish eyes smiling. In fact, it didn't matter if you were Irish, Scottish, German, or "half-breed"—as Miz Eudora referred to those who weren't blue bloods, which was nearly everyone and most especially Mabel. All eyes were full of smiles as the doors closed behind the last customers. The Savant Sisters picked up the brandy snifter from the piano, which was filled with tips, and handed it to the piano player who'd had the longest smoke break in history.

"You can keep those, you know," he said.

"Nah," replied Miz Eudora. "I didn't come here to make money. I came to have a good time and that I did." She gave one of the cackles for which she was notorious back home. "You know, I didn't have a clue what all this talk of late was about when people kept making such a big deal about 'goin' green.' I really like the idea of 'goin' green.' It sure was fun today. I can't wait to do it again." With that, she bid her good-byes to Carly and Peggy, both of whom agreed they should all have another "play date" soon.

She walked out the door, with me following so as not to interrupt her innermost thoughts. As we approached the parking deck of the hotel, where Dirty Harry had allowed us to park during the parade, I caught the faint sound of my neighbor singing. I leaned a smidgeon closer to her so as to make out all the words. Lo and behold, she was singing the chorus to *When Irish Eyes Are Smiling*. In the shadows of the evening, I couldn't very well make out her smiling eyes, but if they were anywhere near the smile on her lips, she was a lovely sight to behold. As Miz Eudora concluded a second refrain with, "In the lilt of Irish laughter, you can hear the angels sing," she did indeed sound like an angel, whose singing was wafting through the night air, combining with the echoes of faint laughter drifting through the city streets.

"That Mabel is gonna be more than *two* shades of green with envy when I tell her what all went on today."

"But she was there …," I began.

"Land sakes! That body of hers might'a been there, but I'll guarantee you she won't remember a thing come tomorrow. She'll be lucky if she even remembers that fan, not to mention that poor old Ira. All I can say is, I hope that stuff he had was as good as Horace's 'special blend' so he won't remember a thing either."

We'd barely gotten a block away when Miz Eudora spoke again, her demeanor totally changed. "Sadie, do you mind driving by Reynolds Square? I'd like a minute in private with Mr. Wesley," Miz Eudora politely requested as I headed toward the thoroughfare to take us out of the city.

"I'll be glad to," I answered, "but are you sure you feel safe out there at this time of night?"

"I'll be alright," she answered solemnly.

When we reached the side of the square nearest the statue, I stopped the car long enough for her to get out. Since I didn't know how long she'd be, and she'd given me no indication, I drove around Reynolds

Square so many times I looked like a hamster on one of those circular wheels. That was alright because it provided me with a view in the dim moonlight of her attempting to look saintly beside the statue of John Wesley. She trotted over to one of the nearby benches, where she sat momentarily and obviously prayed. I guess, for whatever reason, it made her feel her prayer would be more holy and better received were it near some holy figure. Since we'd seen no statue of St. Patrick, I guess she figured this was the next best thing.

After she got back in the car, we rode in silence until I got us out of Savannah. Because it was now in the wee hours of the next morning, I suggested we stop for rest and drive home later in the day. Gratefully, I received no objection. I do believe my neighbor was too busy replaying the entire day and evening in her mind. I'm not sure I'd ever seen her experience such an enjoyable time, especially considering Mabel was involved in part of it.

I didn't know whether it was because of Danny, Ira, Tom, Dick or Harry. *Or even Dirty Harry, Slick Willie or the man with the belly.* All I knew was, for the time being, all was well with the world and I was lifting up my own prayer of thanks for the influence of St. Patrick.

NINETEEN

Rollin' in the Aisles

I HAD HEARD of sleepwalkers, and even encountered a few in the past due to Leon's line of work, but
from what I gathered since moving to Smackass Gap
and attending several of the area churches with Miz
Eudora, there was also a breed of "sleepsitters." Every church had a few. First Church, Smackass had its
own fair share, but one of whom was notoriously
known throughout the congregation. This man—to
remain nameless so as not to embarrass him in print—
came every single Sunday, supposedly because he
loved the music, especially when the choir "tore into
some rip-roarin' old gospel song." That's probably
because that was the only time he was able to stay
awake. Personally, I've always been inclined to believe the reason he fell asleep was either because his
wife snored too loudly at night, or he had a shoddy

mattress, or both. But for whatever reason, he found the church pew a most comfortable place to get in a few extra winks come Sunday morning.

You must also understand his wife never came to church. She was "a good woman and all,"—as the church folk described her—but she stayed home and cooked every Sunday. "That," she told people who asked why she didn't attend, "is my way of worshipping the Good Lord. I get more out of cooking than anything else." One look at her proved she was telling the truth. A look at her husband indicated he was also getting a lot out of her cooking. My only question about that was what she gave back to God for all the blessings He had bestowed on her. I'd heard of people setting a place at their table for Jesus. Even so, I somehow couldn't imagine the Almighty swooping down every Sunday to partake in a plate of food at her table as "His fair share." Besides, the way I heard it, the only extra plate she set was for the dog and it went out beside the back stoop.

Oh, and there's one last thing about the wife of Mr. "To-remain-nameless." She ate promptly at noon on Sunday so if Mr. "To-remain-nameless" wanted to partake in the Sabbath meal, he'd better be seated at the table when it was served. Otherwise, she cleaned up the dishes, put everything away and that was the end of that. She did, however, make enough extra "vittles" on Homecoming Sunday each year for him to share her "worshipping food" with the rest of the congregation. I've decided, during the three years I've been here, that's why Preacher Jake always made sure we were out by noon on Homecoming Sunday. He wanted to be certain the food didn't get taken up at the strike of noon, sort of like Cinderella's carriage turning into a pumpkin at the stroke of midnight.

Enough rambling, though, let's get on to what happened last Sunday. I'm really glad Mr. "To-remain-nameless" chose to come that day, for he had four things going for him, plus an extra little bonus. You see, it was a bit overcast and too hot to do anything but sleep, the choir planned to sing a "rip-roarin'"—which actually turned into "side-splittin,'" by the time it was over—old gospel song (whose title was even befitting of the last Sunday for the choir director who'd faithfully given over two decades of service as she rode out of that position), it was communion Sunday, and he got the most unique wake-up call that had ever gone out in our congregation. And about that extra little bonus, well, it actually turned out to be a pretty big-sized bonus, seeing as how word of it spread all over Clay County by the time evening came. All in all, it was a pretty memorable day in the history of First Church, Smackass.

Oh, and so you understand the full impact of the story, you have to know that if the choir "got a-goin'" with their special music, someone was to punch

Mr. "To-remain-nameless" so he wouldn't miss it, and then when it reached 11:50 on the clock on the back wall of the sanctuary, someone was supposed to punch him so he could get home and in his seat at the table by noon. On communion Sundays, someone simply punched him when it was time to be served and he quietly exited out the back door after taking his bread and wine (which at First Church, Smackass, was nothing more than grape juice).

There's just one other little bit of "housekeeping" you need to know in order to fully understand the significance of this story, especially for those of you who don't attend church. You know how, if you go into certain areas of an inner city, you might run into "the hood?" About as inner city as it gets in Clay County is at First Church, Smackass. We have our "hood," too.

Let me explain. Sometimes in a congregation, certain families have their "self-appointed" seating assignments in the pews, which may go as far as to include a handful of families sitting together in one little area. Like other "hoods," it could be dangerous to venture into them. You don't dare go into a church and take someone else's seat. Heaven forbid! Most churches have them, they're simply not privileged enough to have a specific name for their "hoods." We're no different, except our area where several families flock together is nicknamed "the neighborhood."

It is an area on the left side of the church, about three-fourths of the way down from the back door, next to the outside aisle.

To explain further, churches don't follow the same rule as most tour buses. They don't play the "swap seats" game. Members have their own marked pew, like the neighborhood dog has his marked spot, and they don't stray from that spot. Our "hood" was made up of approximately three families, including their offspring, and their offspring's offspring. Only on this particular Sunday it was a holiday—July 4th, to be exact—so there were several visitors, which means there were some people seated in that area who weren't part of "the neighborhood."

Things were already a little off kilter for Smackass Gap because we weren't having our annual Dam Fireworks Show at the dam on Lake Chatuge. That was about the biggest happening in Clay County besides the annual New Year's Possum Drop, so folks were a bit disappointed. There was no need for disappointment, though; at least not for the members of First Church, Smackass. The youngest member of our "neighborhood" gave us a better show than the annual nightly fireworks and everybody still got home before dark. In fact, they got home in time for lunch, including Preacher Jake *and* Mr. "To-remain-nameless." Here's how it all went down—or up, or even back and forth—as the service progressed.

It was the scheduled Sunday for communion so the person in charge of waking up our renowned sleeper was on standby. Instead of a registration pad for visitors like some churches use, and like we'd had in the past, Preacher Jake decided to try communion cards. He'd decided it would be a fine way to keep up with who was still active in attendance and purge the files of those who no longer participated in the "goin's on" in the life of the church.

While he was giving instructions on the use of the communion cards, I took that opportunity to check out who was "present and accounted for" that day. As I glanced over and saw the head of Mr. "To-remain-nameless" doing "the bob" a couple of times before his chin fell to rest against his chest, I was reminded of a story I'd once heard from one of Leon's minister friends from Emory.

Seems this minister was preaching on Adam and Eve and the sin of taking the bite out of the apple, so he asked the congregation, "What did Eve say to Adam in the garden of Eden?" A woman in his congregation chose that particular instant to give her sleeping husband a friendly wake-up call with her hat pin, to which he reacted by sitting straight up in his seat and yelling, "Jumpin' Jehosaphat!"

The man fell back into his peaceful slumber, and the minister kept going with his sermon. A few minutes later, the minister rephrased his question and asked it again. The wife, more than a little embarrassed by her spouse's sleeping habits and not expecting another question from the pulpit, gave her husband another stick of the hatpin, this time with a bit more force. Again, to the chagrin of both the wife and the minister, the man spouted off with, "What is that thing you keep sticking me with?"

Realizing he was quickly losing control of the congregation's attention, the minister tried to wrap up his sermon as succinctly as possible and still make his point. He was unaware that just when he asked the question for a final time, the wife also gave her husband "the point." The sermon ended and, as the minister had hoped, everyone in the congregation had something to go home and talk about all week, because this time the wife was determined to make sure her husband stayed awake. She gave him such a good sticking that he flew from his seat and exclaimed, "If you poke me with that thing one more time, I'm gonna smack the mess outta you!"

I had to mask my own private chuckle at the recollection of that story. First Church, Smackass, didn't need a woman with a hatpin, although I had no trouble imagining Miz Eudora pulling that same stunt on Horace back in their middle years. In fact, she'd pulled it on her sister-in-law once at Lake Junaluska when it had come time for Mabel to pray. Her stunt got a similar reaction. I was grateful no one in our church, except for Mrs. Azalee who was too sweet to use it, had a hat pin on this particular morning. No need, we had something better. Children … and no children's church due to the holiday, which meant the children were all in the sanctuary with everyone else.

Unfortunately—or fortunately, depending on how you want to look at it—Preacher Jake finished his sermon earlier than usual so he could get home in time for a July 4th cook-out with the other ministers of the area. Therefore, the man on standby to wake up our renowned sleeper had slipped into the men's restroom. That meant when the head usher quietly gave the signal for the standby man to "Wake up Mr. 'To-remain-nameless,'" the standby man's five-year-old daughter had to take care of it.

After giving him her best shot three times in her most polite little ladylike voice, she turned to where the head usher was directing communion traffic and prolifically announced, "He's either dead or frozen 'cause he won't wake up." Her announcement did the trick, for "the bob" started in reverse, along with a wave of soft snickers that went both in forward and reverse throughout the pews.

We also had a bright and precocious young lad with a creative imagination, who was the youngest member of "the neighborhood." It took little to spark that imagination. Today it was sparked by the fact that whoever had placed the communion cards in the pew racks didn't take into account that visitors would be sitting in the hood's marked area. Therefore, there were not enough cards for everyone in those pews, which meant cards were being passed back and forth until each person had one.

The lad, watching all of this very closely, looked at the filled-out card in his mother's hand and excitedly asked, "Is that our ticket out of here?"

He was obviously ready to go, for before his mother could answer or grab "a-holt" of him, he had already managed to get on the floor and was rolling toward the back of the church. It must have been quite an obstacle course, for you could tell where he was according to which pew, or section of the pew, had people squirming, giggling or jumping up in their seats as he wiggled past, rolling all the way. We even had one of our female members to yell out, "Jumpin' Jehosaphat!" *Thankfully without the hatpin.*

When the lad reached the back pew and began his return roll, his mother was prepared to catch him as he passed her. The only thing is, he was also prepared, for he rolled right on across the aisle, skipping her completely, so as to give the people on the opposite side of the sanctuary a little thrill too. I'd dare say that was the first thrill some of those little old ladies had had in quite a while, judging from the girlish smirk on some of their faces as they turned to their neighbors. Had I known he was going to pull that stunt, I'd have paid him extra to give a roll toward Miz Eudora's spot near the front on the right side.

It was right then it came time for the choir to stand up and sing the "special music," which for that Sunday happened to be *Ticket to Ride.*

The piece began with a baritone solo. At least it was supposed to. When the poor man who was to sing the introductory solo opened his mouth to deliver the first line, "Have you got a ticket to ride?" he literally spit out the words, no pitch amidst his chuckling.

That phrase, intended to be the lead-in for the choir, was that and more seeing as how it led to every single one of the choir members erupting into laughter, like a wave going through the choir loft. My mind drifted off to the Sunday Mabel had gotten it "in her craw" to choreograph *The Little Drummer Boy* back at Christmastime, but that memory was cut short by "the wave" currently making its way through the respective rows of the congregation.

Mr. "To-remain-nameless" was not only now fully awake, he was tapping his toes and rocking back and forth to the music, along with most of the rest of the congregation. He didn't even bother to look at his watch to see if he'd missed lunch, which he hadn't since Preacher Jake had finished early. By the time the little guy rolled his round-about way back to "the neighborhood,"and the "side-splittin'" special music had concluded, not a single soul was left mourning the lack of July 4th fireworks, since the bang we'd just experienced was better than any grand finale of sparks I'd ever witnessed.

I'm not sure who had more fun "rollin' in the aisles" that day, the little fellow or the people who got caught up in the laughter of the moment. Anyway, by the time we reached the final hymn, *Rock of Ages*, I determined a fun and memorable holiday had been had by all at the "Rock and Roll" church! I would have bet money that all the visitors, not to mention all the members who had played hooky that day, would show up on the next Sunday. I also figured there was a little extra in the collection plates that went down the aisles during the anthem since the show was so good.

The only thing better than that day was the following Sunday. It appears our little imaginative, precocious fellow "awaitin' his ticket outta here" had spent his past seven days making up his own ticket. I'm not sure how long it took him to concoct the brainstorm that was not only his ticket, but the entire congregation's ticket, out the next week. You see, while the rest of the little boys and girls—dressed in the finest clothes Clay County, and its seamstresses, had to offer—followed their leader to children's church in the adjoining building, he managed to lag behind and apparently hide unnoticed under the back choir pew until just the right moment.

When he thought the preacher had gone on long enough, he appeared running across the chancel area yelling at the top of his lungs, "Fire! Fire!" He was so loud that he proved to be a noteworthy competitor with the blares of the firetrucks' sirens when they arrived.

From the speed with which the congregation cleared out of the sanctuary, you'd have thought they were in their own Fire Drill competition. Once outside, I quickly saw the reason for that. Our older boys—the shepherds who "had come with great haste" to see the baby in the manger at last year's Christmas pageant—had headed up the lines of people exiting the building.

In the meanwhile, Mr. Grover Swicegood had managed to get himself to the back door and was telling everyone he was "sure there was no danger" and to "use caution exiting the building." He was right about one thing. There was no danger except that of getting between the little guy, who caused all this commotion, and his mother, who was ready to give him "a lesson he'd not soon forget."

I wondered if that would mean the end of our weekly entertainment. But, then, when I considered Mabel's taking over the helm—or as was this case, conductor's stand—of our music program commencing the next Sunday, I laid my worries to rest. There would be someone "rollin' in the aisles" come every Sunday … Mabel or Miz Eudora.

TWENTY

You Take the High Note and I'll Take the Low Note

MIZ EUDORA SEEMED more chipper than usual as she bounded up my driveway, whistling a happy tune as she came. The notes were familiar, but not familiar enough to recall their title before my morning's dose of caffeine.

"Good morning, Miz Eudora!" I called out, meeting her on the front porch with her mug already filled to the brim with her usual black coffee and cream.

"Aye," she replied, "and 'top o' the mornin' to you!"

I chuckled, glad to see she was still having so much fun getting "reacquainted" with her Irish heritage, and that her mind was on something other than "disposing of" Mabel. "What was that tune you were whistling?"

Rather than give a simple answer, she began to

hum the notes.

"Isn't that 'Oh, you take the high road, and I'll take the low road?'" I quickly interrupted. Then recalling the words of the next phrase, I added, "But isn't that a Scottish tune rather than an Irish one?"

"Not in this case, it isn't, 'cause I'm the one singin' it!" she quickly and defiantly declared. "Besides, it doesn't matter," she was even quicker to inform me. "What matters is that Mabel's bound and determined to keep on bein' in charge of the choir at the church. After my last attempt at making Horace's 'special blend' to keep her quiet, I decided it would be both a lot cheaper and faster to give Mabel singing lessons rather than risk blowing up another barn."

"Who's going to give them to her?" I asked, with that "I wish I hadn't asked" feeling punching me in the gut, the same reaction that typically accompanied many of my questions to her.

"I am!" she proudly proclaimed, her stance resembling a male peacock showing his full regalia. The shock that rippled through me must have shown on my face, for she immediately added a detailed explanation. "Well, I'm not actually going to *give* her the lessons, as in teaching her to sing. I'm going to *pay* for the lessons. I figure that's a perfectly good use of my inheritance money from Pa, and that he'd wholeheartedly agree. I'm sure he's tired of turning over in his grave every time she opens her mouth and starts that God-forsaken caterwauling."

"Who did you find here in Clay County that offers voice lessons?"

"Oh, it's not here. When I was down to see Preacher Jake the other day, I saw this nice little booklet in his trashcan telling about some week-long class up in Minnesota where they have all kind of singing and choir classes. I took it out of the trash and read all about it. When I asked Preacher Jake if he'd ever heard of it before, he told me it's at St. Olaf College with one of the best choirs in the country, and that if anybody could teach Mabel to sing, those instructors could. So I got him to help me fill out the registration right then and there. I sent in the money with the form and they've done sent me a letter what says Mabel and I are approved."

"Don't you mean accepted?" I asked, wondering whether the Scandinavians would be able to decipher her various expressions, such as "what says." Her gruff grunt of a reply caused a strange realization to ripple through me. Miz Eudora had not once, in her entire lifetime, had to fill out any kind of form. Most of the Rumph or Jarvis dealings would have been done orally, and had there been any signature necessary, it would have been sealed by a handshake. She had grown up and lived during a time when a man's word meant something and a handshake was his honor. "Accepted" and "approved" were foreign words to her, and I decided they should stay that way. She had also taught me about a woman's honor, and what a grunt means, in the matter of a few short seconds.

"What I mean is we're packing up and going to Minnesota in two weeks," she replied.

"*We're*," I repeated to myself. Suddenly the full impact of what she'd just said hit me. "Since when are you interested in learning to sing?" I asked dubiously.

"I'm not. But I'm goin' along just to make sure they really do teach Mabel to sing. Besides, I've always wanted to watch God work a miracle. I figure this is goin' to be as good a miracle as I could ever hope for." She paused for a minute. "The best miracle would be if she packed up and moved back to Myers Park, but since that don't look like it's goin' to happen in my lifetime, I guess learnin' to sing will be the next best thing. At least I can stop goin' cross-eyed every Sunday when she opens her mouth up there in that choir loft. I'll become the saint of our congregation."

I started to inform her that a saint was determined by the number of miracles one received, not gave, but then I decided those words would best be left unsaid. Besides, I knew both she and Mabel well enough to know there was no fear of that happening with either of them. *Calamities, yes; saints, no,* I mused with a silent chuckle.

She slurped a big swig of coffee. "At least all

won't be lost. Preacher Jake says there's this list with a thousand things on it you're supposed to do in your lifetime. One of them is to hear the St. Olaf Choir sing its Christmas concert there. We won't be there at Christmas, but I will get to hear the choir. That ought to be good for half a point."

I knew the list of which she spoke, but saw no need to enlighten her by sharing that it wasn't a point system. Rather, I let her go on as she gave a sly snigger. "It's sure a good thing the council voted down showing our services live on television. Can you imagine the looks on all the faces in the congregation every time the choir would sing with Mabel in charge? I'll bet we'd be the most prune-faced bunch of people ever collected in one place. Wouldn't nobody ever want to come to church … leastways, not ours. Those people out in 'TV Land' could turn her off, but the rest of us would still have to listen to 'er."

A horrible thought suddenly crossed my mind. "Miz Eudora, how exactly do you plan to get all the way to Minnesota with Mabel?" What I meant was how she intended to endure her sister-in-law's presence for that long. I wish that was what she had also taken it to mean, for I was totally unprepared for her answer.

"I was about to tell you that. I hear tell, from Preacher Jake, this college is situated in a lovely little town and is a beautiful campus with lots of places to sit and relax. I was thinking since your husband was a college professor on a religious campus, it might bring back pleasant memories of your man when you took us there."

"Took you there?" I barely manage to stumble through the words, praying all the while I was caught up in a nightmare as I listened to her convoluted reasoning.

"Yes, in your car. I'll pay for every penny of the gas." She smiled graciously.

"Uh-huh," I finally muttered, softly as I hem-hawed in my effort to think of a response. Before I had a chance to take a stand on the subject, she took my "uh-huh" as a "Yes!" Turned out it wasn't a "yes" or a "no"; it was a mournful groan.

"Do you have *any* idea how long it would take us to drive to Minnesota?" I asked, still totally stupefied.

"No, but I'm sure it won't seem like any time at all. I'll pack us a good dinner and we can take some good ole bluegrass CDs like Hattie's got in her Hattiemobile. We'll have us a grand ole time." She flashed me an innocent childlike smile, as simple as her faith. "You realize that bluegrass music came from Ireland, right?"

"I do believe you mentioned that while dancing a jig with those fellows in the park in Savannah," I absentmindedly answered, still lost in the idea of driving this pair all the way to Minnesota. It was bad enough to have to deal with them in Smackass Gap, so I wasn't quite sure how the Scandinavian crowd would take to them. I started to suggest we have our 'grand ole time' at the Grand Ole Opry, reasoning Nashville, Tennessee, would be a lot closer. But then I imagined Mabel singing in that style and figured it would be twice as bad as it already was. Thus it was that I resolved myself to the fact that the three of us were going to Lutheran-land.

AS IT TURNED out, I guess Mabel had the same idea of going to Minnesota. "The only people up there are Lutherans," she complained when she arrived shortly afterwards to butt in on the morning coffee ritual, "and I'm Methodist. I have no problem with going for voice lessons. In fact, I think that would be a superb idea. But why didn't you sign me up for Duke or maybe Emory, since that's where Sadie's husband taught? Emory's only two hours away in Atlanta."

"Because Preacher Jake didn't have a booklet from one of those places tellin' about their good singers in his trashcan. I did the best I could with what was at hand."

Or in the trashcan, I wanted to reiterate, but decided to keep quiet. I had an idea Miz Eudora was saving face, in case she was asked that same question by some of her other non-Lutheran friends. *This way,* I said to myself as I mulled over Martin Luther and the Lutherans, *we're saving "grace!"* My pun was enough to amuse me to the point that I briefly forgot about the long drive. However, in the back of my mind, I made a note to suggest that flying might be a nice alternative. That way, I could stay home. Though I was usually glad to tag along, for fear of missing the comical antics of this pair, this was one trip I would have gladly foregone—a tidbit you need to remember for the next chapter.

"Besides, listening to their choirs at Duke or Emory wasn't listed in the thousand things you're supposed to do before you die," she defended, chugging another sip of coffee. Then turning to me, she added quietly, "I ought to get another two bonus points just for teaching Mabel to sing!"

"HMMPH!" Mabel grunted as she stomped off the front porch. Try as she may, satisfaction was written all over her face that she was going to have the most trained voice in all of Smackass Gap and would be a sure shot for ensuring her tenure in the position of being the Director of the Choir. I'll bet the phone lines were buzzing all the way back to Myers Park the minute she got home.

She wasn't even halfway out the driveway when Miz Eudora reared back in the rocker and let loose with a boisterous cackle. "You know, Sadie, if the voice lessons don't work, I have a back-up plan. From what I hear, that Martin Luther fella had his own brewery in his basement in Germany. One of them Lutherans can surely teach me how to make home brew, and with their founder bein' German, their recipe ought to be "pert near" close to the one Horace's dad used, him being German and all, too." She cackled again, even louder than before. "Just think, if the singin' lessons don't cure her, the brew will." A gleeful look spread across her face. "And if I am lucky, which I ought to be given my Irish heritage, we'll get a double-whammy. Both of the solutions will work and maybe Mabel will head on back to Myers Park." Suddenly the joy in her expression dissipated as she stared worriedly at me. "On the other hand, I must not have been too lucky or she wouldn't have shown up in Smackass Gap a'tall. And rest poor baby brother John G.'s soul, he mustn't have had any luck a'tall nor he wouldn't have got stuck with the thorn."

"I don't think I'd worry if I were you, Miz Eudora. I actually heard the St. Olaf Choir once many years ago and they were superb. Surely you'll get your money's worth."

That seemed to please her enough that the tormented scowl disappeared, replaced by a smug look of satisfaction. Miz Eudora finished the last of her coffee, then went home singing at the top of her lungs. "Oh, ye'll take the high note and I'll take the low note, and I'll get to the end of the song a-fore ye."

I leaned back in my rocker, swaying away my anxieties, as I thought how pleasant it might be if one of them really did take the high road, and one took the low road, and like in the song, they never met again. My mind forced me to quickly lay the sad tale of that song to rest and be grateful my neighbor's concern was notes and not roads. Then, remembering that I'd be the one driving, I decided there would be many high roads, low roads, and roads at all points in between. My rocking immediately halted as I prayed Mabel would see no need to "warm up" her voice on the way there. If so, I feared one of that pair would encounter a long walk.

Well, if that should happen, I reasoned to myself, *at least one of them will be kickin' up her heels and doin' a jig ... all the way to "Lutheran-land!"*

TWENTY-ONE

Minnesota, Here We Come

THE DAY OF Miz Eudora's foregone conclusion—
that I would drive her sister-in-law and her—to Minnesota finally arrived. As it turned out, I was indeed
"foregone" when it came the day to leave for the singing lessons. "Foregone" was a perfectly accurate description, for as we bustled down Mabel's driveway
in the wee hours of the "top o' the mornin'" of the
trip, Miz Eudora wasted no time in giving the command, "Fore!" I laughed to myself, realizing she was
right in one way. My mind was already gone. I'd lost
it the day I muttered "uh-huh" in response to her notion of having "a nice drive" to Minnesota. Of course,
I must admit she did deliver the command with much
gusto, and a wonderfully deep resonance in her voice,
already showing signs of the Scandinavians' ability
to control their voice. *And their accents,* I added. I

secretly wondered if she'd been practicing out in the fields with Clyde, or whether she had possibly convinced the old choir director at First Church, Smackass, to give her a few private lessons. No matter, she was primed and ready to take full advantage of every dollar of Pa's inheritance money she'd spent on this effort.

Thankfully we only had a two-weeks notice about the trip. That meant I didn't have too many days to kick and scream my disapproval, while Mabel had exactly enough time to schedule all her spa appointments over in Young Harris, Georgia (only twelve miles away from Smackass Gap) to "look my best for the instructors." Frankly, I did not see her appearance as a factor in her vocal training, and even if I had, I didn't think two weeks was going to make much of a difference. *At least not in her case*, I told myself as I sneaked a peek in the mirror at her straddled across the back seat.

No matter, at this point there was only one red warning flag going off in my brain. I sincerely hoped we would not return home to have *both* of them singing in the choir, hailing all they had learned, thanks to Pa Jarvis. It would be our poor little church's luck that they'd wind up seated next to each other every Sunday. Preacher Jake might as well ask the bishop to be moved, for no one would ever hear another word of his sermons. They'd be too busy watching that pair.

Oh well, I finally reasoned as I took a firm grip on the steering wheel, *at least it would take care of people sleeping in church, including Mr. "To-remain-nameless." No one would want to miss a thing.* Not to mention it would give everyone lots to talk about over Sunday dinner. With that thought, I asked Miz Eudora to start passing out the "vittles" she'd brought along. I decided I might as well get something good out of this trip. If all else failed, her cooking would make any day a great "top o' the mornin'."

We had barely gotten out of Clay County when Mabel plodded—literally—forth with her "vocalizing." To make matters worse, she began to sing "Minnesota, here we come" to the tune of *California, Here We Come*, stomping her foot with such force on each beat that I decided we should put her in the field behind Clyde while she did her warm-up exercises. She could have the field in front of Miz Eudora's house plowed in double time. *Not to mention the back forty!* When I thought nothing could be worse that early in the morning, Mabel then began to sing one phrase repeatedly, taking it up half a step each time until she was literally screeching in the back seat. *Our "top o' the mornin'" has gone to the bottom in no time flat!* I mused impatiently, wishing she had already "come" to California or Minnesota, or anywhere besides my back seat.

I shot a glance toward Miz Eudora, expecting

one of her curt comments. Instead, all she did was reach down toward the floorboard, where she retrieved a bottle of water from the cooler I'd brought. Following the "see no evil, hear no evil, speak no evil" principle, I decided it best not to look at what else she retrieved while she was bent down into the front floorboard.

"Here, Mabel, you might need this," she offered thoughtfully. "You don't want your vocal cords to get too dry while you're workin' them so mightily."

Had I not known better, I would have considered my neighbor was simply placing stock in her sister-in-law, making the best use of her money, while using this act as preparation for the training to come. Instead, I recognized her ulterior motive; she'd developed a reputation. I watched the bottle being passed over the seat, while praying with the same gusto Mabel thrust into her "caterwauling," that her vocal cords— *and all the rest of her*, I quickly added to my holy plea—actually *would* soon dry up, at least for the remainder of the trip.

By the time we reached Tennessee, Miz Eudora's premonition had paid off. Mabel was asleep—either that, or passed out, and I really didn't care to know which—in the back seat. That was when I discovered my crafty neighbor had sewn a hidden compartment in her tote bag, just the right size for a pint jar—which is exactly how much it took to keep

Mabel quiet for our long two-day ride. While I thanked God for all those ribbons Miz Eudora had won for her many areas of expertise in "craftiness" at the local fairs, I also prayed she had another secret compartment hidden somewhere for the ride home.

THE FIRST THING we saw when we arrived in the Twin City area was a huge billboard that read: "Minnesota: Not Just for Lutherans Anymore." Mabel, whose presence had finally rejoined us, had "chowed down" on the last sandwich left in the cooler and was finishing off a jar of pickled beets. She was again fully alert, at least enough to catch the sign that greeted us. Considering she and I had both earlier made a comment to the fact that Minnesota was full of Lutherans, I decided God truly did have a sense of humor. Either that, or He had gone to being very vocal and open in delivering His messages. I was devoutly hoping Miz Eudora missed the sign, but to no avail.

She immediately piped up with, "See? I told you there were more people besides Lutherans in Minnesota. I had Preacher Jake look it up on that internet thing and there are plenty of other kinds of churches here." She beamed, smugly satisfied with herself, knowing she needed say nothing else on the subject. The sign plainly said it all.

Not sure how the cafeteria food would be on

campus, I suggested we stop for lunch in the town of Northfield, just before we reached St. Olaf. After driving around the block once to check out all the possibilities in each direction, I saw the perfect restaurant, situated directly above the Cannon River. I figured with a name like Froggy Bottoms, it had to be good. *Or at least have lots of atmosphere.* The town was incredibly quaint, with gorgeous facades, in the small downtown area. Even though I knew it had not been inhabited as long as Clay County, what I had seen thus far had already given me reason to suspect there was a lot of history here. I regretted I hadn't taken the time to do a little research on the area before our arrival.

There was no problem in finding a parking place and in no time, we were inside the restaurant, whose charm welcomed us the moment we entered the front door. While Mabel's heels flopped loudly down the steps, Miz Eudora and I were taking in all the frogs, the central element of décor for the establishment, as we made our way down spiral stairs that took us to a dimly-lit restaurant and pub below the street level. The building possessed the kind of setting where imaginations could run wild, which is obviously what prompted my neighbor's first words.

"This place got any good stories?" Miz Eudora asked as we stepped from the stairs onto the floor, where we were greeted by a tall, dark and handsome young man.

"Oh, it's full of stories," he answered. "We've got great food, great beverages and a terrific history here, which involves Frank and Jesse James. There's even tales this place is haunted." He left us with menus, which were part of a small newspaper about the restaurant and the town.

"Well, how do you like that?" Miz Eudora asked, nudging me soundly in the ribs. "If St. Olaf don't do a better job than St. Patrick did, we still got the possibility of one more spirit." She gave a silly cackle as Mabel plopped down in one of the chairs at a small round table, in the corner where our host led us, and delved straight into the menu section of the publication.

I was too interested in the articles of the paper and the fact that guest rooms, two of which overlooked the Cannon River, were available for rent on the upper floor. The long drive was already off to a good start, as far as I was concerned. From the look on Miz Eudora's face, she was equally pleased with our choice of stops. According to the publication, the area's motto read, "Cows, Colleges, and Contentment." *There's something here for each of us,* I noted, thinking the cows would keep Miz Eudora content, the colleges would be down Mabel's alley and I would gladly love to experience the contentment. *Maybe this will be a vacation after all.*

"You ladies know what you want yet?" asked

our tall and extremely muscular waiter, who looked like he could have taken out any "haints" who spooked the place. Come to find out, he was actually a football player with a full scholarship. I was pleasantly surprised that he had a real summer job, giving me cause to be already duly impressed with the work ethics of the Lutherans, since he attended one of their institutions of higher learning in the area. (That opinion was based on my former acquaintances of students with full scholarships who saw no need to work.)

"We'll all have some of that good food the other guy said you have," Miz Eudora shot at him before either of the other of us had a chance to respond, "but you'd better give Mabel water to drink. She's had enough 'beverage' on the way here to last her for a while."

"May I suggest the pulled pork?" he asked, using his best manners, which I concluded were a stark contrast from the treatment he gave those he encountered on the field.

I gave him a nod and told him he'd better bring us all water, considering Miz Eudora had never tasted tea that wasn't sweetened. Fearing her arteries—not to mention her frank opinion—couldn't handle the lack of sugar, her rebuke was an experience from which I wished to save the staid Lutherans.

"Frank and Jesse James!" exclaimed Miz Eudora, as if food was only a secondary reason for darkening the doors of this place. "I can hardly wait to tell Hattie and Theona. Sadie, do you think we can use your cell phone to call them later? They'll never believe how much excitement we've already run into."

"HMMPH!" roared Mabel. "I cannot believe I am in the presence of two grown women who relish being in the company of such common outlaws," Mabel stated emphatically as our server walked away.

"Common outlaws," repeated Miz Eudora. "Land sakes, Mabel! Don't you know nothin' 'bout the Wild West? There wasn't one thing common about Frank and Jesse James. They ranked right up there with the best of 'em.

"P'SHAA! Common outlaws, I reckon!"

Considering each of these two women considered the other to be an out-law rather than an in-law, I figured they both had plenty of experience in the judgment of outlaws. However, I failed to bother to offer an opinion, for as the saying went in the south, "I don't have a dog in this fight." *Nor an in-law or out-law*, I surmised with great humor. I was grateful that, at that very moment, a man from the table next to ours piped up to give us the whole run-down of the shoot-out that happened between the James-Younger Gang right out in the middle of the street in front of the Froggy Bottoms.

"Frank and Jesse managed to get away, but some of them weren't so lucky. Two of the outlaws were killed in the street, and from what I understand, were brought to the morgue, which at that time was said to be in this building," he informed us. It turned out his whole table was filled with members of the Historical Society who were able to give us all kinds of tidbits of history from that notorious outlaw encounter. "Their raids went south after that incident," he said. Then realizing he was talking to a group of southerners, quickly added, "In a manner of speaking."

"How about that, Sadie? We'd have missed all this fun and history if you hadn't come along with us and brought us to the Froggy Bottoms." All ears, Miz Eudora focused her attention on what the locals had to share.

Mabel sat there, stewing over Miz Eudora carrying on an intelligent conversation with learned folks of the community, while no one seemed to notice her fine upbringing and position in life, nor gave a care that her husband was "the" Dr. John G. Jarvis. The situation did nothing but worsen with the entrance of three more hungry patrons, all women we soon learned.

"Miz Eudora? Miz Eudora Rumph?" I heard a female voice calling from the bottom round of stairs. She'd obviously recognized the voice.

"It has to be her," said one of the other two, spying the coat. "No one else would have a purple fopher coat like that."

"Or would wear it if they did," stated Mabel

emphatically, turning her chair to get a glimpse of the three women headed in our direction.

"It *is* her!" exclaimed the third one of the group.

"They must be outlaws too," blurted Mabel. "Who else could possibly know Eudora Rumph here?"

My shock of Miz Eudora being recognized here was as great as hers, although I disagreed with her prediction of who the newcomers were, considering that here in the land of the Lutherans—and all the rest of the churchgoers who lived there—it wasn't like we were among a great big heathen community. Miz Eudora stood and hugged the three women like they were her long lost friends.

"What a pleasure to meet you here," offered the one who had first recognized her.

"It's mighty nice to meet you ladies here, too. Who are you?" asked Miz Eudora, stupefied.

As they all exchanged names and pleasantries, we learned that all three of the women were secretaries in United Methodist Churches. *So much for Mabel's outlaw theory*, I mused comically. To make a rather long story as short as possible, one of them had run into Miz Eudora while we were on the Paducah trip a couple of years earlier. Since you don't meet someone like my neighbor every day, news of her—and the outlandish outfit—spread to the woman's other friends. Pictures were shared via the internet, so much so, that they spotted her immediately. The other two were quick to introduce themselves, both having seen and heard of her. "We'd love to have you come to Minnesota sometime," invited one of them.

"Well, I think I'm here now," Miz Eudora replied, causing them to laugh outright.

"I just can't believe you're from a place called Smackass Gap," said the other.

"Believe it," replied Mabel dryly. "Where else do you think people would let her live?"

"Did you say …," began the man at the table beside ours.

"Yes, she did," Mabel answered curtly, cutting off his question.

The three women took seats at the table across the aisle from our corner spot and immediately became engaged in the conversation, much of which found its way back to the outlaws. "There's even a celebration called *Defeat of Jesse James Day* the weekend after Labor Day each year," said the man from the Historical Society. "It commemorates the September 7th anniversary of the event. Townspeople reenact the whole thing in a seven-minute show that runs throughout the weekend."

"We've had as many as 100,000 people come to see it in a year," added another of the society's members.

Mabel, noticeably annoyed by this entire scenario, stated, "I cannot believe that a town in such a cultured community has a festival to celebrate out-laws. How utterly absurb!"

"My dear lady," replied the man, whose name we learned was Wylie, who had been so informative about the history, "we are *not* celebrating the virtue of outlaws. We are celebrating the defeat of the outlaws. You see, those notorious men who had yet to be stopped by the lawmen of the day were halted by the simple citizens of our fair community.

"P'SHAA! Utterly absurd, I reckon," stormed Miz Eudora. "You have to excuse Mabel. Everybody in Smackass Gap sure does. That's why we're here, but I won't go into all that. She's not nearly as int'restin' as all this talk about what happened in your town all them years ago. Please be goin' on with your story."

That was like an "Open Mic" invitation to Wylie. He stood from his chair and, using his hands and arms to help set the stage as he spoke, said, "It was like this. It was a beautiful day in Northfield. The sun was shining and the nearby farmers were thankful for the day's work they would accomplish on this seemingly perfect day of September 7th in 1876. All of a sudden," he paused to provide a bit of intensity to the story as the crescendo of his voice added to the dramatic effect, "the people in town heard the loud clip-clopping of horse hooves coming toward them. They knew that meant only one thing.

"The citizens banded together and let out the yell, 'Get your guns, boys! They're robbing the bank!' Men took off for their guns and ammunition while the womenfolk rushed inside and made sure the children were hidden out of harm's way. It was only moments later when they saw eight members of the James-Younger Gang, led by Frank and Jesse themselves, heading toward the First National Bank of Northfield, gunshots filling the sunlit air. Bedlam and gunfire instantaneously replaced the brightness of the day." He left us hanging for a moment, piquing our interest for the rest of the story. Even Mabel was leaning a bit forward in her chair.

"When it was all over, there were two of our townsfolk and two of the outlaws lying dead in the street. The rest of that gang made a run for it, but they were either captured or killed in Minnesota. The James' brothers managed to get away, but their unsuccessful bank robbery here in Northfield is what led to their demise, putting a huge damper on the reigns of their criminal acts." His arms went down to his sides as he sat back in his chair. "It was our brave citizens who made sure that James-Younger Gang got an early retirement. And although it went down as a fateful day in history, it gave our brave men a claim to fame, one that we still hold onto proudly today."

"Land sakes!" exclaimed Miz Eudora. "That's just about the most excitin' tale I ever did hear. I can't wait to go home and tell Hattie and Theona. I might just ask Preacher Jake if I can stand up and tell about it from the pulpit during the announcements on the Sunday after I get back home. Thank you folks for sharing all that."

"Haven't you ladies ever heard the saying, 'Get your guns, boys!'?" Wylie asked. "It has become a famous call to arms."

"Oh, I've heard it plenty of times," answered Miz Eudora, "but it was always when somebody had seen the revenuers roamin' about. I never give a notion to the fact it come from up north, much less from a bunch of Lutherans."

One of Wylie's group gave a vivacious laugh. "Lutherans made their share of brew, too, only a different kind. Martin Luther had a brewery in his basement." I could tell his comment affired Miz Eudora's Plan B.

"And don't forget," reminded one of the ladies, "we Lutherans use real wine in communion."

"Well, do tell!" exclaimed Miz Eudora. "I reckon them folks who started you drinking wine at communion gave you a chance to taste the fruits of your labors a-fore puttin' it on the market." With that, she reared back in her chair and gave a huge Smackass-style cackle.

The ice had certainly been broken between these two communities of faith, culture, demographics and backgrounds. There was nothing left but a trail of water, proverbially speaking. Each person from the Historical Society had something to add now that there was a live "all-ears" audience. By the time we left, Miz Eudora knew the names of most everyone in the place, including the two owners, who were a father and son. "You ladies come back," the son cordially invited as he shook her hand.

"You can be sure of that," replied Miz Eudora, beaming and waving as we ascended our way back up the spiral stairs.

Mabel, on the other hand—or foot, as the case was—flopped her heels on every step, harder than she had on the way in. She added a "HMMPH!" on every fourth step, making her exit resemble the sound of a human drum corps. I was grateful our next stop would be for her gratification. Much more of her attitude and I'd have been ready to reach for a bottled water in the cooler myself. *Along with the contents of the secret compartment!*

There's one thing that could be said for our arrival at the home of "not just the Lutherans anymore." We'd begun the trip with Mabel singing, "Minnesota, here we come." I figured Miz Eudora and I should end it singing the words, "Minnesota, here we are!"

TWENTY-TWO

He Touched Me

AS WE DROVE onto the beautifully serene campus of St. Olaf College, you could sense the majesty and devout heritage that served as the foundation for this institute of higher learning—which I prayed would not fail at "learnin' Mabel how to sing," as Miz Eudora put it. Both my heart and soul were filled with an indescribable awe, unlike anything I'd ever experienced with Leon on the times I'd visited campuses where he made guest appearances. *Perhaps because you never had so much at stake at one of those places, Sadie Calloway. It's going to be a long ride home if they do anything short of a vocal transplant with Mabel.* Trying to ignore that pressure, I focused back on the scene around me. My southern roots—and Methodist husband—lent cause for me to be familiar with Duke, Emory, Southern Methodist and many others of the impressive universities and seminaries, some of them overly foreboding in their gothic design for my taste. Yet, I had never sensed the same simplistic peaceful- ness masked around all the stone buildings at any of those places. Perhaps it was the unpretentious setting of Minnesota's pleasant rolling hills, with a vision of expansive farms in the background. One farm in par- ticular, the one most visible, actually reminded me of Miz Eudora's except that all of its outbuildings were immaculately clean and white, like they'd just been painted or whitewashed. I truly felt, as I gazed at that barn and the impeccable neatness of the lush green grass of the meadows and fields that surrounded me, I was in a foreign country. I wondered if this topogra- phy had given the Norwegians who originally settled here a sense of being back home.

Regardless, this was to be our home for the next six days. I left my admiration of the grounds, height- ened by the gargantuan windmills turning high above the trees, to get my two passengers registered for their "singing lessons"—which I learned was actually a full- blown conference on worship, theology, music and arts. Next I got them checked into Ytterboe Residence Hall and prayed they didn't have to pronounce it should they get lost. Mabel took it upon herself to read aloud the entire syllabus for the week, along with every point of information, while I toiled at getting all her "stuff"— to put it nicely—out of the trunk.

Miz Eudora also must have noticed it, for she wasted no time in bellowing, "Land sakes, Mabel! Why in tarnation did you haul all that stuff up here? All you needed was your voice and it was attached somewhere in all that padded body of yours." She paused, and from the look on her face, I could tell she was trying to figure whether Mabel had actually come equipped with a voice when the Good Lord made her, or if all that padding was what was keeping it from working properly.

Frankly, I felt the urge to tell her Mabel's "pipes" worked just fine. I had no problem hearing them across the gap back home, or from the choir loft at First Church, Smackass. However, at that moment, Mabel came to the list of courses being offered during the week and I was suddenly "beholden" to her for her mighty voice. My focus turned to her words, for I was most impressed to hear her state they offered a class on literature that would include the works of, among other great Christian writers, Flannery O'Connor, my favorite author. That bit of information put an extra kick in my step as I double-timed it through the rest of getting them settled, The minute I got the baggage— including the women—unpacked, I headed back to the registration desk to see if there was any possibility of getting an on-site registration, which I happily did. Suddenly my grave drudgery had turned into excited self-indulgence.

As I walked back toward the dorm, the blades of the windmill in its background reminded me of how our lives keep turning. No matter what is thrown in our paths, the world keeps on turning and we keep on going forward, even when oftentimes it seems backwards. Nonetheless, each day of our lives is another step forward to our journey's end. I recalled a hymn I dearly loved, *Day by Day*. *From Sweden*, I recalled as I hummed its tune, its words flooding through my mind as they seemed "at home" in this place of Scandanavian roots.

What a great opportunity and experience I would have missed had I not agreed—or actually gotten kowtowed into— driving Miz Eudora and Mabel here, I mused. I had considered the time at Froggy Bottoms as great fun, but even that paled in comparison to what I felt at this moment, a moment I truly felt God's presence at work and moving through my very being. Never before, in all my life, had I felt so touched by the Holy Spirit. My last few steps back to Ytterboe Hall were taken slowly and languidly as I thanked God for the blessings He had poured in my life, many of them unrecognized until this exact moment, but most especially the one I considered greatest, that of being "Live in Smackass Gap."

Little did I know that, before the end of our stay here, I would not be the only one of our threesome who would be touched as never before.

THE WEEK TURNED out to truly be a time of luxurious self-indulgence. From the masters at the Boe Memorial Chapel's pipe organ, to the professional musicians who had come together to "as one" hone their skills, to the direction of some of the finest choral conductors in the business, to the rich overtones of the bells in the hands of tremendously skilled ringers, to the worshipfulness of the many services, to the word given at each of the services, my soul was uplifted in ways I had never known possible.

Of course, the hefty portions of wine served at communion each day didn't hurt when it came to dealing with Mabel and Miz Eudora. Thankfully, they got placed in two different sections of the women's ensemble, and since their eyes had to stay glued to the choral director, they had no chance to roll eyes at each other, or even keep a check on what the other was doing.

I could get used to this life, I told myself by the third day. The biggest grievance I'd had to encounter was the fact that Mabel had considered "comfortable walking shoes" to be her lowest-heeled pumps. Her feet got as much of a work-out as her voice but, thankfully, she was so engrossed in taking such good care of her voice, using it only to sing, she kept her complaints to herself. *Most of the time.* That was partially prompted by the good looks and uncanny humor of the young man who was their choral director. Having already made a name for himself in the world, she was determined to keep up a good appearance in front of him.

She made up her mind at the get-go to be his star pupil—or chorister, as the case was. I'm not sure about being the star, but when he moved the women of each section of the SSA ensemble around to get them where he could pull out the best blend of voices, she got moved more than anyone else. I had a hunch it was because he was trying to place her where her voice would be hidden by the strongest voices in the group. That hunch was confirmed when he took her aside after the first rehearsal, and quietly shared that "since your voice is so distinctive and powerful, why don't you cut it back a few notches? And since our worship services will be taped for anyone who would like to have them, I'm sure the others would be greatly disappointed if they didn't hear their voices too on the recordings of our performances at the various services this week."

"Oh, my!" she exclaimed. "So you think I have an extraordinary voice?"

The young conductor cringed uncomfortably as he tried to find exactly the right words to respond to her loaded question. Looking down at the floor, I suspect his words were swayed by the sight of the heel on her shoes that might have hit him upside the head had the wrong answer been given. "Madam," he said with a professionally sincere expression, "you have a voice unlike any I've ever heard in all of my travels around the world."

She jumped up and fell back down, into his arms, when her high heel hit the polished floor with all her weight on it. "Oh, my!" she exclaimed a second time. Fortunately for the young director, a group of men from the SATB choir entered the room at that precise moment and helped him stand Mabel aright.

With a flushed face, and the makings for an aching back, he politely and quickly excused himself. I couldn't tell if his reddened cheeks came from the men seeing him with Mabel in his arms or whether she had taken the wind right out of him. I came to the conclusion that it was due to the latter of the two possibilities, which was a great feat in itself, considering how much breath control his truly exceptional voice had mastered. I'd heard him during the women's rehearsal and was duly impressed. He verified my thought when he exited the room, muttering under his breath, "That woman can sure pack a wallop!" I also noticed he had not added his signature proclamation, "Rock on!" for when something he liked happened. That sealed my verdict.

I'm not the only one who's been touched today, I said to myself with a loud chuckle, thinking back on my inspiring experience from earlier in the day.

Mabel headed straight toward Miz Eudora, who

was right outside the door where she and I had been inconspicuously watching and listening this entire time. "Our conductor is enamored with my voice," she shared. Retrieving a fan from her purse to ward off her developing "hot flashes," she added, "I do believe he is enamored with the rest of me, too. You should have seen the way he held me in his arms."

I winked at Miz Eudora, who graciously—and much unlike her—kept her mouth shut. My fear was she'd shatter Mabel's bubble with, "He had no choice but to hold you in his arms that way. One tiny movement, and he'd have wound up on the floor under you." But, as it was, I think she had already considered this story would get a better response if left to the ears of the members of First Church, Smackass. In fact, I had a sneaking suspicion I might be reading about it in the next issue of *Clay County Progress*. At that thought, I really hated I didn't see her land on top of the young conductor, although I was grateful he wouldn't miss the final concert and everyone in attendance would be able to reap the rewards of his labors. *Which includes Mabel's voice*, I frightfully recognized. *Perhaps it's too bad he didn't fall on* her! *But, then, that would have been a far worse scenario for him, especially when she'd have started blaring, "AHH-WHOOP!" at the top of her mighty lungs!*

With that dreadful thought, I decided things happened in the best way possible as I wondered whether Miz Eudora would also get a chance to be touched before the week was over.

THE WEEK PASSED all too quickly for my liking. Not only had I enjoyed wonderful company from intellectuals and artistic persons from around the country, and even one from Taiwan, I had engaged in a rare cultural and educational experience second to none. That's not to say I don't experience culture and the arts in Smackass Gap, but here was merely a different kind of culture and one I'm sure is not for everyone, anymore than the culture found in Smackass Gap is for everyone. I, though, happened to be fascinated by both.

Beauty abounded all around, again no more than in Clay County, but it was a completely different realm from the majesty I enjoyed daily at home. All in all, as far as the surroundings went, there was really nothing there I didn't have at home; it simply came packaged in a different format.

There was, however, a noticeable difference between this place and home, one I would have liked to package. *And possibly sell back at home!* I surmised jovially. It was that Miz Eudora and Mabel weren't constantly going on at each other with aggravated complaints. Ironically, both of them were all smiles for the most part. Mabel was in her element, or so she thought, and as long as she thought that, that's all that mattered. Miz Eudora was as pleased as punch with the manner in which she had chosen to spend a part of Pa's inheritance left to her. What she had not disclosed to anyone—including me until much later—was that Mabel's registration fee had actually come out of John G.'s trust, which she was still able to partially oversee. 'I knew he wouldn't mind, and since he's the one what married her and therefore was responsible for us having to spend that money to rectify his wife's voice, I decided it should come from his fair share,'" she defended when she made me aware of that small tidbit *after* we'd gotten back home. But it didn't matter, Pa Jarvis would have surely been proud to see his only daughter and the spouse of his only son getting along so splendidly.

Just when I thought the entire week had passed without any mishaps, I found I had made that assessment a wee bit early. The week didn't end with a BANG, or anything like it. What did happen was not much more than a simple nod, not unlike the ones that happen from various members of the congregation of First Church, Smackass, each Sunday, as with Mr. "To-remain-nameless." It was actually a matter of the placement of the nod rather than the nod itself that caused the disruption. Maybe I'd better just give you the explicit details rather than letting your mind go on wandering needlessly.

I'd just finished my soda and fun-size package of chocolate-covered peanuts for a quick "pick-me-up" before I went into our last class for the day, a choral reading session. Since the three of us were going to have to hit the road for home early the next morning, this would be our last class period. In reality, it wasn't even what you'd call a class. People merely packed into an average-sized concert hall to read through the latest choral compositions, directed by the duo of the school's two most noted conductors, one of whom was the young man into whose arms Mabel had already fallen.

There are two things here of which you should take note. When I say people packed in the room, I wasn't exaggerating. Every person who could fit in the concert, plus a good many more, vied for one of the comfortable padded seats, not to mention the free music. The biggest lesson I learned there is that "free is free," no matter whether it's packets of choral music or what. You can always trust the word "free" to get some action, and also some backsides in a chair. Such was the case. The second lesson learned was that I should never eat the last of the chocolate-covered peanuts. Someone else might need a burst of energy more than I. Now on with the story.

Miz Eudora found herself an out-of-the way seat in the section running down the side of the room. Even though she was smack-dab in the middle of the row, she was carefully hidden behind a big support post where she could remain inconspicuous. *Not that her purple fopher coat and red-plumed hat provided much camouflage!* But in her mind, she wanted to be where she could keep close tabs on Mabel in case there was anything else she wanted to jot down in her little note-book to go back and report. I found it amusing that the contents of the free packet were bunches of "octa-vos" like the ones she'd complained about Mabel buy-ing for the choir at home. Miz Eudora wasn't the least bit interested in the contents of the package, though; she was merely using them as a cover-up.

Unfortunately, so many people showed up for the reading session that they ran out of free packets of music. The dedicated stayed; the undedicated didn't. Sadly—or humorously, depending on the way you look at it—the man who took the one remaining seat in the entire auditorium, which was beside Miz Eudora, was dedicated. It's too bad he wasn't also alert and still in control of his voice. Until that day, I never realized that voices were like bladders. When you've lost con-trol, you've lost control.

That wasn't the only thing that lost control on that late Thursday afternoon as people were dwindling down, hungrily and sleepily looking forward to the dinner hour in ten short minutes. Ten minutes can be a dreadfully long time when you've lost control. Such was the lesson learned by many individuals in that auditorium.

Miz Eudora, being her Southern hospitable self, offered to share her music with the man who'd taken the last seat beside her. To her, it was no more than offering a guest a slice of pie or glass of iced tea— sweetened, of course. That was the first, and only, time I'd ever wished she hadn't been quite so much of "a broken mold of a genuine mountain woman," which was how I often referred to her. The sharing of music wasn't the problem, or maybe it was, as what happened after that kind act was a classic case of a chain reaction.

At first, Miz Eudora held tightly to the music while leaning it toward him, still allowing herself the option of using it as a cover-up but, at the same time, allowing him to read the words and music. Or so she thought. When she saw his head bobbing in all directions as he tried to see the music, she held it a little closer to him.

"Thank you," he acknowledged in the kindest, but also the lowest, second-bass voice I'd ever heard. "I've been coming here for over fifty years. I hope I can still sing the tenor line, but my voice has dropped a little over the years. I may have to try the baritone notes."

Good luck! I wanted to say. *Maybe I should give him the four-leaf clover I have tucked away in my wallet for emergencies.*

"I was a boy soprano in choirs in Italy during my childhood and early adolescent years." His comment was warranted by his distinct Italian features. "When we moved to New York shortly after my voice changed, I became known as an Irish tenor. I inherited that from my mother's side of the family. That was nearly seventy years ago."

Wondering if anyone had informed him on how many times his voice had changed since then, I saw an abnormal, yet endearing, star appear in Miz Eudora's eye. With my brow furrowed in question, it dawned on me the reason for her admiring gaze. She had told me about John G. being an Irish tenor. *This man is bringing back memories of her 'baby brother' she loved so much.*

"I moved to California, after studying eight years in New York, and then sang there professionally for several decades."

And he's seated beside Miz Eudora for a reading session? My mind ran rampant with dreadful thoughts of what he would think should she open her mouth and try to sing. *But then, her dress should hint she is not a singer.* With that, I recalled some of the musicians I'd known when Leon and I lived in Atlanta. *On second thought ...*

The star in my neighbor's eye was getting brighter. Doing the math, I began to have another dreadful fear. *He's older than her ... his mother was*

Irish ... he was an Irish tenor. I froze in place. *Don't tell me she's falling for him.* I watched closely as they continued to chat, noticeably enjoying each other's presence. *Maybe I should switch seats with her*, I decided. But as I stood, I remembered I was there to keep an eye on her, who was there to keep an eye on Mabel. I couldn't give my pretense away so I reclaimed my seat before someone else grabbed it, which was a good thing for that was the minute the conductor chose to begin the session.

My concerns about the man's shock at sitting beside such an untrained singer evaporated into thin air the moment he opened his mouth. His pitches and lyrics were leaping all over the page, more so with every passing octavo. Miz Eudora, noting he couldn't read from that distance, held the music even a little closer in his direction.

Now she was unable to see it, a dilemma noticed by the woman seated next to her, who in turn held her music toward Miz Eudora. When the woman next to her also *heard* what was going on, she leaned away from the man's direction, which caused Miz Eudora to also lean farther to the left. This, in itself, was a spectacle to behold as the two women were both leaning sideways, with Miz Eudora's head tilted in a high, uncomfortable-looking position toward the other woman's music when she was, in fact, merely trying to keep an eye on Mabel. The man, also leaning, kept stretching his neck lower and lower as he tried to make out the words, much less which lines and spaces the little black dots were on. By this point, his words were unrecognizable, for he was making them up as he went, in what I could have sworn was a mixture of English and Italian texts. The problem with that was they sounded like some crude guttural sound rather than the text of a lyrical Christmas lullaby, which was the piece they were reading at the moment.

I honestly sensed a deep pity for him. I couldn't imagine what it must have been like for him to be trying so desperately to be a part of what was once so easy for him. None of that was an issue, for a couple of minutes later, he *was* what was going on, or at least going down. While I was busy feeling sorry for him, it appeared he was feeling sleepy as a result of the lullaby. That's when I realized he was so engrossed in the music, and what it sounded like in his head, the gentle flowing melodic lines put him right out.

No longer did I need fret over Miz Eudora falling for him. It was he who fell for her, or rather, *on* her. He was leaning so far toward her seat to see the music, which because she was leaning so far to the left, had shifted. His head, shifting with it, was right over her chest when it dropped against her bosom.

In total shock, her breathing literally stopped as her eyes scanned the situation. The younger of the two conductors saw immediately what had happened for he had been staring in disbelief at the owner of the dourly wrong notes. You couldn't blame him for laughing because it was hysterically funny. I don't know that I've ever seen that kind of distress on Miz Eudora's face. The biggest part of her quandary was due to the older conductor, who was more foreboding that the one who led her women's ensemble. I guess you can say the rest of the story was his fault because he'd begun the reading session by giving the order, "There shall be no talking in this room, only singing!"

Therefore, when his eyes questioningly shot in her direction after she raised her hand to get someone to help her out of her embarrassing pickle, she suddenly remembered his words, "No talking, only singing." Her hand immediately shot back down and she finally took a breath, which she needed for her next move. You see, she also took matters into her own hands by singing at the top of her lungs, "He touched me." It wasn't to the tune some people connect with those three words, but rather to one she made up for that decisive moment. She at least had the decency to sing it using the beautiful resonance she'd learned during the week from the young conductor.

None of that mattered though. What did matter was that she was no longer hidden behind the support post, for every pair of eyes in the room was now glued to Miz Eudora Rumph instead of the renowned conductor. I couldn't help but laugh aloud, harder than I already was, when I saw the expression on the face of the younger conductor. He'd been teaching the women's ensemble all week regarding vocal sounds and how dependent they were on the placement of vowels. This was placement alright, but I don't believe it was exactly what he had in mind.

And there were no vowels or consonants involved in this situation except for the ones included in the giant "AHH-WHOOP!" that Mabel let loose from the center-stage front row seat, the one she'd taken to make sure she got the most possible from the reading session. I'd say she was successful in her effort. She got a birds-eye view of the "goin's on." The only one with a closer view was the man resting on Miz Eudora's chest. It was the first time I'd ever seen Mabel in such shock that she was unable to utter a single word.

It was Mabel's loud yell that clued me into the fact that the man was as deaf as he was off-pitch. *Poor thing. No wonder he couldn't find his way out of a bucket*, I sympathized. *Or off Miz Eudora*, I surmised, igniting yet another uncontrollable bout of laughter.

Mabel's unnerving yelp was also all it took to put an end to the reading session. Her condescending glare caused Miz Eudora to jump up, which in turn caused the man's head to bump loudly against the unpadded arm rest between her seat and his. Looking down, but paying no attention to the condition of the man's head, Miz Eudora's tirade began.

"This is all your fault, Mabel! If you hadn't demanded to take over the choir, I wouldn't have had to use Pa's hard-earned money to pay for you to be here, and then I wouldn't have had to be here, and Sadie wouldn't have had to drive us here all the way from Smackass Gap!" That accusation was enough to kindle a room full of guffaws, but she didn't stop with that. "And if I hadn't had to come here to watch you, I wouldn't have had to hide behind the music, and this poor man could have had his own packet of free music. Then I wouldn't have had to be leaning over so far to try to make sure he could see, and he wouldn't have been lulled to sleep by the beautiful music, and therefore he wouldn't have touched me."

Oblivious to anything that had just happened, the bump on the armrest jarred the man to the point he woke up and shook his head for a moment to get his bearings. Remembering where he was and what he was doing, he opened his mouth and let loose with his own sound, which was unfortunately a two-octave ascending stretch on the word "down." Ironically, that had been the last word he had seen, and was preparing to sing, on the page before he "took the plunge," landing him on Miz Eudora. It had been in a phrase of the Christmas piece the group had been reading at the time about the nativity, based on the carol of *Away in a Manger*. However, his ill-fated attempt at finding the right note sounded like the cow—known for giving up its sweet-smelling hay for the baby—had given birth instead of Mary. It certainly added a different dimension to the Christmas story.

With that, the conductor—who had also lost control—threw up his hands and shouted, "Session over!"

"I thought he said we could only sing in here," Miz Eudora noted, a bit huffy that he didn't follow his own rule.

The younger conductor raised his right hand forcefully in the air as a sign of approval and in Miz Eudora's direction yelled, "Rock on!"

When all was said—*and sung*, I joked with myself—there wasn't a person in the concert hall who hadn't been touched in some way, even if only with a burst of energy. The lethargic faces of ten minutes before were full of life as the room emptied and people headed toward the dining hall, in a much jollier mood than I'd witnessed all week, I must admit. No one could complain. Not only had they received a free packet of music, they'd also received a free show. *And a good one at that*, I determined, privately wagering most of them had never had the privilege of dealing with something that bizarre in their choirs at home. They'd come here to learn; they'd without a doubt learned how to handle the situation should a similar ordeal ever occur in their own churches.

I had only one contention with the "tizzy" Miz Eudora had exhibited. In her round of all the many ways Mabel had been responsible for the chain reaction, she mentioned the poor man being "lulled to sleep by the beautiful music." Unquestionably, Mabel's voice had improved noticeably, but it still wasn't to the point I would have called it, nor any of the music that came from it, beautiful. And since Mabel had been singing up until the time of the incident, she, in effect, had nothing to do with the beautifully aesthetic quality of the music. Therefore, I dismissed that part of Miz Eudora's "hissy fit" as invalid.

The evening's service, which immediately followed dinner, was to focus on Epiphany. Several people involved in that service had, no doubt, already experienced an afternoon epiphany of their own, including Miz Eudora, whom I ventured would never complain about people having their own individual copies of music—or octavos—again at First Church, Smackass. I missed half the service because I was busy, hastily and fervently praying I wouldn't also be reading about this little episode in the next issue of *Clay County Progress*. I had to admit the "AHH-WHOOP!" was delivered with a much more pleasant and soothing tone than usual, so all was definitely not lost in Pa's inheritance money.

WITH THE LAST of the suitcases, and all our acquired materials, in the trunk the next morning, I took one last look over the farm and rolling hills that had called to me so endearingly upon our arrival.

"Sadie, do you ever feel like God sends you somewhere for a reason?" asked Miz Eudora as she slowly trailed along behind me.

I knew that feeling exactly. It is what I had felt at St. Olaf all week, and now regretted having to leave so soon. That's how I felt about Leon and I happening upon Smackass Gap, which led to me eventually moving there following his death. "Yes, ma'am, I do," I answered with a sincere smile.

"I've always regretted the fact that my baby brother never became a professional Irish tenor, for he had such an incredible voice. And I've regretted worse that he died such an untimely death, which I've often blamed on Mabel. But after being here this week, and experiencing the things I have, and especially that elderly gent in the reading session, I must admit I'm glad John G. did not live to that point, nor that he had to go through having his voice go awry like that man's. I don't believe I've ever felt so sorry for anyone in my entire life, not even Leland when he used to go and sing every day to his own 'wild Irish rose.'

"Maybe it wasn't just Mabel who was intended to come here," she concluded.

"Maybe you're right," I replied, taking her arm

in mine as we walked back inside Ytterboe Hall to make sure we'd left nothing behind. I laughed to myself. *We've left plenty behind here.* Reflectively, I added, *But we're taking a lot more with us.*

I PULLED TO a halt at the final stop sign before exiting the campus and looked longingly in my rearview mirror at all the beauty that lay behind me. My sixth sense, so strong I felt someone was tapping my shoulder, alerted me that we would return to this place. We had all been moved—*touched in one way or another,* I jestingly mused—and I knew this was not our last trip here. *I just hope we fly the next time,* I said to myself as I pressed the gas pedal and headed for one last look at Froggy Bottoms before hitting the major highway.

I was reminded of the slogan Wylie had shared with us: "Jesse James slipped here." For the sake of Miz Eudora and everyone else in Smackass Gap, I prayed we would no longer be listening to Mabel slip through the cracks of the piano keys. Otherwise, I feared a sign might appear in the choir loft that read, "Mabel Toast Jarvis slipped here." It would be interesting to see how long the effects of Pa Jarvis' inheritance money would last. It would also be interesting to watch Miz Eudora's face the next time the congregation sang *He Touched Me.*

TWENTY-THREE

Peace in the Valley

MIZ EUDORA HAD finally accepted the fact that Mabel had her "foot and all the rest of her" firmly planted in the position as Director of Music at First Church, Smackass. I had to give her credit. She had not simply lain down and taken it, but rather stood and put up a good fight. In the end, though, she did the honorable thing and presented a peace offering.

I discovered all of this quite by accident. What tipped me off on this particular day, on which I was watching her from her front porch before I knocked, was the way Miz Eudora was parading around her house with a square piece of cloth like she typically used to cover a fresh-baked pie or a dish of something on the table that she'd cooked for dinner and wanted to stay fresh until the next meal. I'm not sure whether it was the fact that—instead of a piece of an old flour sack—this square piece of cloth was purple and edged with red lace, with a red tassel sewn in the center of the top, or whether it was the piece of paper, entitled *The Language of the Fan*, lying on her sewing machine that alerted me to the fact something was amiss in the Rumph household.

I peered through the open front door, where I could see through the screen, for a few moments longer. What first struck me was the way Miz Eudora was slinging this "fan" around. It looked more like a matador slinging his red cape around in front of the bull to catch its attention before taking both ends of the cape and holding it out for the bull to run toward. There was no doubt the bright red lace and pompom would have definitely caught the bull's attention. I quietly snickered to myself, musing as how Miz Eudora would come closer to catching a bull than a man with this fan.

That's when she whipped around with the fan and spied me at the door. "Sadie, am I ever glad to see you! I was debatin' comin' over to your house to show this to you a-fore I present it to Mabel."

A great weight of worry was lifted off my shoulder. "What is it?" I asked, not admitting I'd been watching her for a while now.

"It's a fan. It does double duty. She can fan with it a while, and dab her face with it a while. I've even made her a little chart with some new motions. I'm sure the men she's giving fan signals will understand these as well as they understood those other cock-eyed ones she used."

It's odd how I happened upon her right then. I'd decided to pay her a visit under the pretense of bringing her a plate of cookies, hoping to cheer her since Mabel was obviously at the helm of the choir to stay. Considering I was taking cookies to the best cook in the county—or at least the one with the most blue ribbons for baking on her back porch—I should have known that excuse was an obvious farce. But the minute she opened the door, I realized "the Good Lord" had sent me there. Her face indicated I was not a moment too soon. She was terribly deep in thought and those thoughts seemed to take voice as she laid the fan back on the sewing machine with the little paper telling how to use it.

"Sadie, I have a confession to make, and it concerns you, so I'm glad you're the person I'm a-gettin' to tell."

I prayed I deciphered the rest of her words easier than I deciphered those as she took the cookies to the kitchen and motioned for me to take a seat.

"I'm sure I always knowed this," she continued as she joined me and took a seat opposite me, "but traipsin' through all those old graves at the cemetery, many of whose names I knew and lots I'd heard tell of as a child, I've come to one conclusion. When those people reached that cemetery, their burdens were over.

Actually their burdens were over before they reached the cemetery. They were over when they finished their last breath. And all those people I've worried about so long, why, they ain't sufferin' no more. They found perfect peace when they were laid to rest. Why, even Ma and Pa. I was so all-fired concerned about them, Pa especially, turnin' over in his grave at the thought of Mabel livin' up here on his mountain. But he don't care. He's havin' a wonderful time up there, or wherever it is, in gloryland."

The only time I remember actually "touching" Miz Eudora was the day Horace died and I gave her a hug. And maybe the evening after his "celebration" when Mabel and I "rescued" her in Hotlanta from the Red Hatters who had mistakenly kidnapped her. That one I'm not even sure about, but if I did hug her, it was out of sorrow for the ordeal she'd had to deal with, thanks to her "blamed ole sister-in-law." I felt the urge to reach out to her now, but I felt an even greater urge to let her finish this confession.

"You know, Sadie, you've done a lot of good things for me since you've been here. In fact, every time I read that little plaque up there on the wall about doing good, I think about you. You're a living example of that saying and now look at the change you've made in me." About the time I was ready to interrupt and jump in with a correction to that statement, she took care of it herself. "It wasn't actually *you* who changed me, it was the Good Lord Himself. But it took some- one like you to be the culprit that carried me from despisin' that blamed ole Mabel to realizing she's one of His creations too. And after all, my baby brother John G. did marry her. I ought to be nice to her out of respect for him, if for no other good reason."

I could have sworn I detected a tear in her eye as she uttered that last statement. She paused for a moment and gave me a smile, one whose joy matched the shining glimmer in her eye. All that was missing from her angelic glow was her halo, and I kept watch- ing to see if it might appear atop her horns, which I was sure were sprouted somewhere atop her head.

"When you first got me started in all this gene- alogy, I wasn't too sure about it. But Mary and all her fine helpers over at the library was so nice to me that it was like havin' a whole pile of new friends. It didn't only connect me to all the dead people buried in all them cemeteries we visited, it connected me to lots of live folk who've been here and around me all the time. I've decided to make a weekly venture of goin' to the library and visitin' those women. Maybe take 'em a cake or something, or check out a book." She snick- ered. "I must admit that sittin' in my rockin' chair overlookin' Smackass Gap with a good book would be a lot more relaxin' than hikin' up all them hills of the local cemeteries lookin' for dead people.

"Now don't get me wrong" she went on, while

searching my eyes as she spoke for fear she'd insulted me or my idea. "I really do like researchin' all this genealogy stuff. It's made me come to realize that my baby brother and I weren't so different after all. He might have been a fancy, high-fallutin' doctor and all, but we do share the same roots. The only real difference between us is that I'm interested in all the begats and stuff, you know, the beginnings and him bein' a proctologist and all, he was interested in their ends."

There was no way to smother the laugh that erupted due to her analogy. "Miz Eudora, you surely have learned a lot, and taught the rest of us a lot, through all this research of your ancestry. You've even given me a desire to look into my own background. But more than that, you've come to terms with Mabel, and the situation of the music director at the church, and you've taught all of us a great lesson about 'letting go and letting God.'"

"Yeah, I do feel better. I just wish I could let God give Mabel this fan instead o' me havin' to do it." She smiled a wicked smile and I knew she was going to be alright.

As I reached out to give her the hug I'd been contemplating, my action was interrupted by the giant "AHH-WHOOP" that came flying up her driveway, along with the silver Buick and a cloud of dust. We barely got all the doors and windows closed—as had become the habit when we heard Mabel coming in a blaze, so as to keep all the dust out of the house—before she jerked the car in park and hustled up the steps. Her arrival was highly reminiscent of the day she made the proclamation that she had decided to take over the music program at the church. I prayed she didn't suck out all the good that had just radiated from the living room.

"Eudora," she called, surprisingly in a congenial tone. "I have a confession to make and I thought you should be the first to hear it." She turned to me. "It's alright if you hear it too, Sadie, because I intend to go and share it with Preacher Jake as soon as I leave here so he can inform the whole church."

I had to pinch myself to make sure I was awake. It was highly out of the ordinary for Miz Eudora to be in the frame of mind she was, but Mabel being civil too? I was "half-a-mind" to look outside to see what aspect of the harmony of the cosmos was floating around in the air and had so affected their behaviors, which was typically total chaos.

"After going to Savannah and then Minnesota," Mabel began, "I was reminded how much I always enjoyed traveling. If I am to accept the position of Director of Music, I would be accepting a huge responsibility. I would be required to be there every Sunday, and then there would be all the planning and rehearsing to get the choir ready for each week. If I only had to contend with my own voice, it would not be a problem. But I am forced to consider that I would have to work with voices like that of Hazeline, who doesn't know a blue spruce from a loose screw, not to mention that couple of brothers, the tenor and the bass, who between them can't find a single pitch in your big black wash pot."

She gave a hint of a reflective smile as she let out a sigh. "All things considered, I've decided not to be the Director of Music for First Church, Smackass. I'm sure the former director would be willing to carry on a few more weeks until a suitable replacement, although lacking my fine qualifications, can be found. That would also mean Mrs. Azalee could continue in her role as the pianist."

With that, Mabel ended her pronouncement. She reached inside her purse for a hankie and when she did, her fan—which she'd recently been using on Mr. Whitmeyer, the church's latest, and only, widower—fell to the floor. Unknowingly, that one slip of the hand proved what I had been suspecting throughout her entire confession. The way Miz Eudora pursed her lips and rolled her eyes told me that she, too, perceived the real truth behind Mabel's words.

It wasn't that Mabel was not interested in being in charge of the music. It was that she was more interested in keeping an eye on all the "goin's on" in the congregation, which she couldn't do from the choir director's seat, and continuing to fan the flame with whatever eligible widower might be in the line of fire. *Or more specifically, in the line of fanning*, I corrected myself with a smirk.

Miz Eudora took that opportunity to give Mabel the fan. "I made it for you as a gift since you were the new Director of Music. It was meant as a sign of congratulations, but now it can be a sign of good ri … best wishes!"

I could tell she immensely enjoyed the opportunity God had let her have to personally present the fan to her sister-in-law.

Wiping away an imaginary tear, Mabel replied with, "I don't know what to say." She read the directions for using the fan, trying out a couple of the new motions, and immediately recanted her statement. "Actually I do know what I wanted to say. For my encore as the Director of Music, I am going to sing a final solo on Sunday. I've decided to sing *Peace in the Valley* to let everyone know there are no hard feelings and that I'm all about following those words on your sign there." She pointed to Wesley's quote.

I didn't know whether to thank Miz Eudora or John Wesley, or even Rob Tiger for having had the sign in his front window down at Chinquapin's, but it seemed the combination of the trip to Savannah and the founder of Methodism's famed words truly did resolve the current problem at hand in Smackass Gap. *No thanks to St. Patrick nor all those fancy singing lessons,* I noted silently. *Although those singing lessons may make Mabel's rendition of* Peace in the Valley *a bit more peaceful, or at least pleasant, to our ears on Sunday or any other time she decides to hold forth with that powerfully mighty voice of hers.*

For the first time since Horace's passing, it seemed all the residents of our area might actually enjoy a little "peace in the valley." Our lion and our lamb had finally "laid down together" as the words of the hymn said, although I was still at odds about which one was the lion and which one was the lamb. In fact, there were days I felt they were more accurately described as the bear and the wolf the hymn mentioned. But whatever they were, they were at peace for the moment, which was indeed a pleasant rarity for our little corner of the world.

Mabel exited the driveway calmly, with not a mite of dust raised by the tires of her silver Buick, as she went to break the news to Preacher Jake. I never did give Miz Eudora a hug, but instead walked home in silence to allow her time to wallow in the success of her venture and enjoy the peacefulness of the moment. *And pray for the peace of Mr. Whitmeyer.*

"There will be peace in the valley for me," I sang, my voice slightly off-key, as I crossed Highway 64. "Someday," I sang to conclude the phrase of the hymn. *Seems "someday" is today,* I mused, not bothering to query how long that "someday" would last.

TWENTY-FOUR

In a Pickle

ALTHOUGH I WAS certain the harmonies and rhythms were nowhere near the way George Frederic Handel had composed them, there was a multitude of the heavenly hosts—otherwise known as the members of First Church, Smackass—singing a chorus of "Hallelujahs!" on the following Sunday morning when Preacher Jake announced Mabel had turned in her baton. A wave of "Amen"s also broke out in rounds throughout the sanctuary.

"I'll not be turning in the robe, mind you," added Mabel, standing from her choir loft perch, "just the baton, so you'll still be able to hear me sing every Sunday, and I'm sure the person who takes over the position as Director of Music will still want me to sing solos for your listening enjoyment."

The wave of "Amen"s stopped.

Now I'd heard of the choir doing such a good job there was no need for a sermon. I even remembered one particular Sunday when Miz Eudora met Preacher Jake at the door, following a rousing old gospel hymn, with the words, "You ought to have just pronounced the benediction and let us go home after that choir special. That was a good'un!" That seemed to be the same feeling throughout the congregation on this Sunday.

I knew Miz Eudora would have something to say on the way home, but even I wasn't expecting, nor was prepared for, what came out of her mouth. Heaven only knows why; I'd known her for how long now? It was such a celebration—"bigger even than the one at Horace's passin'," Miz Eudora later said— that I drove Hattie and Theona with us just over the state line to Young Harris, Georgia to eat at Brother's, my favorite restaurant in the nearby vicinity. "My treat," I told them.

"Well, I'll tell you one thing," Miz Eudora said the minute we got in the car and were barely out of earshot from the church parking lot. "We won't have to be puttin' up with any more of them fake "Hallelujahs" and "Amens."

As opposed to what? I wanted to ask, but promptly determined it safer not to know.

Too bad Theona didn't share my opinion on being safe rather than sorry. Instead, she opened the door widely for discussion. "Fake 'Hallelujahs' and 'Amens'?" she repeated, expressing the same bewilderment the rest of us, except for Miz Eudora, shared.

"Yeah. Don't you remember that Sunday when Mabel decided to sing *Ivory Palaces* and some woman jumped up and starting yellin', 'Hallelujah' and 'Amen'?"

"Vaguely," I answered, "but how could you tell it was fake?"

"Land sakes! You'd have had to be a sinner and a half not to tell that."

So much for me getting into heaven, I mused with a smile. *If that's the measurement for getting in the front gate, I guess St. Peter's going to tell me I was two whole sinners and give me the boot!*

"First off, *Ivory Palaces* is not a 'Hallelujah, Amen-in' kind of song. It's a sit back and think on your heavenly reward kind of song. And if that wasn't enough, you could tell," Miz Eudora informed us, "because she was holdin' her wig on with one hand and shoutin' with the other raised up in the air. Had she been doin' the real thing, she wouldn't have been thinkin' 'bout holdin' onto no wig nor nothin' else! It t'would'a been the Holy Spirit that had a-holt of *her,* and she'd have been shoutin' with *both* hands up in the air!

"P'SHAA!" she exclaimed, more fanatically than usual while shaking her head. "Jumpin' up and shoutin' 'Hallelujah' and 'Amen,' I reckon!"

Okay! I'm glad we got that off our chest, I laughed to myself, debating whether I was possibly *three* whole sinners for not picking up on any of those clues.

"And then there was the subject of speaking in tongues," she went on, still shaking her head. "If she wanted to do that, she should'a taken up bein' the choir director down the street at the church what does that."

Guess there was still more on her chest, I surmised, preparing myself for another round of ranting and raving, which once again was aided by Theona.

"Speaking in tongues?" asked our peacemaker, who at the moment was creating more disturbance than peace. "I've been at church every single Sunday and I don't remember anybody speaking in tongues. I think I'd have noticed that because my people always knew it when people were speaking with a forked-tongue."

"There wasn't nothin' forked about this," replied Miz Eudora. "She had the choir doin' all that Latin and German and stuff didn't nobody round these parts of Smackass Gap understand."

Should I tell her they could understand Mabel's "speaking in tongues" as well as they could understand her terminology? A wave of guilt swept over me. *Her terminology is what she grew up with, Sadie, just like your terminology is what you grew up with. The mountain people understand her just fine. The*

"Latin and German and stuff," they don't.

That voice that always made me stop, step back and rethink did it once again. *And Mabel didn't grow up with Latin and German in her terminology.*

So once again, just like that voice, Miz Eudora made me stop, take a step back and rethink. Her words all made perfect sense to her. As for the rest of us ... well, all we needed to know was that on this Sunday, the people of First Church, Smackass, made a joyful noise ... each in their own languages. *Or at least in their own ways.*

A WEEK PASSED and Mabel's retirement was still the topic of discussion around Smackass Gap. Miz Eudora was so excited she used her *Live in Smackass Gap* column to invite all of Clay County to help the church throw her sister-in-law a "Going Away" reception. "It will be held immediately following next Sunday's service, which will feature *real* 'Hallelujah's and 'Amen's," as she put it.

As for me, I was ready to put this whole matter of Mabel taking the choir over to bed. Between trips to Savannah and Minnesota, I was looking forward to "the end of this song." *After all, the fat lady has sung* how *many times?* Looking back over all that had transpired in our little community, simply because of a conducting baton, I had to lay blame where it belonged.

It seemed all the "to-do" over the past few months (which was the quintessential example of "much ado about nothing") was Miz Eudora getting "all fired up" about something that was out of her hands anyway. But as for the "Going Away" reception, a good bit of what happened with that was the result of Miz Eudora getting herself in a pickle. If you know anything at all about Eudora Rumph, you'd already know that she pretty much stayed in a pickle. But on this particular day, the day before the reception, she literally *did* get herself in a pickle. A sweet pickle, to be exact.

Usually people found themselves in a pickle when they were in the throes of some undoing. This particular pickle came about when the throes were past and the silver lining was in sight. You see, Mrs. Grover Swicegood had happened upon a "sweet" little place in Kannapolis, North Carolina, one day while visiting some of her kin. It was a "sweet" little place because it was a bakery and its cases were filled with some of the most enticing delicacies ever to be mixed with sugar. Not only that, but its name happened to be The Sweet Pickle Bakery & Delicatessen.

It also happened the bakery was known for its oversized, overstuffed cream horn (called "cream horm" by Mrs. Grover Swicegood, who happened to love them no matter how you pronounced them). While Mrs. Swicegood purchased a regular sized one for herself, she took a picture of the oversized one with her cell phone and sent it to me with a message to show it to my neighbor.

Miz Eudora went on to do exactly what both Mrs. Swicegood and I figured she would. *No, she actually did what I thought she would do*, I corrected myself. Mrs. Swicegood figured Miz Eudora would do the sensible thing and have her bring one back for the reception to celebrate Mabel's retirement. I, on the other hand, knew a road trip to Kannapolis, North Carolina, was eminent. Although I had a weakness— or fetish, depending on how you wanted to look at it—for bakeries, I'd never driven five hours to get to one (although I did fly to Europe and visit one on the North Sea once, but I was already there at that point, so it didn't count).

Both Mrs. Swicegood and I were right about one thing though. Miz Eudora decided the giant "horn of plenty" would be a most appropriate way of "offering thanksgiving to the Good Lord for the 'good riddance' of Mabel." Accordingly, at the reception, in walked Mr. Grover Swicegood bearing a huge box filled with the lightest, most delicious cream-filled concoction you've ever seen. On its side was written "How Sweet the Sound," a suggestion made by Mrs. Swicegood and one I agreed was most apropos.

"It's too bad they didn't have one of these things back in the days of the wisemen," uttered Miz Eudora as she watched those in attendance clamoring to get a piece of it. "The little community of Bethlehem would have loved this with a big ole pot of coffee about the time the shepherds broke the news to ever'body."

I wanted to say something back to her, but how does one reply to a statement like that? She was probably right. *Had* there been coffee, and *had* there been cream horns back then, the community of Bethlehem would have probably loved it.

There is one more thing you need to know before "the end of the song," or at least the end of this volume of "The Winsome Ways of Miz Eudora Rumph." You all know the saying, "It ain't over 'til the fat lady sings." In this case, Miz Eudora's opinion was, "It ain't over until the fat lady sings it right."

You see, while we had been enjoying lunch and sampling many of the baked goods at the Sweet Pickle, a group of individuals from Germany entered the shop and sat at the table next to ours. It seemed odd to me that Miz Eudora couldn't understand the anthem Mabel had the choir do in German, but she had no problem calculating that group was from Germany. Like with everyone else with whom she comes in contact, she had no problem striking up a conversation.

She did, however, have a problem deciphering the conversation, which was about biotechnology. Yep, you guessed it. She was lost in space … or could just as easily have been. *Literally!* By the time I'd tasted "near 'bout" all the things there were to taste in the glass counters, the Germans, who were visiting research scientists, had explained they were visiting the North Carolina Research Campus, which deals with biotechnology as well as many other facets of scientific research. I never understood exactly what they were doing at the campus—teaching, learning or simply observing. Instead, I was more interested in learning and simply observing how they were teaching Miz Eudora what biotechnology was.

I'm not sure how much of what they said she understood since they were, after all, "speaking in tongues" part of the time, but she did understand enough that she asked them to do some "artificial selection" and "hybridization." She was "bound and determined" they could give Mabel a new voice box that would enable her to sing on pitch and "quit warblin' like a turkey buzzard." Her choice of words were equivocal of her "speaking in tongues" to the German research scientists, so naturally they were enormously intrigued by "warblin' turkey buzzards" and "sick voice boxes." Within no time, the entourage from Germany was working on a grant proposal for their latest quest ... Mabel.

I found myself grateful the young man who had seated us upon our arrival placed us in the back corner where none of the other customers could hear our conversation. It was like being in two pickles at one time, one Sweet and one sour. *And I'm sure you can guess which was which!*

Oh, and there was one other invitation. Miz Eudora also extended one for all her "colorful" friends and their hats to join her at the Sweet Pickle at a later date. All I can say about that is, if you're going to get yourself in a pickle, then that's the way to go!

TWENTY-FIVE

Christmas in August ...
Smackass Style

"SADIE!" I HEARD Miz Eudora calling enthusiastically as she came bumbling up my driveway as fast
as her legs would carry her. A peek out the front door
showed me her arms were bent at the elbows and going round in circles like the wheels of a locomotive,
visually making it appear she was picking up speed as
she came. *The little engine who could*, I observed. I
wasn't sure whether to lock the door and hastily hide
from the runaway locomotive, or open the door and
let her in before she knocked it down on her way in
the house. "Sadie!" she called again. "Wait 'til you
hear the idea I came up with this morning!"

That was all the answer I needed. I reached for
the wooden door to close it, but she was faster than I
was as she pulled the screen open and wheeled right
in. Wishing I could have had a pair of ear plugs handy,

I prepared myself for the news I was about to receive. Whatever it was, knowing who it was coming from, it couldn't be good. I closed my eyes and bit my lip, waiting for the morning's shock.

"Sadie! You're not gonna believe the idea I came up with this mornin,'" she announced.

One eye dared to sneak a peek at her for that was definitely a true statement.

"You know when I wanted to take Mabel to Savannah for a mission trip, only my mission didn't pan out?"

The other eye jerked open, for I remembered that foiled mission trip only all too well.

"Well, in the midst of all that whoo-ha, God gave me an idea for a way to make something, or at least something besides all that fun we had with all those women, a meaningful mission."

Okay, she's got me, I told myself, opening my eyes wide and biting her bait instead of my bottom lip. I wasn't ready to tell her to count me in yet, but I figured if God had something to do with her idea instead of Hattie and Theona, it might be halfway safe. "Why don't you take a seat on the front porch? I'll bring out some coffee and you can tell me all about it."

Somehow I felt a little more at ease with this human locomotive on the front porch rather than in my front room, in case steam started coming out of the boiler like the first time I'd seen her rolling up my driveway in this manner. *That fateful morning she first announced Mabel being a snake in the grass,* I reminded myself, *which spawned the idea of the first mission trip.*

She didn't even give me time to hand her the mug before she started sharing her idea. "I've been rackin' my brain ever since church yesterday to think of something we could *really* do to celebrate Mabel going back to sitting in the choir instead of bein' in charge of it. A real mission to benefit people."

Surprisingly, I deemed the controversy we'd suffered over the past several months as highly beneficial. Now everyone in Smackass Gap, or at least in our congregation, was happy Mabel was simply back in the choir. They'd learned the hard way that it surely beat the alternative of her being in charge of the choir.

"We're going to have Christmas."

I nodded, but with my head going around in circles, instead of up and down, in my confusion. "As opposed to *not* having Christmas?" I asked, puzzled.

"No, we always have Christmas. But this year we're going to have it twice." Her answer left me just as puzzled. Therefore, the only response she received was a perplexed glare. It was still enough of a response to keep her going. "Remember on the way to Savannah when we stopped at Shirley's Sole Food Café in Toccoa, Georgia?" Without waiting for a reply, she kept blowing steam, full-speed ahead. "Well, I've had a notion to do something to help her out with that mission of hers ever since that day. This morning, I knew exactly what I was supposed to do to help that nice Shirley. Lady Roadrunner sent me a photo of me in Savannah, running down the street in that 5-K race wearing those crop pants I made out of that rose-printed flour sack. It's on the nightstand Pa made me for a wedding present, the one that sits right beside the bed Horace's Pa made us for a wedding present. Anyway, I see it ever' mornin' when my feet hit the floor, but this mornin' when my feet hit the floor, the picture hit me."

She gave an excited chuckle. "Well, the picture didn't really hit me. But it sure 'nuff got me to thinkin' about all those fun Georgia women and how I'd like to see them again. And then it made me think about Shirley and all that good food and how she was using her talent in the kitchen to make a home for all them people she's helpin' with her homeless shelter. So God smacked me upside the head the same as He'd hit me with the picture and all of a sudden, I got this notion to invite all those women, and all their friends, to come to Shirley's for a meal to help her raise money for her shelter.

"We can do it in August when I've got a break between the summer gardenin' and the fall gardenin' and since we're doing something special to help give those people a place to live, we can call it Christmas in August ... Smackass Style." Without taking a breath, she asked, "What do you think?"

She'd spit out so much at me that I was still trying to chew on having two Christmases, much less digest the rest of it. "I think I'd better drink at least two cups of coffee to get me up to speed with where you already are this morning," I finally managed, wishing I could close my eyes and start the morning all over. But she was so enthusiastic with her idea and had such a good heart about helping Shirley, I had no choice but to jump on board with her. *Runaway locomotive and all,* I mused in a private joke.

But then, giving no more thought to the matter, it seemed I was hit upside the head the same as my neighbor had been earlier in the morning with the picture, for suddenly I had a clear vision of the same mission. The only words that came to mind were the very same ones Shirley had used when we were talking about *When the Saints Go Marchin' In* and God's "saints" marchin' into heaven. "Miz Eudora," I replied just as resolutely as Shirley had that day, "that's one march I want to be in."

Although we were talking about a mission event instead of a march, she knew exactly what I meant. Her face broke into a big smile as she finally sat back in the chair and took a healthy-sized sip of her coffee.

"I still have all the addresses for the invitations

we sent for Savannah. I'll start making cards today."
The dread I had felt that day, working on invitations
to Savannah, was now met by an equivalent amount
of joy at the idea of working on invitations to a Christmas party in August to help Shirley and the homeless.
*Wait until I tell Lady Roadrunner what that one little
picture started!* I knew hers would be the first invitation to hit the mail.

Then the list grew faster than I could keep up
with it as I mentally named off Carly, thinking how
great it would be if the Savant Sisters could play car-
ols. *Especially* Rockin' Around the Christmas Tree!
*They'll have that place rollin' in no time. Then there's
Smokin' Barb and Do-It-All Deb, not to mention those
two nice ladies, both named Doris, who live in the
Toccoa area. And Miz Eudora loves that one Doris'
husband,* I recalled. That's when I told her it needed
to include spouses and friends of all the ladies.

"The more the merrier!" she exclaimed, helping me with the invitations. It was the only time I'd
ever agreed with her when she'd stated those words.

Later that morning, as I watched Miz Eudora
waddle happily back home, I pondered whether she
had a flour sack, stored back somewhere in "that
blamed ol' cedar chest," that by chance had poinsettia
flowers embellishing it.

WHEN THE DAY finally arrived for the big Christmas in August event, I wasn't sure whether to be "a-feared" like the shepherds, or excited like the angels, at how Miz Eudora would decorate Shirley's side room to make it look like it had come right out of Smackass Gap. Either way, I could hardly wait. In fact, I suggested Hattie and Theona help her get the room set up while Mabel and I took care of the items that had been donated for the reverse auction we'd planned. While working with Mabel, I neglected to mention that a private concert, to be given by her at the location of the winner's choosing, was the main auction item. I figured that announcement would set off enough sparks to equal the fireworks of either the July 4th Dam Fireworks—which we had consequently missed—or Clay's New Year's Possum Drop. *Oh well,* I humorously commiserated, *at least that part will be akin to life in Smackass Gap!* I smiled. *Not to mention that it will probably wind up in the next installment of* Live in Smackass Gap*!*

With the help of the two ladies, both named Doris, and the Traveling Queens, Shirley's had been transformed into a haven of Christmas in no time. I had no clue how Miz Eudora managed to come up with enough, and I dared not ask, but each table's centerpiece was a chamber pot filled with artificial poinsettia flowers. Instead of napkins, Miz Eudora had made enough of her fabric fans for each person slated to attend. Or at least the women; the men each received a handkerchief that looked identical to the fan. *Minus the lace and tassel*, I noted.

"This way," she said with great pride, "there should be no shortage of restrooms. And should there be, I've got my motorized outhouse parked out back." Not one of the helpers dared say a word, but lots of strange glances ricocheted off the walls.

While Miz Eudora didn't show up in an outfit fashioned out of a poinsettia-print flour sack, she did prance in sporting a pair of "new used" purple leather sandals she had picked up at the Goodwill store. On the top of each shoe was crafted an intricately-designed sparkly flower in the shape of a poinsettia, having come that way straight from the shoe factory. I was absolutely stunned; apparently I wasn't the only one. As if the pair of sandals didn't warrant enough interest in and of themselves, Mabel added to the attention they ultimately received.

"I cannot believe you would show up in such trashy shoes," Mabel spouted at the top of her lungs. "Where did you get those? At the same Goodwill store where you got that ridiculous outfit you wore to Horace's funeral?"

"One and the same," confirmed Miz Eudora proudly. "But they're not trashy. They're brand new," she announced, taking off one of the sandals to show its scuff-free sole.

Mabel shot an uninterested glance in the direction of the sandal, but her eyes suddenly grew the size of saucers. "Italian leather!" she gasped, reading the shoe. "You found brand new Italian leather sandals in the Goodwill store?"

"Land sakes, Mabel! Just because they're foreigners, you don't have to hold that against 'em! These shoes have as much right to be here as you do.

"P'SHAA! Italian leather, I reckon!"

While everyone else, men who had tagged along with their wives included, was now busily admiring the expensive "new *un*-used" Italian leather sandals, I was in awe of the antique corsage pinned to Miz Eudora's purple fopher coat. It was exactly like the one my grandmother had worn year after year when I was a child. It had silver-colored foil leaves outlining it and small red glass balls, grouped in a center cluster, attached to it. My heart was instantly warmed by the memory it produced, and I realized there was more to this mission than simply helping raise money for the homes provided by Shirley's Soul Food Cafe. It allowed each person in attendance to revisit a Christmas of the past, one in a simpler time, when stockings held a few pieces of fruit, nuts and peppermints, and the one or two presents were those things necessary for everyday living. For those who were fortunate, there was possibly one inexpensive doll or tea set, or a ball or small train.

And speaking of simpler, the Traveling Queens, Do-It-All Deb and Smokin' Barb, who'd shown up to act as hostesses for the event, had traded their usual elegant hats for red-and-purple tu-tus on their heads. Where their crowns usually sat, a red poinsettia was on top of each of their heads in the tu-tu's opening.

"HMMPH!" barked Mabel. "Christmas is a time for the *Dance of the Sugar Plum Fairy*. I should have known you'd show up with the *Dance of the Tu-tued Red Hatters.*"

Personally, I thought it was a great idea. No Christmas was complete without a visit to *The Nutcracker.* These characters simply wore their tu-tus on their heads, which was better than some things I'd seen them wear on their heads! And instead of the Rat King, we had all these Traveling Queens. *What more could one want?* I asked myself.

Once the room filled with guests, Miz Eudora stood to welcome everyone to Smackass Gap, "via Toccoa," she said. "I must admit I can't take credit for tonight. That goes to Mabel. In fact, I reckon I owe her a great big debt of gratitude, 'cause it was her doing what gave me this wonderful idea of a little something to make for all you friends what showed up."

She went into a demonstration, followed by an explanation, of the fan. "And if the fannin' don't work out so well, you can dab the sweat with the fabric. I call it my 'no-fail hot flash swatter.'"

It was immediately decided she'd hit upon a delightfully unique idea, with an even greater delightfully unique name. And in the process, she'd paid tribute to Mabel, which in turn, kept "the blamed ol' sister-in-law" quiet for the rest of the evening while she sat proudly puffed up in her own little world. You had to hand it to Miz Eudora, she did figure out a way to keep Mabel out of the way which, in my opinion, was more unique than her "no-fail hot flash swatter." Her treatment of Mabel still reminded me of the song I'd loved so much in grade school about Snoopy and the Red Baron on Christmas. No matter how gruff my neighbor sometimes seemed, she still had a heart somewhere underneath that purple fopher coat.

I did have to give Miz Eudora credit on one count though, a count for which Mabel had no claims. She had indeed pulled off a Christmas … Smackass style, one like she had experienced as a child, and one that probably invoked familiar and pleasant images to a lot of the people who attended the event. As we packed up at the end of the evening and prepared to go back home across Helen Mountain, I was grateful Miz Eudora had unknowingly showered me with a gift I would "ne'er long forget," in her words.

The evening had been so miraculous that I found myself wishing Christmas could be every day … *Smackass style.*

TWENTY-SIX

Yes, I Want to Be in That Number

A FEW MORNINGS later, I sat straight up in the bed and looked at the alarm clock, which was rarely set as life in Smackass Gap rarely needed an alarm clock. This morning was no different, except for my internal alarm clock going off and telling me to jump up, put my feet on the floor and get moving. I have "no idee" what prompted me to "rise and shine" an hour earlier than usual on this particular morning, but I awoke amazingly rested and ready for what the day held in store. That's when I became frightened and wanted to crawl back under the covers. I had learned early on—since my time of being Miz Eudora's neighbor—that few days went by that didn't hold *something* in store. And given the fact that a few days had passed idly by without more incident while Mabel was occupied with her fanning and her hopefully-to-be flame, I guess I was subconsciously anticipating, or fearing to be more realistic, a new chapter—or in the case of these two, a whole book—in the next installment of "The Winsome Ways of Miz Eudora Rumph." So to wake up forewarned, there was "no tellin'" what would transpire involving either Miz Eudora or Mabel—or worse, both—before my feet again nestled their way between the comfortable covers of my bed, which had indeed become a haven of rest at the end of each day with those two.

There was no doubt Miz Eudora would be rushing to my house for our morning visit before long, but since I'd obviously been awakened by some external force other than my own, I decided I'd better get myself up and going, and "high-tail" it across the road. When I arrived there, she was sitting dreamily in her front porch rocker, her fingers tracing around the edges of a legal-sized business envelope.

"You know, Sadie, when you first suggested I look into genealogy, I was right a-feared of what I'd find. Then I decided it seemed more like something Mabel might do, diggin' around in her ancestry tryin' to find some long lost queen or king lurkin' back there. Or at least some piece of inheritance awaitin' her. But now, I can't tell you how much I appreciate you helpin' me find my int'rest in researchin' all our roots. It was like diggin' 'round in the dirt lots of the time, 'cause I come up with plenty of that too on all them people I was learnin' about. In fact, I spent more time in the dirt than I did anything else, but it sure was fun, and lots more int'restin' to boot!" Miz Eudora gave that infamous cackle of hers.

"Well you know, Miz Eudora, there's a lot of dirt in all our ancestries. I guess that's why people refer to it as 'digging up their roots.'" With that, we both gave a big laugh.

Miz Eudora's laugh then faded into a philosophical gaze as she stared down at the legal-sized business envelope, her fingers still tracing around its edges. "You know, I really am grateful that I turned my time from diggin' in my garden this past spring and summer to all this 'diggin' up bones,'"—which is what she'd grown fond of calling her research. "It was worth every minute we spent lookin' at people's tombstones and final restin' places to find all these missin' leaves on the limbs of my family tree. Otherwise, I'd have never found the person what sent me this nice letter."

"What nice letter?" I started to ask, but refrained, knowing its contents were exactly why I was seated on the front porch of Miz Eudora's house instead of finishing my last hour of beauty sleep in my bed. *Which makes this letter* not *so nice in my book*, I quickly decided.

"This one what tells me that I'm the last in a long line of Peays and that I'm the rightful owner of a house on the outskirts of some place called Las Vegas. This man what sent me the letter mentioned somethin' about 'the Strip,' so I'm assumin' it must be near some peninsula or somethin'."

"How did this man find you?" I inquired, finding it hard to believe—not to mention of great dismay—that I was the instigator of her learning this shocking news.

"That nice young lady what works at the library with Mary helped me trace some of my relatives who moved out west from here. After some ramblin' 'round for awhile, like all them wanderers in the desert with Moses, a few of them wound up in the western part of Texas, but then there was this one who must have ventured out on his own. Since this letter speaks of 'the Strip,' I reckon he had a hankerin' to be near water since he went and found himself a peninsula."

I would have stopped her to inform her that the one on "the Strip" was more likely the one "wanderin' in the desert," but she didn't give me time.

"From what I can tell from this letter, I'm the last of his descendants. Seems when I was pokin' 'round tryin' to learn somethin' about one particular branch of my tree, I thought I ran into a dead end so I gave up. It appears I did run into somethin' dead alright, but it was a dead branch and I'm the last one livin' what's related to it."

If you'll recall, I felt like I was caught up in one of those old westerns when some old cowpoke comes in the bar and orders a round of drinks. Now I felt like all that was lacking was Gabby Hays or one of his contemporaries standing next to me scratching his head. And if he wasn't scratching his, I was surely scratching mine because it was like Miz Eudora had taken me on a long circle to get back to where we'd started from. Her reasoning made perfect sense...*if* you could keep up with her rambling. At the same time, it made me wonder whether I had been trapped in a dream, set in the Old West, during the entire saga of this volume in "The Winsome Ways of Miz Eudora Rumph."

"This Mr. Proctor who sent me the letter wants me to contact him at my earliest convenience," she went on, pausing for a moment to open the letter and read its exact words, "in order to set up an appointment regarding the settling of the estate, which includes the house."

Miz Eudora stared at me with dazed eyes, which I was sure were met by mine that were just as dazed. It wasn't St. Patrick's Day, there was no need to wear green, but I was pinching myself anyway. I wasn't sure whether it was to make sure I was awake or to see if I'd heard correctly. It didn't matter. All I could do was gawk blankly at her.

"So you see, Sadie, this might be a bigger bumper crop than Horace ever made in all his years of farmin' this land. All he got was a bunch of corn. I got myself a house nearly all the way across the other side of the country. Land sakes! It might even have a waterfront view bein' on that Strip and all."

Now, if you've gotten this far through this book—and particularly if you've gotten through the rest of the books in the series about Miz Eudora Rumph—I'm sure you can envision this neighbor of mine "makin' her way" down "the Strip" in Las Vegas. What's worse, I'm sure you can also imagine Mabel "struttin' her stuff"—and fan—there, as well. Not to mention Hattie or Theona, whom I'm sure she'd never leave at home while she traveled that far. I wondered how far I'd get with the excuse that "I have some sort of stomach bug" on the morning of that trip. My sense of adventure killed that thought instantly, though, as I realized this was *not* to be one of our "anything but typical" *road* trips. We were going to take to the air. Given my already established love for flying—which I had not partaken in since before the death of my dearly departed Leon—I wasn't about to miss the episodes of this crew on a jet. I only hoped the jet's crew was ready for the Smackass Gap crew.

The rest of the morning was spent sipping on iced tea—sweetened, of course—while we discussed all the many blessings that had come out of the past few months, the two most notable being Mabel giving up the notion of taking over the choir and Miz Eudora inheriting a house near "the Strip." It was funny that she called them blessings; I called them incidents. *Most of them should have more correctly been termed accidents!* I reasoned.

We spent the rest of the day on the back porch leading down to the cellar, the home of the infamous "special blend," stringing the second season's round of green beans for her to can. That one act solely showed how much Miz Eudora had taught me since my move to "the Gap." She'd taught me the fine art of stringing beans. She'd brought me to realize the beauty of all the green—planted and natural—that surrounded practically the entirety of Clay County. *With the exception of kudzu, which was highly akin to Mabel.* You worked on the back porch, which is where all her blue ribbons from the fair hung, and you rested and visited on the front porch. And now, I had learned that my simple little unassuming neighbor was going to be the proud owner of both a home in "the Gap" and near "the Strip." *How much better could life get?* I asked myself, but not sure I was totally convinced.

Having put the letter's contents behind us, we chatted about everything and at the same time, nothing. There was no mention of limbs or branches, either dead ones or live ones, although we did come up with a few good ideas for her next few installments of

Live in Smackass Gap. The day brought me to one conclusion. I was most happy "to be in that number" of people who were lucky enough to call this place home. And the music to *When the Saints*, as it played in my head, was definitely "hot," just like the rest of me that had worked up a good sweat from the sultry hot, end-of-summer day while stringing beans, which would most assuredly win Miz Eudora another blue ribbon come the fall.

When I finally retired to my haven of rest and nestled my feet and the rest of my body snuggly between the covers, my mind was whirling with all the preparations that would soon need to be made. I sensed my body's natural alarm clock would wake me even earlier on the next morning than it had on this morning, given all the reservations I would need to arrange. As I closed my eyes, laughing inside at what I had feared would be the end of a horrible day, I found myself giddy at the "prospect" of what was to come. That's when my whirling mind questioned whether I should rent a "whirly-bird" for our crew rather than buy plane tickets. I never got an opportunity to answer my own question, for my mind—like the rest of my tired body—had already fallen into a pleasant slumber, graced by a dream of all the "saints"—and sinners—of Smackass Gap "marchin'" into the Strip. The last thing I remembered was a vision of Miz Eudora dressed in one of those t-shirts similar to the ones in Las Vegas, or other popular spots, that reads: "What happens in Las Vegas stays in Las Vegas." Only this shirt said, "What happens in Smackass Gap" on the front with the same caricature of my neighbor that was on the rest of the Smackass Gap shirts. The back of the shirt bore only one word: "happens." The word was accompanied by a sketch of Clyde, wearing Miz Eudora's red hat and proudly smiling as he stood over a fresh pile of …well, you get the picture. In the background, I heard the church choir "singin' to beat the band"—as Miz Eudora called it when the choir "got a-goin'"—with Hazeline on all the right words and the tenor and bass brothers on the right pitches, "Oh, I want to be in that number when the saints go marchin' in."

WHEN THE SAINTS GO MARCHIN' IN

We are traveling in the footsteps
of those who've gone before
But we'll all be reunited on a new and sunlit shore.

CHORUS: Oh when the Saints go marching in,
When the Saints go marching in,
Oh Lord, I want to be in that number
When the Saints go marching in.

And when the sun refuse to shine,
And when the sun refuse to shine
Oh Lord I want to be in that number
When the Saints go marching in. CHORUS

When the moon turns red with blood
When the moon turns red with blood
Oh Lord I want to be in that number
When the Saints go marching in. CHORUS

On that hallelujah day
On that hallelujah day
Oh Lord I want to be in that number
When the Saints go marching in. CHORUS

Oh when the trumpet sounds the call
Oh when the trumpet sounds the call
Oh Lord I want to be in that number
When the Saints go marching in. CHORUS

When the revelation comes
When the revelation comes
Oh Lord I want to be in that number
When the Saints go marching in. CHORUS

ABOUT THE PHOTOGRAPHER

Photographer Mark Barden is no stranger to capturing images on the mission field. Since 2000, when he became the Director of Mission/Outreach for the Western North Carolina Conference of The United Methodist Church, he has used his telecommunications background to tell the stories of people all over the world. After becoming the WNCC Director of Communications in 2006, Mark continued to feed his passion for missions by volunteering on various mission trips, always bringing home a plethora of stories and photographs. From the jungles of the Democratic Republic of Congo and Sudan to the rice paddies of Cambodia to the snow-capped mountains of Armenia, he has continued to interweave the two of his greatest loves, missions and photography, into a tapestry that tells the story of God's love for humanity.

Born into a Methodist parsonage family, and a grandson of Methodist missionaries, Mark grew up with the church touching multiple aspects of his family's life. With a committed faith, along with degrees in communications, he followed God's calling into broadcast journalism and eventually college teaching at the University of Mississippi and Murray State University. Eventually his desire for parish ministry led him back to North Carolina to complete ministerial studies at Duke University. Before joining the conference staff, Mark spent 15 years as a pastor in local churches in the Western NC Conference.

After 11 years at the Western North Carolina Conference office of The United Methodist Church, Mark is pastor at First United Methodist Church, Elkin, North Carolina. He is married to Barbara Jean Barden, Minister of Education at Myers Park United Methodist Church in Charlotte, N.C. They have one son, Chris, a student at High Point University in High Point, N.C.

ABOUT THE AUTHOR

Catherine Ritch Guess is the author of twenty-three books, all of the inspirational genre, including fiction, non-fiction and children's titles. In addition, she is a composer and a frequent speaker/musician for a wide range of conferences and events. She has served as an Organist/Minister of Music for over 40 years, and is appointed the Circuit Riding Musician through the Western North Carolina Conference of the United Methodist Church, a position which allows her to serve globally through her writing, speaking and music.

One of the FACES of *Interpreter* magazine in 2004, and the Profile of the UMC for September 2009, Catherine spends much of her time reaching out to others around the world. Her newest non-fiction, *Because He Lives,* has been selected for the 2012 UMW Reading List, and she is currently researching her next missionary book, as well as her next Miz Eudora comedy.

Her most treasured activity is spending time at home in North Carolina with her family. Catherine lives near her childhood home, filled with memories of her grandparents who were natives of the Great Smoky Mountains (not too far from Smackass Gap), and whose Appalachian wit and wisdom inspire many of her stories featuring her beloved Miz Eudora character.

www.ciridmus.com
www.mizeudora.com
www.catherineritchguess.com